Second Chances

Books 1 & 2
Second Chances...at Love

Dale Mayer

SECOND CHANCES BOOKS 1 & 2
Beverly Dale Mayer
Valley Publishing Ltd.

ISBN: 978-1-988315-78-2
Print Edition

About This Book

Go ahead. Take Charge of your life. Move forward…if you can…

Changing her future means letting go of her past. Karina heads to a weekend seminar and discovers the speaker is the person she needs to move on from. But she soon realizes bigger issues are facing her…

Brian has moved on, at least he'd believed he had… until he sees Karina in his audience…and realizes he's been lying to himself.

Passion pulls them together, love binds them together, but a revengeful enemy determines to keep the two apart…and destroy them both.

Sign up to be notified of all Dale's releases here!

https://geni.us/DaleNews

Second Chances

Book 1

Second Chances...at Love

Dale Mayer

Chapter 1

HER HEART RACING, Karina pushed open the glass double doors and walked into the almost deserted pub. Her breath quickened as she searched the faces of the few patrons inside. *Had he left already?* Or was Brian Saunders somewhere here, drowning his sorrows? Wendy, Brian's girlfriend of two years, had broken up with him and taken off for Europe, or some such thing. Karina knew she should feel sorry for him, but instead her mind wouldn't stop pestering her.

Here's your chance. One last shot to make him notice you before you go home and never see him again.

That the timing sucked wouldn't stop her.

Besides, if anyone asked, she was just here having a drink. And she could use one. Her last exam was done. She'd finally finished school and damn if she didn't feel like crying instead of cheering.

"Hey, Karina, thought you'd have booked it by now."

She waved at one of several friends having a good time at a nearby table. Most of the students who'd finished exams had already left, and the few stragglers writing tomorrow were either cramming or here trying to forget about writing in the morning.

"Nah. Leaving in the morning. It's a long drive and I *so* don't want to deal with that tonight. Or the ferry."

That elicited several nods. Anyone who lived on Vancouver Island knew about ferry woes to the mainland. She'd tossed around the idea of staying on the island, had even looked for work, but nothing had come of it, so she was heading home to Vancouver. Victoria, and the university in particular, would stay a happy memory. And, in some ways, a tough one.

She ordered a draft at the bar and turned around to take another look. Maybe she'd missed Brian in her first skim.

Shit. Ian Blackburn was here, too. And he'd seen her. Shit, shit, and triple shit. He'd always been super friendly to her, but there was something about him that gave her the creeps. And then last week she'd seen another side of him altogether. A professor in one of the classes they'd been in together had given Ian a poor grade on an assignment. Ian had lost it…big time. Someone had even called campus security to get him out of the lecture hall. He'd turned into something that terrified her and probably every other student there. She shuddered at the memory.

Karina turned around and glanced the other way, deliberately putting her back to Ian.

And there he was. *Brian.*

Her heart sighed even as it started to pound. She should go over to him. He looked sad, like he'd lost his best friend. Which, after the end of a two-year relationship, she guessed he had. But Karina told herself she was still a friend, right? Albeit a casual one, but still… They'd had classes together, the odd beer-and-pizza night as part of a group. That kind of thing. He had no idea that she'd been in love with him for a long time. She'd been careful to keep her feelings hidden. He hadn't been free and she wasn't the type to break up relationships.

She checked out the other half of the bar before her gaze zinged back to Brian. He lifted his beer bottle and poured the remaining golden liquid down his throat. Slamming the empty down, he reached for the spare, waiting. Damn, she hated to see him like this.

All right. She was going to go over there. Just a sip of beer for courage, first. She raised her glass to her lips.

"Karina. I'm glad you're here. I was hoping to see you before you left. May I sit?"

Ian. Shit. He'd somehow evaded her awareness and seated himself on the barstool next to her without her knowing. This was what she got for being nice and polite to a guy who mistook it for encouragement and, frankly, gave her the willies.

She attempted a smile behind her glass as she drowned a big gulp. She had to get away. Now.

"Sorry, I came here to meet someone." She said it lightly, dismissively. She'd planned to wait another minute or two before approaching Brian, but Ian's crowding was forcing her hand. "Oh, there he is. Brian."

She got up and waved in Brian's direction, tossing a good-bye smile at Ian.

His brows came together in a dark vee and his lips thinned, the expression causing her smile to falter and her stomach to heave. His thick nose and heavy brows might indicate a Mediterranean ancestry, but the darkness in his eyes gave her the spooks.

"I hadn't realized."

Keeping her face averted she took another big step and cast a glance back, relief washing over her when he didn't follow, but instead walked back to his seat.

Well, she'd started down this road, so…

"Hey." She slapped a bright, friendly smile on her face and sat down across from Brian. Now that she was safely seated her unease over Ian abated, even while her heart lurched at the deep unhappiness on Brian's face.

He looked up at her, a lopsided attempt at a smile peeking out. "Hi, Karina. I'm not good company right now."

"Oh." She didn't know what to say. His pain was a palpable thing. Impulsively, she reached across the table and laid her hand on his. "I heard and I'm sorry."

Surprise lit the dark depths of his chocolate eyes.

When he didn't say anything, she stood. She'd intruded on his private pain, and that wasn't right. She turned to leave.

"Wait." His husky voice reached out to her. "Please, don't go."

She smiled warmly at him and sat back down.

She stayed there for several more rounds as they talked deep into the night. Once or twice she glanced over at Ian. Every time she looked he appeared to be seething with anger as he stared toward her and Brian. She shuddered.

"This place is closing soon." She tugged Brian to his feet. "Come on, you look ready to drop."

"I'm not that bad," he protested, but allowed himself to be shuffled out the door. The cool night air hit them and snapped some of the buzz away. Karina looked at the stars, her heart full and happy. Not exactly a dream date, but it was Brian…and her…alone.

"Let's go to my place. I think I have a bottle of wine," he suggested.

"You're going to fall asleep before you ever get it open," she scoffed as she fell into step beside him.

He looked at her, his little-boy expression pleading that

it couldn't possibly be bedtime already. "I don't want to be alone tonight," he admitted softly. "Please come share a bottle of wine with me." There was only a slight slur to his voice and she'd had just enough to drink to feel the same.

Besides, she didn't want the night to end either. It might not be the wisest move but she couldn't come up with any convincing reasons why she shouldn't spend the last few hours with him.

She gave in.

He grinned at her, wrapping an arm around her shoulders. "How come we didn't do this before?" His sloppy grin made her heart laugh. "We should have. I've always liked you."

Magical words.

They walked toward his room, arms around each other, talking, murmuring in low voices. The heat of his voice, the tenor of his words, the glow of moonlight, Brian's touch – it was magic. And she wanted more. She wanted it all. Tonight.

THE COUPLE WALKED down the path, sliding in and out of view. He'd hidden in the trees thinking to see where Brian was taking Karina. And hoping his instinctive guess was wrong.

But no; there she was. Ian thought he'd missed her leaving. But no, she'd left with Brian. Why? *Why Brian?* Brian was nothing. And he had a girlfriend. Or he'd had a girlfriend. According to the gossip, he'd just been dumped.

How could Karina do such a thing? It's not like Brian was in any shape to enter another relationship right now. Had she no respect. For him? Or for herself?

He stood in the shadows of the trees that darkened the path and watched them make their way to Brian's dorm. Anger simmered inside.

Brian had many girls fawning all over him. He didn't need Karina. He'd only cast her off later.

Karina deserved better. If she weren't so blinded by Brian's flashy looks, she'd realize it. She'd be sorry later.

Damn Brian to hell.

SATISFACTION THRUMMED THROUGH Karina's body as she collapsed beside Brian in the wee hours of the morning. Her skin was damp and her body buzzed from their heated lovemaking. "Who'd have thought?" she whispered into the darkness.

A deep rumble rolled out from his chest as he attempted to speak but couldn't. She grinned. She'd brought him to this. She'd been the one he'd turned to tonight. Not Wendy, but her – Karina. Maybe she shouldn't have jumped at the opportunity…but she'd needed the chance to show him how good they could be together. How perfect.

And given that exams were over and all students going their separate ways, it had been now or never.

It seemed she'd loved him for so long. Always an acquaintance, never quite a friend and always superficial, kept on the outside…the last place she wanted to be.

She could no more stop blurting the words than she could stop the tidal wave of love that swept through her, giving the words their freedom.

"I love you," she whispered and dropped a kiss on his bare chest, before nestling her head on his shoulder and falling asleep.

MORNING DAWNED BRIGHT and clear. Karina woke slowly, her body still warm and achy from the night's activities. She bolted upright as memories flooded back. *Brian.* She'd had the most wonderful night of her life. She grinned and bounded out of bed.

Wrapping herself in the sheet, she walked out to the communal room, grateful that Brian's roomies had already left. *Empty.* She stood in the middle of the room, dread forming a sinking ball of steel in her stomach. An engine started outside.

She raced over to the glass doors, stepping out onto the small verandah in time to see Brian's car disappearing down the drive at a good clip. *He was coming back, wasn't he?* She stood there, waiting, for a long time after his car disappeared from view. As her heart broke into a dozen tiny pieces, hope faded away. The small sedan was gone.

And he hadn't once looked back.

Chapter 2

10 years later

IAN BLACKBURN GLARED down at his cell phone sitting in its dock on the car dash. "No, no and no! For the last time. I won't go out for dinner. There's no reason you can't cook a meal at home. Like you've done every night since we've been married."

Hot sun beat down on traffic. Ian transferred his glare to the cars moving at a snail's pace around him. Rush hour in Victoria, BC. What a joke. There was nothing rush about it. He hated all the traffic. It was so much worse these days. What happened to the good old days when the trip home was less than fifteen minutes? And when his wife listened to him. Understood that he knew best. *And never friggin argued.*

He pounded the steering wheel and yelled at Mary. "What's wrong with you? Ever since you went to that stupid seminar you've been whining to go out all the time, wasting money on stupid things like getting your hair dyed at the salon. What's wrong with doing it a home like you always did?" he snapped, his voice reaching through the open window. He heard someone snicker and realized a passenger in a convertible beside him must have heard.

Ian flipped him the bird and drove forward finally reaching the corner where he turned left onto his street. "You look like a boy with your new haircut. You've wasted money on new clothes and now you're talking about changing jobs. Just stop it, all right? That's enough already." Another corner and Ian pulled into the driveway. And parked the car.

He almost didn't hear what she said to him on the phone because he was pulling the phone out of the holder.

"No it's not enough. It's never going to be enough again." Her voice, sad but defiant, put his back up and made his stomach knot. "I wanted to go out for a meal somewhere quiet where we could talk. A neutral meeting ground."

He slammed the car door shut behind him and stared at the front door of his house, an ominous foreboding filling his gut. "Neutral ground?" he said his voice flat and cold. "What does that mean?" He strode forward. *Damn woman.* "What have you done now?"

She gasped.

His heart stalled, then hardened as his feet picked up the pace and he raced to open his front door. "Mary?" He called into the phone. "Are you still at work?"

"No," she said in a barest whisper. "I'm not." She took a raspy breath, then with that same new defiance she declared, "I quit."

"What?" Ian jammed his house key into the lock.

"I've moved out. At least for a while…"

And Ian heard a sharp click on his phone and she was gone. The key stuck in the damn door lock but he shook it loose and kicked the door open. He raced inside. Where he stopped, relief sending shivers down his back.

It looked the same.

Then maybe not. Pictures were gone from the mantle. He raced into the bedroom. "Mary?

Ian stared at the empty closet in shock. She'd done it.

Mary had actually left him. *How? When?* There was no way she'd have picked up and left him on her own. She wouldn't dare.

He rushed to her dressers, ripping the drawers off their runners in his panic. Empty. They were all empty. He walked around the small home like a zombie. Inside, he was empty. Cold. Icy cold. Angry.

She was gone. *For good?* No. She'd said for a while. This came back to something else she'd said last week. A separation she'd said. A trial separation. What the hell did that mean? He'd blasted her good at the time, thinking she was just playing him.

But she'd left. As far as he was concerned that made this as real as it could get – and it looked like there was nothing temporary about it.

He shuddered. He didn't dare go down that road. This had to be temporary. Anything else wasn't doable. Or acceptable. And damn her.

Damn it. She belonged at his side.

Anger and pain warred deep in his gut.

Sure, Mary hadn't seemed all that happy…at least lately. After that last tune up he'd given her, she'd settled down some. But then she'd attended that damn motivational workshop by that asshole Brian Saunders. *Take Charge of Your Life,* it was called. Become authentic to the real you or some other idiotic garbage.

If he'd known beforehand that the speaker was the same bastard he'd hated at university, well, he'd have put his foot down and made sure Mary hadn't gone.

Instead he'd laughed at her for wanting to go. He'd bugged her about the money she'd thrown away. And he'd had fun dissing the drivel she'd spouted on her return.

Well, what the fuck? He sure wasn't laughing now.

No. Now he was pissed. The hurt he crushed deeper down, cauterizing the open wound with the fire of the wrongfully treated, letting it rise and fuel his anger. There was no goddamned way he was going to let Mary just walk out of here and leave him and everything they had together.

But he had to find her first. He had her cell number but that was it.

What happened to his sensible Mary? She'd gone from being a good wife to a defiant woman talking about changing her life. After one goddamned weekend.

Mumbo-jumbo bullshit.

And he knew who he had to thank for that.

Brian Saunders.

Three weeks later

KARINA SAT QUIETLY in the nearly empty seminar room. Her nerves had taken such abuse getting here, they'd finally gone numb. *Thank God.* Now if only the endless rollercoaster of doubts would stop as well. They clogged her throat and fed the butterflies in her stomach.

She needed answers. Her workplace had taken her eight years of loyalty and flushed them down the toilet when they laid her off several weeks ago from her bookkeeping job. After the anger had come the fear, and then the sense of bewilderment. What did she do now?

Maybe this weekend's self-help seminar would help. With some much-needed urging from her two best friends, Cat and Serena, Karina had signed up to attend the weekend self-help sessions.

Run by one Brian Saunders. Her one-night-stand Brian

Saunders.

"It's like killing two birds with one stone, right?" she murmured softly to herself. Her friends were right – she needed to do something to sort out her mundane life…and it was also an opportunity to clear things up with Brian.

This could be her way to move on, both in the professional and personal sense. To clean the slate so to speak. She hoped.

She'd chosen a seat dead in the middle of the huge conference room that had chairs laid out in all directions. The seminar had sold out, which she'd learned, was typical of Brian's popularity. He'd really built a name for himself these last few years. For the zillionth time she questioned her sanity. She hadn't seen or heard from Brian since that fateful night together so long ago. Afterwards, he hadn't contacted her to go out, or to meet to talk… Of course, neither had she tried to contact him.

Over time she'd settled into her life. There was only so much rejection she could handle. But that hadn't stopped her from starting to follow his career when he popped up on her radar several years ago.

And it hadn't stopped her making her friends sick with comments about him. She was here alone, so what did that say?

There were just a few minutes left before the evening started. A quiver of excitement rippled through her. Would he remember her? Or had he been so drunk that night, so long ago, that he'd just forgotten?

She hadn't been able to forget the joy of being with him, or the pain of loss when he drove away. She shook her head and shifted on the hard chair. There was one other issue.

Would he even recognize her? And if he did…then what?

The opening of the double doors caught her attention. The announcer's voice echoed from the hallway, requesting that all guests take their seats in the seminar room. Her stomach did a somersault.

Excited voices blended into confused chaos as a crowd of people moved into the room, eagerly searching out the best seats. Groups of newly made friends formed and reformed, shifting and settling until finally the lighting lowered, and everyone's attention was glued to the stage.

Brian stepped onto the platform, smiling broadly. The crowd cheered and applauded, the noise swelling until Brian Saunders laughed and held up his hands for silence.

Karina couldn't help it; she grinned with the rest of the crowd. God, he looked better than ever. Her heart, traitor that it was, stuttered and stalled before picking up and taking off at a flat-out run. His confidence and dynamic presence instantly affected the crowd.

"Good evening, everyone. Welcome to the 'First Day of the Rest of Your Lives,' our seminar on creating the future you want for yourself."

At the sound of his voice, Karina leaned forward. His voice had changed over the years. Deepened. Strengthened. She studied his features. His hair was shorter and a bit thinner than she remembered, even from his book jackets, maybe a little lighter. The suit changed him, too. God, it fit him like a second skin, shaping and defining the broad shoulders she remembered so well. A hair over six feet, he was a well-built animal. Not that her hormones cared about any of that; they were simply jumping up and down singing "Hallelujah."

Lord, did she have it bad. After ten years… How sad was that? She'd hoped to see him, realize he was nothing to her now and move on. And she hoped to utilize what she'd learn through his seminar to do just that.

Not get stuck in another time warp of attraction.

By the time they'd reached the Q&A section of the evening, she'd finally focused on the material Brian had been handing out, but every time he moved across the stage, she became totally sidelined by his panther-like grace. Her nerves stretched taut as she bounced between succumbing to the pull of his sexuality and succumbing to the wisdom of his advice.

This was *so* not how she had envisioned her weekend.

"You should all have a copy of the schedule. If you don't, my assistant, Mark, has spares," Brian said, motioning toward a large bear of a man with a full beard standing off to one side. "Please look it over and if you have any questions, feel free to contact either one of us." He walked to the small table on the side of the stage and took a sip of water. "Now, let's move on to the questions."

A beautiful blonde, dressed with corporate killer instincts, waved her dainty hand in the air. "Are you married?"

Oh, good question. The general laughter from the audience eased the intrusiveness of the question.

The blonde turned her attention to the audience. "What I really want to know is, if he *is* married, do his wife's views match his? And, if they don't, how do they work around it?"

"I was married, and I have a little girl, but am now divorced," Brian answered seriously. "Does my ex-wife share my views? Yes, to a certain extent. My work was not the cause of our breakup. Does that answer your questions?"

Daughter? She couldn't help wondering how old the girl was.

He directed his query back to the blonde with a warm

smile. At her satisfied nod, he moved on, his gaze skimming over the crowd. Karina's heart thumped as Brian's attention whispered over her to the end of the row, stalled and zipped back to her. His gaze held her locked in place, and she forgot to breathe.

Heads turned as the audience tracked the reason for Brian's stillness.

The intensity of the moment burned. *Oh, God.* Heat washed over her as if he physically touched her, raising her temperature.

Christ, it was as if he'd laid her soul bare, brought all of her inner thoughts and emotions up to the surface. Heat arced between them.

Then he released her, his gaze moving over the audience as if nothing had happened.

She shuddered and gasped for breath.

Well, that answered that question.

He remembered. And how.

KARINA YAWNED WIDELY over her steaming mug of rich Columbian coffee. She'd talked late into the night, first to Cat and then Serena, trying to convey both her excitement and her trepidation over her reaction to seeing Brian again and that silent exchange they'd shared. For all the soothing support of her friends, she'd barely slept. And when she had, she'd been tormented by erotic dreams of Brian. Before going to sleep and since waking, she'd thought about and analyzed that shockingly intimate glance many times over.

Damn. The feeling of being so exposed, so vulnerable, had made sleep impossible. She needed to deal with Brian and move on.

She wanted to be free. To find a partner, have a family, grow old with someone. Not be alone forever, yearning for something she couldn't have and that wasn't even real.

Taking a deep breath, she slugged back her coffee and refocused on her homework assignment in front of her. She'd been at it for almost an hour and the restaurant was starting to fill up.

This assignment required a list of the areas in her life that caused her unhappiness. On the opposite side of the page, she was to assess the whys. After this, she was supposed to list the changes she'd like to put into place. All of this constituted the basic groundwork for change. With partners, they would be sharing their lists and looking at what they could do to create change.

She wondered, wryly, if she could just put down one item on the unhappiness side – her life.

"Good morning. May I join you?" a deep, quiet voice asked.

Karina looked up, startled. John, a soft-spoken, middle-aged teacher she'd met at last night's coffee meeting, stood uncertainly beside her. Flustered, she set about to organize her papers to create space for him.

"Sure," she mumbled. "Sorry. What you see here is a last-minute attempt to complete our first assignment. Please, sit down."

John settled his impressive bulk. "I know what you mean. I've done the assignment, but wanted a minute to reread it." He placed his own notebook on the table.

He turned to the approaching waitress, and ordered coffee and the breakfast special.

"Have you eaten yet? Or are you going to live on coffee?"

She grinned at the mischievousness in his voice. "I was up early, unlike some other people, so I've already eaten," she teased him. "I'm struggling with our homework now." Gloomily, she propped her chin on her hands and stared out at the gray scene outside of the window. The sun might manage to shine today, but even if it did, she wouldn't get a chance to enjoy it. The seminar schedule was intensive with workshops, lectures, luncheon and a social hour. By evening she'd be exhausted, with one lecture still to go.

"May I take a look?" John asked.

Karina nodded, then turned her attention to the world outside the window once again.

"You've taken a serious look at your life. Although you may not like the results, they do show thought and intention. I'm not sure he can expect more from us at this stage." He tapped the paper in his hand. "Frankly, I don't think I've done half as good a job as you have putting it on paper," he admitted.

"But doesn't all that really say I'm unhappy with everything in my life?"

"Isn't that why we're here?" he pointed out. "You'll probably find that as you start to make changes your list will change, too. Maybe dissatisfaction with a couple of major areas is coloring the rest of your outlook."

She pondered that bit of wisdom. "It's possible, I suppose. I'll think it over." She stood up, tossing enough money to cover her bill onto the table as she collected her papers. "I'm going to head into the seminar room. See you later."

In hindsight, she should have had more coffee. The morning damned near killed her. Her nerves were on extra-sensory alert and she was super aware of Brian's very presence. With the attendees organized into groups, he'd moved freely throughout the room, checking in with each team.

Except for hers. Thankfully, she'd gotten caught up in the exercises they were doing. Brian might have been on her mind when she arrived but it was the valuable knowledge she was gaining that kept her focused.

At break, she found herself needing to be alone. She slipped out to the hallway and headed for a quiet, empty space.

She stopped by a long window and stared out. Bending her neck, she took several deep breaths and let some of the tension slip off her shoulders.

"Karina."

Jesus. She closed her eyes briefly.

Slowly, she turned to face Brian. God, he looked good. She stared up into steady, curious eyes that were only slightly wary. Softly she answered, "Hello, Brian. It's been a long time."

He reached out to clasp her shoulders as if not sure whether to hug her or push her away. "I couldn't believe it when I saw you here last night." He grinned a huge smile, maybe tinged with relief. What had he expected? "Damn, you look good."

She shrugged. What could she say? "Thank you."

They stared at each other in silence. So much needed to be said, and everything was left unspoken.

After a long moment, he said, "It's wonderful to see you." At her questioning look, he smiled quietly. "Really."

And she believed him. Warmth unfurled inside. Nerves bounced then calmed now that they'd finally made contact. "Good." And she meant it. Her smile brightened. "I'm really enjoying your seminar. You're very knowledgeable."

He went as if to say something. She leaned in, hoping…

With a regretful smile, he straightened, reached out and put a friendly arm around her shoulders. She lowered her gaze, willing him to pull her in closer. Instead, he turned her toward the door to the seminar room. "Good. Then let's get back. The next set is due to start."

Karina walked back to the seminar room, her nerves feeling as though they were being tossed on the high seas. Relief warred with irritation and the first stirrings of old anger resurfaced. She had a right to be angry. *Didn't she?* He'd left *her.* Only they weren't in a relationship and they'd made no promises. It had been for the one night only. She'd known it then. So why was the sense of betrayal rearing its ugly head now?

Because she'd wanted that night to turn into so much more. She'd wanted to mean so much more to him.

And it turned out he hadn't wanted her – or cared in any way.

It didn't matter that she'd known *that* going in, or that it had been pisspoor timing for him back then. She'd known the risk and gambled and lost. And now…what?

Brian showed her to a seat up at the front. The weight of his hand seemed to linger on her shoulder. Or maybe that was just wishful thinking. She couldn't be sure. But her heart was ready to believe he'd wanted to prolong the contact, as a sign, and that just confused her more. She smiled shakily as he walked away. He was, as always, the one who walked away. Damn him anyway.

The next part of the workshop required people to form groups. They were each instructed to explore one area of their lives that they wanted to change, and ask the rest of the group for suggestions on how to go about doing so. Mark, Brian's assistant, supervised this session.

"Many people get bogged down with responsibilities and forget what makes our lives worthwhile. Find something you want to do. Set a goal to work toward. Remember to plan to insert some fun into your changes. Now choose a new partner and talk about what your goal might be, and how each of you might achieve that goal."

"Karina, will you work with me?" the woman seated next to her asked.

"Yes. Please." Karina jumped at the offer. Susan was facing the conflict of going back to work now that her children were all in school. Like Karina, her problem was that she had no idea what she wanted to do. On the plus side, however, Susan had a supportive husband with whom she was still madly in love.

Despite being physical opposites – blonde, elfin Karina versus statuesque, brunette Susan – and in different stages of their lives, the two women had connected instantly.

"All right, let me start. I adore my husband, but I want more for myself. I just don't know what that *more* is." Susan laughed self-consciously. "I'm not making any sense, am I?"

"Yes, you are. You aren't happy with yourself and therefore aren't happy with your half of the relationship. Getting your self-confidence back by finding a purpose or a job that you love will help you to learn to love yourself," Karina offered.

Susan's expression was incredulous. "If you can figure that out, why are you here?"

Karina laughed ruefully. "I need help, that's why. With my career, for a start. I'm tired of believing employers really care about their employees. Some just don't. I'd love to have my own business, but haven't a clue in what area." And that was only the beginning. There was so much more that she couldn't even go into. And she was having trouble focusing. Part of her was tracking Brian's movements throughout the room, anticipating when he might stop in at her group to check on their progress, her heart pounding whenever he seemed to be heading in her direction.

"This seminar has been difficult." Grimacing, Karina added, "The more I see change required in one area, the more I find other areas that need change more. Are you noticing the same thing?"

"Yes, definitely. Seeing the well-dressed people here reminds me how I've let my personal appearance slip. Staying home with the children meant that I didn't need good clothes. It's been an eye-opener to come here." She added a little glumly, "How can my husband stand to be around me?"

"He loves you and has gotten used to your changes the same as you have." Karina changed the subject. "We're supposed to break for lunch soon. Are you going in with the crowd?"

Karina wanted time alone but she knew the best thing would be if she stayed busy. If she were part of a group she wouldn't have time to think. Or feel.

She was off-balance already from her confused emotions. It wouldn't take much for her to fall even farther.

SUSAN SOUGHT HER out again before the start of the afternoon seminar. Karina perked up when she saw the other woman.

"Hi there. You look better," Susan remarked. "John's holding a couple of seats for us. I'm going to grab a coffee to take back in with me. Do you want one, too?"

"Are you kidding? Just point me in the right direction." Karina laughed. She followed Susan to the café where they each ordered large coffees.

They found John easily in the crowd and slipped into their seats with a few minutes to spare. John laughed when he saw the large cup in Karina's hand. "You can't even make it to break time without a caffeine fix, can you?" he teased Karina.

She smiled at him before inhaling deeply, closing her eyes in sensual delight as the rich, dark aroma smoothed over her senses.

"Now that's an intriguing smile! I'd love to know what you're thinking?" asked a dark, velvety voice.

Karina opened her eyes to find Brian's assistant standing in front of her. Mark's warm, brown eyes smiled at her.

"It's a secret. Don't use your Barry White impression on me."

Mark chuckled. "Brian's about to start and you definitely want to listen to this part." He continued down the aisle to where Brian stood at the front of the room.

Brian greeted them.

"Good afternoon. Is everyone rested and ready to go again? Good. Let's get started."

For the remainder of the afternoon, Karina sat entertained and fascinated by the man in front of her. He led the audience where he wanted them, yet kept them well informed on their way. Instead of finding aspects of his personality not to like, she was quickly falling from infatuation to attraction. He was a dynamo.

When the talk ended, Karina was relaxed and allowed herself to go with the flow of people, naturally becoming part of a group of people heading into the workshop portion of the afternoon. This sense of belonging eased her into the next set of exercises. As she settled, her natural chutzpah showed up and her sharp wit wove through the conversation, placing her firmly at the center of attention.

Susan said, "I'm really looking forward to this next session. It's on our innermost desires."

Karina laughed. "I'm so not sharing mine!"

"Come on, please Karina," said Rob, one of the younger single males. He waggled his eyebrows.

Quick repartee flew back and forth, keeping their group in giggles. Their enjoyment attracted envious glances from the other seminar members.

It also caught Brian's attention, bringing him up to their hysterical group.

"Well, I'm glad to see you're enjoying yourselves," he commented, curiosity in his voice. "Karina, as I recall you always did have a great sense of humor. Care to share the joke?"

Karina couldn't answer for the mirth that bubbled through her. She spoke up quickly. "Sorry, our humor ran away with us. We'll try not to disrupt the rest of the class."

She grinned, inviting him to join in the fun.

Pure male appreciation gleamed in his familiar response as their gazes caught and held again. A bolt of awareness shuddered through Karina. The answering glint in his eyes spoke volumes and offered an invitation of his own. Attraction surged once again between them.

Memories of skin sliding across heated skin, his lips caressing hers and whispered murmurs raced through her psyche.

Flustered, Karina broke the connection. Heat bloomed on her cheeks and her heart jumped inside her chest. My God. She didn't dare look at him again – afraid of what she'd see…or not see. What was happening here?

Susan smoothly stepped in to cover the awkward silence. "Karina's a natural comedian. Her one-liners have kept us in stitches for the last half hour." She added, "We're working on the assignment as well. We promise."

Smiling back at the other woman, Brian said, "Good. It's nice to see everyone having fun. Carry on the good work." With one last lingering glance at Karina, and a small smile, he headed over to check in with a different group.

BRIAN FORCED HIS legs to move him away from the woman that had been driving him crazy all morning. *Jesus.* He'd never thought he'd see Karina again. He'd kicked himself many times over the years for his actions back then. By the time he realized he needed to pick up the phone and apologize it was so late that he rationalized that she'd be better off not being reminded of that night. God she looked good.

And damn if that chemistry wasn't exactly the same as it had been years ago.

Still tiny with wild, untamable blond curls, she was a delight with her ready smile and quick wit.

His body didn't give a damn about explanations. It wanted to play…and how. Karina was a trip down memory lane, and a difficult one in many ways. His relationship with Wendy had just ended – a relationship he'd thought was going to last through time. He'd planned on drinking himself into oblivion at the pub when Karina had walked in. Available. Interested. And so alive and caring, he hadn't been able to resist.

That one night had blown him away. Two years of memories with Wendy – gone in a heartbeat. It had been a hell of a lesson. A lesson that had scared him into backing off. How could he trust anything after that one night? A night that erased two years of friendship – turned it into something much more – as if in an instant?

He'd been immature. Shocked even. He hadn't planned to leave without speaking with her that morning. He'd gone into the bedroom to say his good-byes but found her sleeping. She'd been so beautiful. So exhausted. Perfection.

And that had shaken him.

But her declaration during the night of love had terrified him even more than the attraction he'd felt. He'd run.

Heading home had provided an opportunity to avoid the situation, her, his own overwhelming emotions, and especially the incredible shift in his world…and he'd taken it. Coward that he was.

There. He admitted it to himself. He'd been scared of

the emotions coursing through him. The speed of the disintegration of his relationship with Wendy. The speed of the developing relationship with Karina. Off balance, and afraid he was on the rebound and not thinking rationally, he hadn't been able to trust his emotions or the lightning-quick shift in his desire. He did not appreciate the perfection of that evening.

And now, she was here. At his seminar. Deep inside, his soul cried out to connect with her – again. Karina had indeed rocked his soul years ago, had remained in his thoughts and dreams over the years, and now she'd reentered his world. Surely, if she despised him as he thought she would, she wouldn't have come to the seminars…

What was the universe tossing at him this time?

He'd almost cancelled this seminar after the rash of threatening phone calls and especially the menacing letters he'd received recently. The police hadn't explicitly told him to, but in a serious manner they'd asked him to consider at least postponing the seminar.

As a concession he had doubled his security, warned the hotel to stay extra vigilant and had proceeded with careful watchfulness. That had been his focus, his primary concern, until he saw Karina sitting there. So close that if he took a few steps he could touch her. And he wanted that.

His focus had shifted to the beautiful woman from his past, and he was very glad he hadn't cancelled.

Look what he'd have missed if he had.

A thought flashed in his mind and wouldn't let go. Did he deserve a second chance? A chance to see if they truly were connected in the way it had felt when they'd talked into the wee hours and made tempestuous love so long ago. A chance to put to rest the regret and the 'what if' he'd lived with for so long…

Probably not. He'd learned all about what he didn't want in life. Had focused on that cleansing. But he finally had his shit together…and felt desire for the first time in a very long time. Desire to make things right at least. And maybe more…

KARINA BASKED IN the warm glow of heightened self-confidence for the rest of the afternoon. Even as the exercises took her through some heavy storms in the emotional arena, the glow stayed. Approval often did that for a person. She finished the afternoon in high spirits, her hopes restored and her heart singing. There was…something…still there between them. She'd felt it. The connection. It was just a matter now of finding out what that something was.

"Wasn't this afternoon great?" Karina asked, as she and Susan made their way to the hotel's revolving doors. "Working together the way we did, sharing. It was wonderful."

"Absolutely. I really felt like I belonged in our group." Susan paused on the sidewalk outside the hotel, and the two women looked at each other. "So. Where to?" Susan asked.

"Ladies. Could we join you for dinner?" John walked up to them on the sidewalk, accompanied by Andrew, another member of their afternoon group.

"Of course," Karina said with a smile. "We're just trying to make a decision on where to eat."

"How about a vote? Who wants Chinese? Italian? For myself, I'd love some Thai food," Susan suggested.

"Thai or Chinese works for me," John offered. Andrew nodded agreeably.

"Does anyone know the city well enough to point us in

the right direction?" Karina asked.

"I do," supplied an amused voice behind them.

Brian and Mark had walked up to the group during their discussions. "We'd just decided to head for an excellent Thai restaurant around the corner. Would you care to join us?" Mark suggested cheerfully.

With a genial smile, Brian seconded the invitation, his gaze lingering on Karina. She met his gaze confidently, and the warmth in his eyes grew heated.

It took mere seconds to reach total agreement. Karina's heart bubbled with happiness. Falling into step between Brian and Mark, she stuffed her hands in her pockets and tossed back her curls. Good friends, good food, and a chance to spend time with Brian. Life was good.

The group hurried along under a rapidly darkening sky. A heavy downpour had been promised, but that in no way dampened the spirits of those rushing into the busy restaurant. Heavy drops began to fall a few minutes before they reached the door.

"Just in time," remarked Brian as he removed his overcoat, gently shaking off the raindrops. He hung the garment on a large coat rack then turned to help Karina with her coat. It wasn't waterproof and now moisture suctioned the material to her blouse, and it was difficult to remove modestly. The touch of Brian's fingertips on her shoulders sent tingles down her arms, and Karina's heart pounded in her ears. In an attempt to keep the mood lighthearted she laughed as they struggled with the unruly lining of her jacket. And after all these years, Brian's sexy, soft chuckle thrilled her to her toes.

The others were already following their hostess to a table. When Karina and Brian reached the group, she eyed the three empty chairs in a row before grabbing the middle one. She smiled impishly across the table at Susan, the only other female in the group.

"If we sit opposite each other then we can share the men between us."

"With such handsome men along, I think that's a fabulous idea," Susan said with a grin.

"In that case, I'm sitting beside Karina," Mark interjected with a wink. "We should have invited a few other women to balance things out."

"But as this isn't a matchmaking service and as some of us aren't single, it won't matter." John took the seat next to Susan. "The 'attached' ones are here, making yours the 'unattached' side."

"Works for me," said Brian as he took the seat next to Karina.

Andrew just smiled and took the last seat on the married side.

"Are you married, Andrew?" Karina asked, trying to include the shy gentleman in their conversation, all the while doing her best to ignore Brian's overwhelming presence on her right.

"I was for ten years, but we divorced three years ago. Then I got lucky and met up with my current partner, Pam. What about you? You must have a boyfriend, don't you?" Brian asked.

"No, there's no one special in my life right now," she said, flushing. She turned her attention to Susan across the table. She appeared to be watching Brian very closely. The quick, secretive grin that flashed across her expressive face sparked Karina's curiosity. What was that all about?

"Where do you live, Mars? Obviously, not here. Men in

this city aren't so foolish," joked Mark. His hand was in the air trying to get their waitress's attention.

"I gather you're hungry, Mark," Brian teased. "Did you even take a lunch break today?"

"I'm starving. My stomach remembers this place. Have you all decided what to have?"

"No point in even looking, when I don't know how to read the names and have no idea what the dishes are." John nodded at the still-closed menu in front of him.

Karina opened her menu and saw what he meant. There was no shorthand explanation to go with the names of the entrees. Nor were there pictures of the dishes.

Brian turned to Mark. "I have an idea. You know the food. Why don't you pick six dishes for us to share? That way, everyone can try a little bit of each."

"Easily done." Mark tilted his head toward the tiny woman now standing beside him. Together, they discussed the choices. The strange-sounding names combined with the singsong accent added a touch of far-off magic to the evening. Karina appreciated that they were in for a treat.

"Mark lived in Thailand for several months," Brian said. "He's quite a connoisseur."

"Wonderful! We're so lucky that we get to enjoy his expertise. A friend of mine would love meeting you." Karina rubbed her hands together in anticipation. Serena loved Thai food. Always willing to try new foods, Karina had only had Thai cooking a couple of times before, so to have an expert advise them on their meal was fun.

She glanced sideways at Brian and caught him staring back. She felt the heat rise in her cheeks and saw his appreciative and knowing reaction in his sparkling eyes. He was enjoying making her squirm. Thank God he couldn't read her mind completely because even at this distance, she couldn't help noticing how square his cheekbones were, how attractive he was. *God, those dimples.* She didn't remember those. She turned away before she lost control of her compulsion to reach over with her fingertip to stroke the natural recesses. She caught Susan's observant eye. With a toss of her head in the direction of the back of the restaurant, Karina silently suggested a trip to the ladies' room.

Susan jumped up at the idea, her expression smug. She appeared bursting with the effort of holding back a secret. Karina followed closely behind.

"What are you smirking about?" Karina asked, certain she already knew the answer.

"Don't worry. I don't think anyone else noticed."

"Noticed what?"

"The attraction between you two. You obviously think he's cute."

"God, he's gorgeous. But I have to confess… We have a history. Not much of one, but it seems like time hasn't dulled the attraction." Karina collapsed in an exaggerated swoon against the counter. They both burst out laughing.

When she'd regained control, Susan said, "And it appears he's available. He's let you know that. In many ways you complement each other."

"Really?" Karina said, her voice sounding a little desperate to her own ears. Disbelief warred with hope in her voice. Did Susan really see something? And more importantly, did she want to go down that path again? "He's confusing the hell out of me."

"Duh, meeting him again has obviously stirred things up. For both of you. Why not let it develop?" Susan bent closer to the mirror to check her makeup. "You two would be good together," she reiterated firmly. "See where it goes."

Karina wasn't so easily convinced. She'd spent years trying to forget Brian and wasn't so sure she wanted to go down that road again, no matter how attractive he was. He'd been attractive then. And that hadn't stopped him from running away. Who could say if he was different now?

"Let's head back before the men eat everything." With the door half open, Susan motioned Karina to move in front of her.

"Then we'd be hungry and have to find another way to appease our appetites." Karina leered comically, as her ribald sense of humor made an appearance. "Instead of sharing dinner with the men, let's have the men for dinner."

Susan chuckled and lightly elbowed Karina in the side. "I'm on a diet, remember?"

"That's okay. I wasn't sure I wanted to share anyway!"

Still giggling, Karina retook her seat.

Mark sighed. "*Now* what are you two laughing about?"

The women shook their heads, grinning madly at each other.

Brian leaned in close. "Karina, I've listened to your laughter all afternoon, but nobody's let me in on a single joke. So, come on – give over. Please?" A wheedling tone entered his voice as he waited, his face within kissing distance. Tempting her... She licked her lips and considered...

Susan broke the spell by jumping in to answer. "She was just commenting on having a man-sized appetite." Then she burst into peals of laughter at her inside joke.

"Well done, Susan." Karina smirked. "We'll make a comedian out of you yet."

The men just watched and shook their heads, before

everyone turned back to the food that had arrived as they sat down again.

By the end of the evening, the warm cozy ambiance and atmosphere of the restaurant had a bonding affect on the whole group. They were reluctant to call it a night.

Together they strolled back to the hotel, replete and relaxed. Karina barely noticed that the light drizzle had turned to rain.

The street around them was quiet, devoid of both traffic and pedestrians and their laughter filled the night. Empty storefronts seemed to wait for them in the gloom, watching them pass with dark, fathomless eyes. Despite the pleasant chatter happening around her, Karina felt a chill of nervousness run up her spine and looked around for a reason. Nothing stood out. She chided herself silently for being foolish; their group was large and fairly noisy. Nothing bad was going to happen to them. But then why did she feel such a sense of misgiving?

On the way up the long path to the hotel's entrance, Karina noticed a man skulking along at the same pace, on the opposite side of the street. When they stopped he stood motionless in the downpour, staring up at them as they stood in front of the well-lit building. Rain pattered off his hat, dripping from the brim in a steady stream. His face was hidden in shadow, but something about him was familiar in a creepy kind of way that made Karina hesitate.

"I noticed him a couple blocks back. I wonder what he's doing?" Karina jerked her chin in the man's direction. At that moment he turned his head, and she caught a glimpse of his profile. Yes. There was something familiar about it… The others, only intent on making it inside, barely glanced his way. "Maybe he's lost," she suggested, squinting into the darkness.

"If he's lost, he can ask for help at the front desk." Brian held open the door for her. "Come inside and get dry." He cast a glance at the stranger then shrugged. "Mention him to the hotel staff, if you'd like. He'll probably be gone before they even approach him." His palm landed gently on her back, ushering her inside, out of the rain.

Looking over her shoulder one last time, Karina realized that she could no longer see the man.

The stranger had already moved on.

ANGER FLASHED, OLD and sharp, scraping Ian raw as it rose to the surface.

Was that Karina? From university? What was she doing here? He'd never forgotten her. He couldn't. He'd wanted her something fierce back then. She'd only had eyes for Brian.

The same old bitterness choked him. *Brian again. And now with Karina. The bastard.* He snorted. Both had made his life miserable.

And both appeared to be happy.

That observation brought his wife, Mary, to mind. His stomach twisted. Things were bad between them. She wouldn't even answer his calls now. Said she needed more time and to not bother her.

His pain burned. He slammed it down deeper.

And sneered. *Brian and Karina, huh?* His research hadn't brought any hint of a relationship in Brian's life. No mention of Karina anywhere, and he certainly would have noticed.

He had a score to settle with her, too. Now that he'd

seen her here, he'd dig deeper and see what he could find.

The thought that the two of them were happy *together* twisted in his gut.

She hadn't given him the time of day back then. Wouldn't even give him a decent chance. Especially that last night when she'd left the pub with Brian. He'd watched them leave, had followed them to Brian's place – had stayed outside and waited.

She hadn't come out.

Apparently that relationship hadn't worked out back then. And Brian had married and divorced in the meantime. And didn't that thought bring a smile to his face. Brian didn't deserve to be happy. Not after what he'd done.

And neither did Karina. Ian had hated her back then. Hated Brian, too. But his emotions back then were nothing to what he felt now. Sure, part of that was due to Mary having walked out, but it seemed that Brian was responsible for Ian losing both women. Karina years ago and now Mary – after she'd attended Brian's seminar. Brian had ruined Ian's marriage. There's no way Ian would let Brian have Karina now too. Not again.

Chapter 4

KARINA PRESSED THE elevator button to head up to her room for the night. Warm, mellow and flushed from good wine and great company, the world looked bright and rosy.

"Karina?"

She stilled as butterflies fluttered in her stomach.

Brian.

Turning to look at him, she couldn't help the intimate smile from blossoming forth. *Why not? They were alone.*

"Are you going up to your room or will you stay downstairs for a while?" Brian pointed to the open elevator door.

Flustered, she shrugged.

"Actually I thought maybe we could talk? Catch up on the last decade." A slow, sexy smile formed on his lips. "Come have a drink with me in the bar, please…" he wheedled.

His words reminded her of the last time they were together. When she'd pursued him. Did she want to go for a drink? Did she want to spend time with him now? *Hell, yes.* The silky tone of his voice and barely hidden suggestiveness slid into her blood, heating and speeding it as it thrummed through her system. She wanted to breathe. She would breathe. In a minute. When her world righted and her imagination calmed. Christ, he could still send her sideways like no other. Whatever they'd had in the past had nothing on what was happening now and would happen…

If she let it.

His desire to spend more time with her felt sincere, and this time it was his idea. Why not?

She nodded and watched Brian's smile widen.

He led the way to the bar, choosing a quiet, discreet corner at the back. They chose seats across from each other. He studied her quietly for a long moment. "I know I said it before but it is really good to see you."

She managed a lopsided smile. "Is it?"

His gaze warmed, making her insides shiver. "Yes," he whispered, "it is."

The heat in his gaze became unbearable to resist. She looked down briefly, breaking the contact. She took a deep breath and asked the burning question of the day. "Why did you ask me down to the bar?"

"To apologize."

The answer flew back so fast she couldn't do more than stare.

Swallowing heavily, hating the anxiety and fear that clutched at her insides, she sent up a silent prayer to the universe. *Please don't let him apologize for the best night of my life.*

"For what?" She couldn't manage more than a whisper.

"For not being there in the morning. And…" He frowned, staring down at the black marble tabletop. "And for not contacting you afterwards."

She shuddered. After a moment, she managed to get out the words choking her throat. "Why didn't you?"

His regretful sigh reached across, deep into her psyche. "There's no excuse. I was dumb and I was scared."

She blinked. That so wasn't what she expected to hear. "Really? Why were you scared?"

He slouched back in his seat, his hands folded together on the table.

She narrowed her eyes. Then she saw his uncertainty. He was squeezing his hands together so tightly his knuckles were turning white. Good. She watched him struggle for control and sat back to listen.

"I wanted to wake you up and… But I was confused and we were headed in different directions then. I'd just come out of a bad breakup of a relationship I thought was strong and steady. Then out of the blue you were there. I knew you, but…I didn't really know you. I hadn't seen you…really seen you, until that night. And that night was so strong, so passionate… I regret that you woke up alone…" He stopped. He ran a hand over his hair, sighed deeply, then said, "It's as if everything I'd known and believed had been tossed upside down. I didn't know what was real and what was fantasy." He took a deep breath and added, "Then you said you loved me. And that was too far, too fast…and way too deep for me at that moment." He gave a self-conscious shrug. "I took the coward's way out. I ran. Since then I've often wondered, 'What if?' and lived with that regret." He caught her gaze and held it. "Please forgive me."

Never could she have imagined this strong, confident man admitting to such behavior. Neither could she have ever imagined the reasoning behind his actions. She stared at him. Over the years she'd made a lot of excuses for his behavior. But she hadn't considered this one. It was the only one that could make her feel okay about his actions. Not good, but getting better as she contemplated the depth of meaning and sincerity behind his words.

Strong? Passionate? Inside, her heart smiled. The corner of her mouth tilted. "Fantasy, huh?"

His devastating grin slid out, sneaking into her heart. "Unbelievably great fantasy."

"Then maybe…just maybe I'll forgive you."

His smile winked out as he realized what that meant. "I am sorry. I behaved terribly back then." He leaned forward, grasping her hand gently in his, his thumb stroking, caressing hers. "I never meant to hurt you. I was young and stupid."

"It wasn't much fun." She winced inside and realized if he was coming clean, then… "I'm sorry, too. I knew you weren't yourself that night. In a way, I took advantage of your situation, but…" She laughed lightly. "It was just one of those events. She didn't tell him that if that night didn't happen before she'd headed home from university, she'd have wondered her whole life about what might have been if she'd only taken a chance.

Silence stretched comfortably between them.

He reached for her hand again. "Understandable. And, again, I'm sorry."

His gaze deepened, enveloping her in a special glow of intimacy. "I'm glad we had that time together. I've kept my memory of you close ever since."

Hot, then cold, his words had taken her to the edge and back. So he'd regretted that he'd left her that morning? Thought about her over the years… Yet he'd married and divorced in the meantime. So he hadn't exactly been pining for her. So what did his confession mean right now? For her. She swallowed. Hard. "You never contacted me. So it couldn't have been *that good,*" she added lightly, hoping for something that would make her feel better, but not really expecting more.

Saying that out loud brought back vivid memories of just how good they'd been together.

"It was *that* good." He frowned, staring down at her hands. "I couldn't contact you. I was ashamed of what I'd done. Figured I'd ruined my chance with you." He lifted his gaze to stare deep into her eyes. "Did I?"

The energy in their tiny booth electrified. She wanted to wrap herself around his hard length and drive him crazy…as crazy as he was driving her.

"Karina?" So soft. So sexy. So not subtle.

She shouldn't. There's no way another quickie affair was in her plans. A relationship, yes. A love affair, yes. A repeat of ten years ago, no. *Hell, no.*

Staring into those magnetic eyes, knowing she had to hold true to what she needed this time round, she said quietly, "I'm glad you have the same memories I do. I'm beyond delighted that you are still interested in me. But I won't… I can't…have a repeat of the last time."

There she'd said it.

And again he surprised her. Those eyes held hers, as if caressing her deep inside and promising never to let her go. "Understandable. Trust is a big issue. And I agree. So let's give this a chance, see where this goes, shall we? Friends for now?"

He held out a hand, palm up.

Tremulously, she reached out and placed hers in his. "Yes. I can do that. Friends," she whispered.

THE NEXT MORNING, Karina slouched back comfortably against the hard chair, propping her feet up on the seat in front of her, enjoying the silence of the empty room. She'd woken earlier than anticipated and had ended up here in the seminar room, anxiously awaiting the day's presentation. Anxious to see Brian again.

It didn't matter at all that she was early. In the dimly lit space, she glowed with happy memories of the previous night. Not only had she gone to bed alone and smiling but she'd actually slept. And slept well. Hearing his side of things and making peace with Brian had relaxed her and filled her dreams with rosy thoughts of a possible future.

She'd wanted to phone her friends, but sent text messages, instead. Maybe a phone call would intrude and deflate her amazing little fantasy bubble. Or maybe it had to do with not wanting to jinx things. Regardless, even though she wanted to fill Cat and Serena in on these new developments, she wasn't completely ready to do that.

Even after a decade of angst, Brian tugged at her heart in a way that she couldn't define. She was incredibly aware of him physically. If he'd tried, his words might well have seduced her last night. She desperately wanted to reach out and experience heaven again…with him but she wouldn't settle for another one-night stand. This time, if they connected, she wanted it all. All or nothing. No more being a captive to the memory.

Feminine power surged through her. And that surprised her.

She felt in control of her hormones too, almost primal. Was in control of herself in a way she hadn't felt before…

Lost in thought, the *clunk* of a latch and a movement out of the corner of her eye caught her attention. Someone stood at the double doors, surveying the layout of the room. So still. So silent. Waves of malevolent energy emanated from the figure. Again, she felt a flash of recognition.

She slouched deeper in her chair. Had he seen her? She heard the door open and close. Stealing a quick glance around, she realized the stranger was gone. *Thank God.* From the glimpse she'd seen, he could have been the man standing outside in the rain last night. And she felt the same foreboding as she did then.

Had he seen her? She didn't think so. *Why was he here? Did he realize this was Brian's seminar?* Or was this just coincidence that she'd seen him twice in such a short time? The sudden chill made her uneasy. She sat up to look around again. A quick check of the large, shadowed room did nothing to dispel the sense of wrongness.

Just then the overhead lights snapped on and Mark strolled in, bringing a calming influence back into her world.

Relief swept through her and she greeted him. "Good morning, Mark."

Mark started in surprise. "Good Lord! Karina, did you sleep in here? I thought I saw you and Brian go into the bar last night."

She flushed. Just how much did he know?

"I wanted to spend a few moments alone in the quiet before we start today," she said, shrugging. She walked toward him, slowly stretching the tension out her back. She began to pull out her cell to check the time, but then asked, "Is it almost time to start?"

"Not quite. I needed to bring in today's worksheets and check that everything is ready to go." He dropped the stacks of paper onto the table. Different sets went into different piles. "There, that'll do. And all the chairs are set out. Good." He nodded, as if satisfied that the morning could begin as it should. "I'm going to pick up a coffee before we begin. Do you want to come with me?"

"Let's go!" She walked out with him, the stranger in the shadows all but forgotten.

"Why are you soaked?" Susan asked a little later, as she eyed the raindrops still clinging to Karina's sweater.

Karina laughed. "Mark's as mad about coffee as I am. We skipped out to a little specialty coffee shop around the corner. Just look, a real mocha cappuccino to start my day."

Susan linked her arm through Karina's, shaking her head. "I'll always remember you for your coffee addiction."

"It's not that bad," Karina protested. But after a sidelong look from her friend, she admitted, "Okay, it's bad. Speaking of which, I'd like to stay in touch with you after this weekend. Interested?"

"Of course! I want to stay in touch! Maybe we could even get together on a weekend, too."

"I'd like that." Karina swiftly hugged her new friend.

Later that morning, the women paired up for another exercise geared toward relationship issues.

Susan whispered, "I'm hoping to get my husband's help with my secret dream of going into business on my own."

Karina gasped. "That's what I want to do, too."

With a much better understanding of each other's problems, it made for another productive and fun session.

As they headed toward the luncheon, Karina was overtaken again by a strange sense of foreboding. Her breath caught in the back of her throat as she recognized the square set of shoulders and antagonistic angle of a man's chin, far ahead of them in the crowd. She tugged Susan to a stop.

"Look, Susan. That's the man from last night, the one outside the hotel."

"How can you tell? It was so dark and rainy last night."

Susan twisted, trying to catch a better view of the stranger among the throng of people in the lobby. "Besides, so what if it is him?"

"He came into the seminar room really early this morning too. I don't know what it is about him, but he gives me the creeps." Karina kept shifting to track the man's movements. "He looks like he's searching for someone."

"We can go ask him if he needs help."

"No. I don't want to talk to him, but I'll mention it to Mark or Brian."

"They're both standing over there." Susan pointed out the two men waiting their turn at the buffet. "They probably can't even see him for the crush."

"Let's go." Karina led the way through the sea of people, trying to keep one eye on the stranger's whereabouts. Finally reaching her goal, Karina stepped close and tapped Brian on the shoulder. He turned quickly, accidentally knocking into her. A quick save on his part stopped her from falling.

He held out his arms and, after a quick intake of breath, she walked into them for a short, gentle hug. "I'm sorry, Karina. I nearly bowled you over."

True on so many levels. "It's okay." Karina's eyes drifted shut and she held Brian to her for a heartbeat too long. It was too tempting to stay in his embrace, too exciting to feel the firmness of his chest and the muscles in his back. She gave him a gentle squeeze before withdrawing.

Brian's eyes had darkened with emotion and his expression showed he'd been affected by that embrace as much as she had. *Good.* Karina caught Mark's assessing gaze and warmth filled her cheeks.

"Oh, you were just trying to sneak into line, weren't you?" Mark winked at her, diffusing some of the tension in the air.

She smiled gratefully at the big man. "Not at all," she protested. "But I did want to speak to both of you. Remember that creepy man standing in the rain last night? I think he was just here again. He acted like he was looking for someone."

Brian frowned, and turned to look over the crowd. "Where did you see him?"

"I think he's the guy in the rain outside the hotel last night. He was over by the door when we first came in." Unconsciously, she rubbed her arms as if to ward off a chill. "I think it was the same guy, but can't be positive."

Mark eyed her curiously. "He really disturbs you, doesn't he?" At her nod, he added, "Okay. I'll go talk to him. I'm sure a few answered questions will help you feel better."

"Thanks, Mark." Karina released her pent-up breath. Maybe she was just being foolish. So *not* her normal self. But she couldn't help the way the stranger made her feel. "Sorry, I'm not usually so nervy. Maybe some food will help. Let's find a table and wait for Mark there."

"Not a lot of choice, is there?" Brian said and using his height advantage, pointed to a small table for four off to one side. The seminar crowd was having lunch in one sitting. "There's an empty one that looks good. Quiet and out of the way."

Brian regarded her tired face. "We can take a plate of appetizers with us, while we wait."

"Really, I'm okay. I'm hungry though, so maybe I should grab… Oh look! He's back already." She pointed toward the doorway where Mark was standing. He quickly made his way over to them.

"Karina, the people at the front desk saw him and offered their assistance. Apparently, he wasn't very friendly but he did say that he was meeting someone." Mark shrugged, running his fingers through his dark hair. "They didn't have any real reason to question him further, but they told me, that his attitude was surly enough that they'd keep an eye on him." His voice held some concern. "I'll let our security team know that someone is behaving oddly and for them to keep an eye out."

Brian nodded, satisfied. "Exactly the right steps to take. See if you can try to relax, Karina. With Mark, the hotel staff and security now watching, you can let them take care of it." Brian motioned to the food. "Let's eat now, before I have to go."

Too busy eating to talk much, Karina's group tucked away the excellent food. The men went back for more, but the women opted for coffee as the second round.

Brian checked his watch. "Only ten minutes to go. I'm going to head up to my room for a minute. I'll see you all in a bit."

Susan turned to Mark. "So. You're a warm, wonderful guy. Why aren't you married?"

"There was someone once. We were very close," he admitted, a sad smile on his face. "But she died years ago. Since then, I haven't found anyone else who made me feel the same way." Both women gasped sympathetically.

"Don't feel bad. She's been gone a long time now. We were high school and college sweethearts. We'd planned to marry when college was over. But she died in a car accident during her last year." Mark was silent for a moment. "Since then I haven't found anyone else quite so special."

Karina squeezed his hand gently. "You will, Mark. You're an exceptional man."

Mark just laughed. "You're a fine one to talk. You've never been married."

Karina smiled wryly. "Touché. But never say never, right?"

Still smiling, the trio trooped back into the seminar just as Brian opened up the next lecture.

"We teach others how to treat us. Therefore, in the scope of a relationship, we can teach our partners how to treat us the way we want to be treated."

This was a new, fascinating concept for Karina. She could see in theory what he meant, but she needed him to go even more in depth.

She was concentrating so hard on his words, jotting quick notes in the margins of her handouts, that it took a moment to realize something had changed. And not in a good way.

"You don't have any right to tell these people how to change their lives," the angry voice exclaimed. "You're just going to mess them up. You poisoned my wife with all that bullshit. She sucked all this garbage in and believed it. Figured it would change her life for the better. Only she decided she didn't want me in her better life. Says I didn't treat her properly. What a load of rubbish. I treated her just fine. And now, she wants a separation. Well, she isn't getting it. I told her that and now I am telling you! You shouldn't have messed with her. You messed with her, which means you messed with me and I'm going to make you pay for that."

Oh God. She knew that voice. Then she recognized the face. *Ian.* The creepy guy from university. The one she'd brushed off that same night she'd spent with Brian.

Ian's voice rose to an angry howl as he stormed to the

front of the room. The edges of his trench coat flapped sharply with each step. With his hair standing on end and red-faced temper, he was an uncontrollable force that wouldn't quit. "You and your high-and-mighty, knows-best attitude. You don't know anything about us. We've been married for almost seven years. Now she says she's not happy. Rot! She just doesn't know what's good for her. And neither do you!"

Arms waving angrily in the air, punctuating his sentences, Ian wound more and more tightly into his rage. "I've been listening to you here today. You're not helping anybody! You're just going to hurt someone else!" He turned to face the horrified audience. "Don't listen to him! Everyone go home and get back to your families. He's a—"

Security burst through the closed doors even as Mark reached the man. Mark grabbed at Ian's wildly moving arms and tugged them backwards. They struggled. Ian's fury intensified. Spittle flew from his lips.

"Let me go, you bastard! You're just as bad as he is."

"That's enough. Calm down!"

"Never! I will be heard!"

Several people jumped from their seats, moving away from the struggling men. Chairs fell over as the room erupted into chaos. Hotel security people raced toward them.

Karina froze, her hand at her throat, too shocked to move.

It appeared Ian hadn't changed – with the exception of becoming even more of a loose cannon. He was generally friendly and smooth, unfailingly polite, until something – anything – went wrong. Then he exploded like a firecracker. And if anyone dared to blame him for something? Heaven help that person. Nothing was ever Ian's fault. Ever. Like now.

Karina couldn't take her eyes off Ian. Did Brian remember him too? How could he not?

"Everyone listen to me…" Ian shouted, refusing to be silent. "This man is dangerous, he needs to be stopped."

The three men pushed, shoved and half carried the intruder toward the double doors. His running tirade never ceased.

"You can't shut me up. I'll be back…!"

The door slammed behind the men, barely drowning out the man's explosive ranting.

Silence descended on the room.

Chapter 5

BRIAN STRODE ACROSS the front of the room before coming to an abrupt halt. He didn't know what to say. He ruffled his short hair. What could he say? He hadn't come up against a situation like this before. Thank heavens for the extra security they had put in place.

And damn the necessity of having to do so.

Ian Blackburn. Jesus. He hadn't seen Ian since university. He'd been strange back then, but never as violent as this. Could he be the one responsible for the threats leading up to this seminar? If what Ian had said during his rant was true — that his wife had left him after attending a workshop — then it was quite possible that Ian blamed Brian. It was a logical explanation, though certainly not reasonable, but then Ian certainly hadn't appeared to be in a reasonable frame of mind when he burst through the doors, screaming.

Brian had to salvage the seminar. Somehow.

"My apologies, everyone. I'm not sure what's going on exactly. Clearly, this man is blaming me for an upset in his life."

Brian paused to think about what he needed to say. "This sort of backlash is always a possibility when one participates in these life-altering workshops, although this is the first time that I've come up against it." He opened his arms wide, turning his palms upwards, hoping for their understanding and acceptance. And that they'd take this example as a lesson to look deeper into their own issues. "That's why we try to look at the real issues, when someone says they're unhappy in their relationship. Sometimes, leaving that relationship *is* the best answer."

Walking slowly across to the podium, he chose his words carefully. It was important to deliver the right message. "You need to look at the underlying cause of your unhappiness. When no other solution is possible, then in some cases, leaving *is* the right answer. However, one person's decision in a relationship will affect both people."

He stopped and cast his gaze around the room, looking at all of the intent faces focused on him. "The repercussions can be severe. Not everyone is willing to work out problems and not everyone can accept change. This type of thing," he said as he gestured toward the double doors, "can be the result."

Mark returned just then, quietly closing out the world behind him. Swiftly, he walked over to Brian and spoke softly into his ear. Brian turned to address his audience.

"Mark has spoken with our visitor." He looked directly at Karina, hoping to settle her nerves. Hell, he could use something to settle his own. "He has calmed down. Apparently, his wife attended a workshop several weeks ago and after that, she asked him for a trial separation. He's having trouble dealing with that." He shrugged. "Obviously, this is a difficult situation for him."

Several heads turned to follow Mark's path as he headed back toward the doors. Brian watched Mark pat Karina on the shoulder as he passed by.

She looked up and caught his gaze, offering him a shaky smile.

She looked slightly better.

Everything would be fine. It had to be.

KARINA TRIED TO stay focused on Brian. Instead of feeling relieved, her uneasiness grew. She studied the other people in the room. Was there any change in their attitude? She searched Susan's features. She seemed fine, normal. Honestly, the audience looked as if they had perked up. Margaret, the barracuda, looked even more fascinated, if that were possible. No one seemed phased by that bit of excitement, the 'something more for their money,' a bit of scandal and drama to take away with them.

A hand gently tapped her on the shoulder. She jumped. She'd been so distracted studying everyone else that she'd missed Mark's return. Now he crouched beside her.

"He's left. Everything's fine."

She peered into his eyes. "Are you sure?"

"Yes. Mr. Blackburn was apologetic and seemed both calm and rational. He said he'd just been overcome when he saw Brian and the emotions were too much for him. He went home a few minutes ago."

"You don't think that he'll be back?" She sensed it wouldn't be that easy. Besides, it seemed to her that earlier, Ian had been looking for Brian the first time she saw him here. As if he'd been stalking Brian.

"No, I don't think so. He did finally say that he no longer blamed Brian. It was his wife's decision to leave that had him so upset."

"That's understandable." She spoke slowly, letting go of her uneasiness. She'd only known Mark for a short time, but she trusted his opinion. "His reaction here makes me wonder if she isn't making the right decision by leaving." She gave a small smile.

Mark grimaced and nodded. "I hear you. We're going to take a break soon. After that there'll be an hour's question-and-answer session and then we'll end with the closing address. A scene like this isn't the best way to finish, but it happens." He shrugged. "We'll have to roll with it." He nodded toward Brian. "That's his signal. We're going to break now."

Mark opened up the double doors, calling out light-heartedly, "I don't know about the rest of you, but I'm ready for a coffee and dessert. Everything's ready, let's enjoy."

The conversation level was loud and lively during the break. Mark and Brian had done their best with damage control, but people needed to discuss the recent events. Some things were just human nature.

Karina stood off to one side, unwilling to be drawn into conversation. Susan had gone to get coffee for them both. Excitement permeated the crowd. It was a heck of a way to finish off the weekend. Brian was saying good-bye to several participants who were leaving early.

Susan returned with coffee and linked arms with Karina. Both women sipped their beverages for several long moments.

Studying her friend, Karina decided a change of topic was in order. A new focus. Something to take her mind off Ian and to direct it forward, into the future.

"You know, Susan," she said, half-jokingly, "awhile ago you talked about starting your own company. What do you think about the idea of starting one together?"

Susan looked at her in surprise. "You know, that isn't such a bad idea. I've wanted to open a toy store since I started my own family."

The two women stopped and stared at each other, the idea rapidly sprouting and gathering steam. Susan continued. "You have the bookkeeping and office experience to be able to tackle the business side of things, don't you?"

"Absolutely. You know, I've often wondered why toy stores don't carry much in the way of educational material. There's a huge home-schooling market. You have the parenting and retail experience and I have the business experience. I wonder what this city has to offer right now, along those lines."

Karina stared off into space, turning the idea over and over in her head. She had some money set aside for a place of her own. It wasn't much, but this way she could be her own boss. Money would be tight for the first while; it always was with new businesses. She'd have to crunch some numbers to get a better idea of the project's viability.

"You know, there are a lot of daycare centers here in Victoria. We could see what their needs are. And I wonder where the school board buys their supplies? We could wholesale materials to them and still supply retail to the public." Susan hopped from foot to foot, unable to stand still in her growing excitement. "Just think, I'd be home part-time and could still bring in some money." She stopped for a moment, considering. "Well, maybe. I guess we wouldn't make much money in the first year, would we?"

"That would depend on what our competition is and on startup costs. If we can't make enough to live on, I can't do it. I have a little money set aside but I'd need to draw a salary from the business." Karina's mind buzzed as figures clicked rapidly in her head.

The idea excited her, and that was a first.

"You do realize that we'd both have to work long hours at the beginning," she continued. "However, instead of you having to go home after school to meet your kids or pay a sitter, if our location is right, your children could come to you at the store. If you needed them to, that is."

Susan looked at her, hope dawning in her eyes. "Do you really think we could? I think you're better at making changes than you think."

Was she? This seemed like a good idea. It felt right. But they were a long way from starting.

Karina shrugged dismissively. "How do you think your husband will like the idea?"

Thoughtfully, Susan said, "I think he just might. He'll be concerned about the size of the investment and the amount of time that I'd be away from the family. If the location were close to home and if the children could come after school or maybe part of the days on a weekend, that would help."

"When you have your own business, you get to make some of your own rules. You never know, maybe I'll get married and have a family one day. I'd like to think that the children could be with me some of the time, at least." Karina backtracked a bit. "Obviously it wouldn't work all the time. But if the children know where you are and that they can come to the store if they need to, it might be enough to make the difference. What ages are they again?"

"Sara is eleven and Michael is eight. Which means if they don't come to where I work they both need someone at home after school." Disappointment crept over Susan's face.

"That's not necessarily a problem. I don't know. This has some real possibilities, Susan."

The women looked at each other, hope growing between

them in leaps and bounds.

"We'll have to do a lot of research first," warned Karina "And we'd have to find the right location." A niggling thought popped into her head. "Susan what did you say your husband does for a living?"

"Paul's in advertising! He could be a real help to us. If he wanted to, that is…" She looked over at Karina, determination on her face. "I'm going to talk to him tonight."

"By the way," Karina asked curiously, "why did you stay at the hotel last night? Couldn't you have driven home instead?"

Susan grinned. "Yes, I could have. On Friday night, I did. But with the late lecture last night and the early-morning start today, my husband suggested that I stay overnight. That was my first night away from my family in over a year."

"And did you enjoy it?"

"It was blissful to get a good night's sleep, but honestly, I missed all of them. Sometimes, that's the trouble with family – you can't live with them and you can't live without them." She laughed at herself. With a shake of her head, she added, "I really do love them, you know."

Karina smiled. How lucky Susan was. She had a husband who loved her and two wonderful children. In addition, she was at a place in life where she could choose a completely new path for herself.

Could they make a business work? Did they have what it would take?

Maybe they did.

"Susan, why don't you do the research for any competition in Victoria and I'll do the Internet stuff and some of the money crunching from my place in Vancouver? We can compare notes over the phone in a couple of days."

"It's a wonderful idea! My sister manages a children's clothing store in my neighborhood. You never know what ideas she might have. It's in a neat mini-mall. What a good location that would be." Susan opened her notebook to a clean page, jotting down some of their ideas. "Karina, any idea what square footage we'd need?"

"Need for what?" interrupted a deep male voice.

"Paul!"

Karina turned in surprise to see her friend engulfed in a stranger's arms.

"What are you doing here?" Susan asked.

The tall, attractive man seemed almost embarrassed; he shrugged and pulled Susan tightly against him. "I missed you. Grandma has the kids so I thought we could drive home together. Maybe we could stop for a special dinner on the way home. If that's okay, that is." He peered closely into her eyes. Whatever he saw seemed to satisfy him. He broke into a wide grin and gave her a kiss on the cheek.

"Maybe you should introduce us," he said. "Your friend doesn't look very sure about me."

Reassured by the delighted smile on Susan's face, Karina grinned. Her friend looked very well adored. "You're her husband, I hope." She smiled warmly as she reached out to shake his hand.

Susan just laughed as she introduced them.

"Susan, if I had known that there'd be other beautiful women here, I'd have come too," he whispered loudly. "She's gorgeous!"

Karina laughed. Glancing around, she noticed Mark and Brian were rapidly approaching with questioning looks on their faces.

"Hi guys." Susan beamed up at them. "This is my husband, Paul. He's just here a little early."

Brian held out his hand. "A pleasure to meet you. We've had a little excitement here today. As such, we're being a little more careful about strangers."

Paul thanked him. "Obviously the 'excitement' involved the seminar. I'm grateful to you both for keeping Susan and all of your other attendees safe. Honey, walk with me to the coffee shop. I'll wait there until you're finished." The two walked away, heads together, deep in intimate discussion.

Karina studied the pair as they walked away. Paul seemed so solid, safe. Dressed in jeans and t-shirt, with his jacket tossed casually over his shoulder, he looked very normal and dependable, and the affection he had for Susan was obvious. With a sigh, she turned back to the two men, who were also watching the couple walk away.

"He surprised me at first," Karina admitted. "But he looks like a nice man."

"I only saw him from the back. With the end of the seminar, there could be a lot of strangers coming in to pick up participants." Mark studied the crowd.

"Karina, I'll drive you to the airport once we wrap things up. Just give me a bit after I close this down." Nodding at Mark, Brian touched Karina briefly on the shoulder and headed in.

Mark followed his progress, speculation in his eyes. "Interesting."

Karina looked over at him curiously. "What is? I mean, we do have a bit of a history, but I haven't seen him in a long time."

Mark grinned down at her. "You never know." He tucked her arm through his and guided her through the crowd. "Maybe this time you'll work things out."

Unable to immediately formulate any kind of response,

Karina just laughed. Really, she didn't know what to think. She hadn't come here looking for a happily ever after. She'd just wanted some closure. But after seeing Brian again, and spending time talking with him, she couldn't help but consider the possibility of more.

A BIT RUSHED, and not quite as dramatic as he'd hoped, but enough to disturb the seminar and shake Brian up. *Good.* He hadn't planned more. Just a simple disruption at this point.

Besides, he hadn't really had time to set a plan in motion. His trip to the hotel had been more to see how these so-called workshops functioned, and to identify any significant people in Brian's life.

The outburst in his seminar was to show Brian that he had no intention of bowing out gracefully. He just needed a little time to figure out a way forward. To deliver justice to those that deserved it. Brian couldn't be allowed to ruin all these lives without feeling the repercussions in a personal way.

No one should.

And Ian was going to show him the error of his ways. Karina's involvement just happened to be a bonus. How perfect that they were both there at the same time. Talk about a two-for-one special.

Maybe he'd get some payback after all. Besides, he had to do something while Mary was 'finding' herself. And having a target for all his anger helped. He grinned.

He hoped Brian enjoyed his gift. The reminder that he was still out there.

Watching.

Waiting.

Chapter 6

BRIAN LOVED DELIVERING the closing address. The seminar might be ending but he'd given the participants valuable information to take away with them. Information to help them take control of their lives. To be the captain of and steer their lives in the direction they wanted to go. Not be a victim of uncontrollable circumstances, never finding happiness or fulfillment. To get on with the lives they were meant to live.

This is what he was meant to do. Too bad it wasn't so easy to apply the same lessons in his own life.

He glanced over the audience loving the connections he made, the friendships he started and the touches he'd made in their lives. He spoke quietly, firmly, with confidence as he tried to inspire them to take his message into their lives and own it. And live it. As he needed to work on living his truth.

Another half an hour, then, finally, it was over.

Every time he finished a weekend seminar, he said it would be the last time. But then after only a few weeks of recuperation he was already planning the next one. They exhausted him and they exhilarated him. When he gave the seminars everything he had, he always came away with more than what he'd brought.

This weekend was a little different. The threatening letters he'd received before the seminar, Ian's disruption and the king of all disruptions – or should he say queen of all disruptions – Karina…

The latter, an event that both delighted and unnerved him.

Her presence had been a huge surprise. One he knew would have a long-reaching impact on his.

Listen to him. He hardly knew Karina as she was today. But he remembered who she'd been…and their one night together. Memories that were both a delight and a torment. An unforgettable night and his unforgiveable behavior.

He had much to make up for.

Now that they'd reconnected, he didn't think he'd ever be able to look at her again and not want her. Her upturned nose, those luscious, smiling lips combined with her intelligent, brilliant blue eyes… Hell, they set him off every time. Her tousled curls cried out to be stroked. Bedroom hair is what he'd call it, always looking like she'd just been made love to.

"Good-bye, Brian. Thanks so much for an informative weekend."

He turned to see who spoke, but calls were coming from all around him as people headed back to their own lives.

Good, soon he could leave, too. He wanted to walk his restlessness out on the beach. Hug his daughter, Chelsea, and listen to her laughter. Return to his normal life and think.

A staff member crossed his line of vision and disturbed his musing. The young man walked up to him, carrying a large florist's box. "Sir, this just arrived for you."

That was a first. Reading the nametag on the man's shirt, Brian said, "Thanks, John. Does it say who it's from?"

"No. There's probably a card on the inside. Do you want to open it here or take it with you?"

"I'll take it home. Would you mind putting it over there, with the cartons stacked up by the double doors?" He nodded at the spot. Even from here, he could smell the heavy scent wafting toward him. Roses. Who would send him roses?

He swiveled quickly, searching for Karina. Would she have sent him flowers? He spotted her in the crowd, chewing on her bottom lip again. Damn it. Brian grinned as he realized Karina's eyes were following the path of the box. She was also frowning.

Their eyes met. She said something to the group she'd been standing with and walked toward him. A smile was trying to poke through, but didn't quite succeed.

"A gift from an admirer, Brian?" Her gaze swiveled to the florist's box again and this time she looked a bit worried. "You must have made a hell of an impression on someone."

Again, part of her bottom lip disappeared into her mouth. Damn it, she *had* to quit doing that.

"Maybe. Although not sure on who though. Not Ian, that's for sure," he joked. Then realized he'd made a mistake as Karina gasped in shock, her gaze zeroing in on the box. He reached over and firmly turned her around so her back was to the box. "I'll take them home to my daughter. She'll enjoy opening them."

"How old is she?" Her gaze warmed. "Does she live with her mom? How often do you see her?"

He answered patiently, having forgotten the universal reaction women had to finding out about Chelsea. "She's three, going on twelve. Chelsea lives with her mom, but comes over regularly. Some weekends she stays with me." Love for his daughter carried through to his voice. He adored his delightful tyrant. "You needn't sound so surprised, children are normal in a marriage."

"Sorry." She laughed, backing up a step. "I'm glad you're so close to her. Too many children are growing up without their fathers today. I didn't mean to get personal."

He barely resisted tugging her closer.

"Are you ready to go?" Karina's question brought him back to their surroundings.

"Is it that time already?" He looked around, surprised. When had it gotten so late?

The lobby had the depressing look of the morning after a party. It was deserted, with coffee cups and dirty plates littering the space. Papers and boxes were stacked against one wall. Lonely piles of luggage dotted the lobby. A few stragglers were still saying their good-byes. The hotel even smelled old and stale…empty.

Susan and Paul were making their way over to them. Paul held out his hand. "Thank you for taking such good care of my wife. She plans to attend your evening lectures, so we'll see you again." He turned to face Karina. "I understand that you and Susan have some big plans that she wants to talk to me about. Presumably, we'll also be seeing you again."

"Most likely. We'll definitely be staying in touch."

The women winked conspiratorially at each other and hugged farewell.

"I'll miss Susan," Karina said, her gaze locked on the couple as they left. "Hopefully we can make our idea work. But there's lots of research to do first," she admitted, a hint of worry in her voice.

"What idea?" He glanced down at her curious at the nervous excitement in her voice.

"We're thinking about going into business together."

After that, she volunteered no more. No matter what question he asked. She'd only say that until the research was complete, she didn't want to do anything that might jinx it. How did that work? Worrying about jinxing something that was still in the idea stage. Still he was glad to hear she was doing her due diligence and not jumping head first into a venture without knowing was she was getting into.

Brian turned his attention back to the room, only to catch Mark grinning at him. He glared back. They'd been friends since elementary school and he sensed Mark was up to something. But Mark's grin only widened.

Walking over to join them, Mark smirked. "A beautiful woman beside you and apparently another one sending you flowers. Tell me Brian, what am I doing wrong?" He smiled down at Karina. "Honey, you don't want to spend any time with this guy. You want to spend it with me," he teased. "When are you going to come and visit?"

She smiled up at him. "You're such a sweetie. And watch what you say – I just might move here."

"You're looking at moving here?" Mark asked. Linking arms with her, he added, "Wow! It's a wonderful idea and yes, *we* want you to move closer." Peering down at her, he added, "This has something to do with Susan, doesn't it?"

Brian stared down at her, thrown off-balance – again. *Karina was looking at moving to Victoria?* He was alternately confused and elated. She was making huge changes in her life. Good for her. And possibly for them. It would certainly be easier to get to know her better if she were close by. He knew long-distance relationships were hard.

She nodded happily at the men but refused to elaborate.

"Well, keep us posted." Mark dug into his shirt pocket. "Here's one of my cards. Let me know when you're coming and I'll scout out something new and different in the coffee world." Mark reached out and pulled Karina into a warm hug. "I'd love to have you closer."

Brian watched as his best friend connected with Karina on an easy, comfortable level. A level he wanted to reach but couldn't get to, yet. But he had hopes.

"Take care and email me that you got home safely. Okay?" With that, Mark kissed her quickly on the cheek. "Brian, I'm loading up the car now. I'll give you a call tomorrow. See you." With a jaunty wave at them both, Mark headed out.

"I'm going to miss everyone." Tears were already starting to well up in her eyes. "I've made some wonderful friends this weekend."

"You'll just have to come and visit us while you plan your move." He slid an arm around her shoulder, nudging her toward his stack of boxes. "Or better yet, move here and we can see where this goes. Come on, let's get your stuff."

After he made arrangements with hotel staff for the courier pickup of his workshop materials, they waited at the entrance until Brian's car was pulled around.

"Wow! Here I had you pegged as a BMW man. But a Porsche, now that shows a completely new side to you."

Brian held open her door, giving him an excuse to stand closer. He caught her dark, sexy fragrance as she moved past him and he closed his eyes briefly. Damn she tempted him.

"This is a relatively new purchase. I felt a little more splash in my life wouldn't hurt." Sheepishly he added, "My last car was a BMW."

They both laughed.

Then she surprised him. "That outburst of Ian's today was seriously disturbing. Even though he was a wild card back in university it's hard to believe he was the same man. Although I did witness a few of his nasty outbursts back then. What about you?" He closed the door for her and moved around to the driver's side. He got in and buckled up and drove out of the hotel parking lot.

"Have you even seen or talked with Ian in the last ten years, or was this as much of a surprise to you as it was to the rest of us?"

"No I haven't." He took his gaze off the road to glance over at her. She seemed really concerned. But then she seemed to have seen Ian's uglier side before. "Honestly I didn't even remember him."

"Really? He seemed so angry. So focused on you personally. I wonder if there is more to it than what he spouted off about his wife?"

Brian shrugged. Who knew what someone as disturbed as Ian might be thinking. He'd rather not think about Ian at all, thank you.

She persisted. "Do you ever get hate mail or nasty phone calls or posts on your website or things like that? Did you…" She breathed deep and finished her sentence. "Did you know his wife?"

That question blindsided him. "What do you mean?" he asked. "No. Ian claims she attended my workshop but I don't remember her." He added, "I guess I can tell you that some things have changed recently. I've received a couple ugly emails, even a note or two but I hadn't connected those to Ian. I spoke to the police and took their suggestion to increase security though." He handled the purring car, with quiet confidence, efficiently pulling in and out of traffic as he brought the sports car onto the freeway.

He stole a glance at Karina, loving the way the very

touchable suede slacks hugged her thighs. She had great legs. There wasn't much he'd forgotten about her that way. The dashboard glowed, giving him just enough light to keep his memories alive.

"Do you think they could've been from Ian?"

He took his eyes off the road to look at her. "It's possible but I doubt it. His actions today appeared to be more the spur-of-the–moment kind. Besides the police already have all the letters I've received over the last couple of months. If they are from Ian, they'll find out."

"Glad to hear it." She'd stretched out her legs, crossing them at the ankles. *Damn, she looks good.* Forcibly he brought his attention back to the road. The rain had stopped and the light traffic was calming, making for an easy drive.

"He asked me out several times while in university. But he always gave me the creeps and I tried to avoid him whenever I could." She hesitated, then added, "He was in the same pub as we were that last night."

"Really? I don't remember much about that night. Honestly."

An uncomfortable silence filled the car and he bit back a groan. That wasn't *at all* what he meant. "Let me clarify. I barely remember the pub, but what happened afterward…yeah, I remember every single minute of that."

He gave her a warm smile, relief flowing over him as she returned it, her smile teasing and so real. He couldn't believe his good fortune that they'd reconnected so well. And that she didn't hate him for his actions so long ago.

"As for the Ian mess… I really don't think we'll ever hear from him again."

She slipped off her shoes and turned toward him, folding her legs underneath her. The dusky interior just barely gave form to the dainty feet resting on the edge of the seat. Her knees were inches from his thighs. Her perfume surrounded him in the tiny space. Heavy and aromatic, it hinted at sultry nights of passion. Memories of them together flooded his thoughts. Again.

"Mark mentioned you're getting ready to start another book."

He forced his attention back to the conversation, hoping that would slow his pulse and reduce the painful tightness in his pants.

"I'd like to, yes." He sighed.

She leaned forward. "Is writing new material hard for you?"

"Not really. I start to crave writing if I'm away from it for too long." In the back of his mind, already half defined, was an outline for his next book. He loved writing. There was a sense of accomplishment in knowing that he'd created something that could help others. It made his purpose in life come alive.

Ever since he was a young boy, he'd known he belonged in the world of words. He'd completed his journalism degree and had even worked editing and writing for various dailies. It wasn't long before he struck out on his own.

He pulled up to the airport drop off. "We're here." He smiled at her in the shadowy interior. "I'll grab your bag."

"Thanks." She smiled back.

Outside, the sky was clear and full of stars. He removed her bag from the trunk and placed it on the sidewalk. She walked to the back of the car and stilled.

He followed her gaze. That damn florist box was in the car.

"Brian, would you mind opening it up?"

He leaned on the black roof and peered at her. "It really bothers you? It's just flowers. Most girls get excited when they see a florist box."

She shrugged, the tiny anxious gesture that made him realize how much the box really did trouble her.

He looked up at the duskiness of early evening that had started to lower itself onto the city. There was an alien feel to the world. The airport was normally unbelievably busy, but right now, everything was quiet – too quiet. Silence reigned.

What the hell. Silently, he reached into the backseat and pulled out the long box. He laid it gently on the shiny hood. He might as well do as she asked. Then she'd relax. Besides, he was more than a little curious, himself.

"Okay, just for you." Without looking away from her, he removed the lid. The heavy aroma of the flowers wafted freely into the night.

"Oh, my God," she gasped in shock.

That got his attention. A dozen black roses nestled inside the florist box. A card rested on top. Scrawled on it in bold black writing, were the words: *I'll be back.*

Chapter 7

THE NEXT MORNING Karina was still upset. And afraid. Even her beloved cats hadn't helped much, stalking around her in disdain. She'd cuddled and cried over them, before hauling them, both still indignant, to bed with her.

Once snuggled in, all she could think about was Brian. On the drive to the airport the night before she couldn't stop watching the way he controlled the car, coaxing it to perform the way he wanted. He was so careful, his touch so sure. The same way he'd handled her body so long ago. Chills ran up and down her spine. Passionate memories made her shiver in delight. She wanted him safe.

But their conversation gave her the impression he wasn't taking this Ian scenario seriously.

She'd had to do something so this morning she'd emailed Mark, making sure he knew about the flowers and threatening note. She'd been blunt. Mark had answered within the hour. He'd talk to Brian.

Then she'd emailed Susan to say she'd arrived home safely. Susan's response was still on her computer screen:

Did he kiss you good-bye?

Typical romantic question. Karina had tried to write a reply several times, but the answer only upset her. Because of course, no, he hadn't kissed her good-bye. Whether he'd wanted to or not didn't matter because she hadn't given him a chance. She'd been so upset over the flowers that she'd quickly grabbed her bags and walked inside – alone.

Earlier she'd bitten the bullet and sent Brian an email thanking him for the ride. She'd kept it short but friendly and added her phone number. Now it was a question of waiting to see if he'd respond.

The phone rang and Karina's heart jumped into her throat. *It couldn't be Brian already, could it?*

"Karina? How was the weekend seminar?"

Cat. Karina laughed. "Oh, my God! It was unbelievable." The words tumbled freely for the next half hour as she caught her friend up on the remainder of the weekend. Karina chose to deliberately focus on the positives rather than Ian Blackburn and his strange behavior.

When she hung up, her mood was lighter and happier than it had been all day. That was what friends were for.

Several hours later, she lugged her heavy grocery bags into the elevator then slumped against the back wall as it rose to her floor. It was amazing how exhausted she could be after doing absolutely nothing for most of the day. Finally, she'd had to just get out for a bit, and had run to the store to pick up coffee beans. Somehow that had turned into three full bags of food.

She checked her phone and found there'd been one call but the caller had hung up. Disappointed that there was no message from Brian, she put on coffee and curled up to enjoy it on the sofa.

Rejuvenated by the caffeine hit, she first checked to see if Brian had answered her email. He hadn't. Unfortunately. However, Susan was up and running. She'd made several phone calls to gather information on educational supply outlets in Victoria, even garnering Paul's support for the business idea.

Now it was Karina's turn to do some fun research. Her fingers danced across the keyboard as she started her search, focusing first on educational materials for elementary schools before losing herself for hours on products.

The phone rang while she was in the bathroom. She ran for it, but didn't make it. She checked the phone. Again, no message. Too bad she didn't have call display. Probably just another telemarketer.

When it rang again, she snatched it up.

"Susan, hey." She jammed the phone between her ear and shoulder. Catalogues surrounded her and reams of sheets filled with figures covered her sofa. Mugs, her tabby, had tried sleeping on her lap, but gave up in disgust. Misty, the calico and the smarter of the two, had stayed away from the beginning.

"Karina. You're never going to believe what I found to-day!" Susan's voice bubbled in a continuous stream over the phone. "The perfect location! It's in the same block as my sister's store. Even better, there used to be an excellent toy store there years ago. I spoke with the property owner, who owns close to half the buildings in that mall…"

"Oh, but—"

She never got a chance. Susan ran right over her.

"He's interested in seeing another toy store going in there…" The words poured through the line, and her enthusiasm was contagious, even over the phone.

Karina started to laugh. "I wanted to phone you," Karina said in between her giggles, "to tell you that I found a wonderful store owner who gave me a huge list of suppliers to deal with. She was fantastic. She gave me advice, hints, tips and shared lots of her start-up woes."

There was silence on the other end of the phone. Susan's voice came across, soft and subdued. "Karina, are we going to do this? Is this for real?"

"I think so. Yes. We still have things to sort out, lawyers to see, finances to arrange, but if the financials work...I think we can do this."

Quiet reigned, as both women contemplated the big step before them.

"Susan, I think I'll go and talk to my bank manager tomorrow."

"At least then you'll know what your options are. Paul and I need to talk and maybe make an appointment at our bank, too. I honestly don't know where our finances are."

"True. Look, let's talk tomorrow after we've both sorted through some of the logistics and we'll see where we are then. Can you email me the address of the potential store location you mentioned? I'll Google it and see what it looks like."

"Good idea. Will do. Tomorrow, then."

Karina looked down at the phone. Everything was happening so fast. It scared her, but it also excited her. In a short while, she could be living in a completely new world.

In the same city as Brian. And without Cat or Serena. She was meeting her friends tomorrow at their favorite lunch spot. At least it had been before they'd all been laid off from the same company.

She couldn't help seeing how much her life had changed. Was changing. And how much it was still going to change.

What was she getting into? And could she really trust the changes to lead her forward into good things? A better life? And now that she'd reconnected with Brian, as a friend, could she accept that — not expect and want more?

THE BUSTLE OF the crowded restaurant hit Karina as soon as she stepped inside the door. The lunch crowd had already filled the popular fusion bar and most tables. Hopefully her friends had arrived early, otherwise there'd be no hope of snagging a table today. And she badly needed to sit down and recuperate. Talk about a crazy morning.

"Karina!"

Spotting a tall blonde waving madly at her from the back corner, Karina worked her way to the rear of the restaurant. She grabbed the single empty chair at the table and plunked herself down, so happy to get off her feet. "Hi, Cat. Serena. So good to see you. Wow is this place packed, or what?"

"Serena and I got here about twenty minutes ago," Cat said, tossing back her long blond hair. She looked Karina over then wrinkled up her face. "You look like you've gone through the wringer. Bad night?"

Karina laughed.

"I've considered all the pros and cons. And been to the bank. I'm going to do it." There, she'd said it. She leaned forward and whispered. "I'm moving to Victoria and starting my own business. Well, a business with Susan."

Karina grinned at the blank looks on their faces. The shock didn't last long. In tandem both of the girls' faces lit up.

"Wow and double wow. Well good for you. Victoria is a great spot to vacation. I think we need more wine." Cat didn't waste any time, raising her arm to flag a passing waitress.

Affectionately, Karina studied her friends. Serena

was…well, serene. She preferred the constancy and normalcy of routine. Cat, on the other hand, would have made a perfect action-movie heroine. She had so much stage presence she was hard to overlook. But it wasn't ego. Cat was all about self-confidence.

"Yes, Serena, I've thought long and hard about this. After coming back from the workshop, it's as if I've suddenly outgrown my life and need to move on."

"This is partly about Brian, isn't it?"

"Yes and no. The business has nothing to do with him. Location also has nothing to do with him. Susan can't move, and I have no reason not to. Except I'll miss both of you… The rest? Well…"

Cat lifted her goblet to clink with the other women's glasses. "Welcome to change!"

The others laughed and clinked glasses before all taking big sips of merlot. Serena chuckled. "Here I thought I was the only one considering starting my own business," she admitted. "Although I'm not going to be as fast at it as you, Karina. I've taken a few free government courses on starting up a small business."

The other two gaped at her.

"What? You have?" Karina stared at her friend. "Why didn't you say so before?" She studied her friend's face for a moment, and suddenly knew. "A bookstore, I bet."

Serena smiled.

"In honor of your grandmother?" Serena's grandmother had passed away a year ago, leaving her a nice-sized inheritance. Her grandmother's death had devastated Serena, who'd been raised by the older woman. And her grandfather had been an author before he'd passed on years ago. Books were in their blood and always had been.

Karina's guess startled a laugh out of Serena. "You know me so well."

"Well, this is an opportunity. Why not consider moving to Victoria to be close to me, then. If you can set up anywhere, Victoria is a great location."

Karina turned to raise a brow at Cat. "And you? What are your plans?" Karina considered how different each of their lives were. Serena, although not wealthy enough to do as she wished in life, had enough set aside from her grandmother to be able to live quite nicely for some time. Catherine, on the other hand, came from a wealthy family and had done government contracts in software security prior to her stint at BB Dominos Securities – where Karina had been in the accounting department.

Cat just smiled. "I'm thinking of doing something really crazy for a while. Not the rest of my life. Just a few months' hiatus."

Serena laughed. "Crazy is what I expect from you. Your brain is the most weird and wonderful thing imaginable. So what is it this time? Secret spy stuff? More high-level security contracts? What?"

As she watched her friend, Karina knew Cat wasn't going to give away her plans right now. She'd share when she was ready – maybe. She was perfect for secret spy stuff. That girl never gave anything away. "Just make sure it's safe, please."

The waitress arrived with another carafe of wine and filled their glasses.

"And this is about moving on with your life." Cat held up her glass for another toast. "To new beginnings." She smiled at Karina, and added, "New beginnings and second chances."

Karina raised her glass and smiled back. "To change. Whether thrust upon us, chosen, or wanted, we've reached a turning point in all our lives. Let's celebrate and raise a little hell as we walk drunkenly down our chosen paths."

With that, the three knocked back the rest of the wine in their glasses and signaled the waiter to refill them once more.

SHE HAD HER first nightmare about Ian that night.

Sweat soaked her skin as she lay trembling to regain her breath. Logically, she understood what was happening, but that didn't help her emotionally.

Mugs jumped on the bed, and Karina hugged him, petting him until his contented rumbles filled the air. Still, it took a long while before she felt calm enough to sleep.

Hours later, the persistent ringing of the phone disturbed her heavy dreams.

"Hello?" a disoriented Karina murmured sleepily into the phone.

Heavy breathing echoed over the line. Suddenly wide awake and filled with terror, she bolted upright. "Hello? Who is this?"

"What's the matter, Karina, don't you remember me?"

The phone went dead.

Crap. Not a great way to start her morning.

She stared down at the handset as chills raced down her spine. She closed her eyes, wrapping her arms tightly around her chest. It was Ian. It had to be him. She didn't know how he'd gotten her phone number, but with the Internet these days anything was possible. The fact was, he had it.

Now what did she do?

The phone rang again, startling her. She stared at it.

Should she answer? A flare of anger spiked through the fear. If it was Ian again, maybe the call could be traced or something. She picked up the phone but waited.

"Karina?"

Her breath gusted out at the familiar voice. "Hi Brian."

"Are you all right, Karina? You don't sound like yourself."

"No. I mean, yes. I'm sorry. I just had a disturbing call." She quickly told him about it. "Instinctively, I want to say it was Ian but I don't know for sure."

"And why would Ian call you?"

"I don't know," she admitted softly. "But he could have recognized me at the seminar."

There was a thoughtful pause on the line; she could almost see the wheels turning in Brian's head. "I'll call the police here and tell them. Meanwhile you could have the number blocked if you have it on call display, or notify the authorities if you're really worried. You might get a call from the police here after I speak with them. At least they'll be in the loop."

"Thank you." And she meant it. She no longer felt so alone. An unruly yawn slipped out. "I had such a bad night and that was before Ian's call."

"Nightmares?"

"Yes," she answered slowly. "Susan and I are making headway on opening a store together and it will mean a move to Victoria. Something I was looking forward to, but…"

"But it's a big change. A lot of upheaval in your life. Yes, I can see that might trigger nightmares."

"I'm female. Worrying is part of our general makeup." She laughed lightly to cover up the struggle to find the words to express what she wanted to say. "Brian…" Her voice trailed off.

"What?"

She had worried about the roses and the note Brian received, and now the mysterious hangup and phone call that came to her directly. "Do you think he could be *really* dangerous?"

"Ian is an unhappy soul and needs to accept the changes in his life. In that way, he's no different than you or me."

"You always seem to have it so together. It seems impossible that you could have anything to work on."

"Not true – everyone, everywhere has something to work on. Just because I write books and teach seminars doesn't mean I don't have issues. If anything I'm more conscious of the issues and how much I *do* have to work on."

Karina winced. That had to be difficult to admit. "You must always be under pressure to be a little better than everyone else."

"Which, of course, I'm not. However, people see me in that light, which adds pressure, yes – but I can't let that rule my life. Anymore than you can let Ian and his warped nature rule your life."

"I know," she answered soberly. "I guess I'm worried." Her voice dropped to a soft whisper. "I'm glad you called."

"Good. I called because I wanted to hear your voice." She could hear the smile in his voice. "Now tell me what you and Susan are up to."

AFTER THAT NIGHT, things moved at breathtaking speed.

It took several weeks for everything to fall into place. Several weeks in which she received three more suspicious, nerve-racking phone calls – all silent. Three more weeks of coffee dates with Serena, hashing over business stuff, and luncheons with Cat. And extracting promises from both friends that they'd come to visit.

Now that her apartment had been sublet, and was empty, her car was packed, and the cats caged and strapped in the passenger seat. She was almost ready to go.

Susan and Paul were expecting her to arrive at their place that afternoon. They were going to work together over the next few crazy weeks. Several orders for merchandise had already been paid for and were on the way. Opening day was in a month's time and they still had a lot to do. Cat and Serena were delighted for Karina and wished her success though they would miss each other. She reminded herself for the dozenth time that they weren't going to be that far away. Victoria was only a few hours' drive or a short flight. And who knew where they were going to end up? She could only hope it worked out for them, too.

Mark had called one night too. That was a surprise, a pleasant one. When he heard their plans he had volunteered to help with the painting and handyman stuff. But that was Mark.

Brian had been a calm, rational sounding board helping her to work through many of the business issues. His schedule was going to be crazy because he was out of town much of the next few weeks.

Karina realized just how much she was enjoying change. These last weeks had been both cathartic and energizing. She felt so in charge of her life. Dynamic and strong in ways she never could have imagined.

And here she was putting all those plans into place.

The arrangement was to meet Mark at a Starbucks just inside the city limits. He was bringing her a city map and said he'd provide easy directions to Susan's place. She'd already Google-mapped it and had directions printed off, but who was she to decline an invitation for coffee? She doubted that Brian would be there, but she hoped he might be.

She'd thought a lot about him since his seminar series and their time together. She wasn't a bit conflicted about what she wanted, regarding him. She just wanted to make sure the approach was right this time.

Hours later, she pulled her silver Toyota Matrix into the busy parking lot. She was exhausted. The cats had howled in tandem for the first hour. She'd tried to drown out their screeches by turning up the radio. But her eardrums had pounded back in retaliation. She'd given up and with the help of Tylenol she'd managed to ignore them for the remainder of the trip.

She got out slowly, leisurely stretching her back and rolling her shoulders to loosen up the tension. Although she was a few minutes late, she'd made good time. *Was Mark here already?*

She turned and scanned the area. And saw… *Brian!*

His car was backing out of a space behind her. His face turned away from her. She walked in front of his car to get his attention and then continued around to his side. His face brightened, a light coming into his dark eyes.

She'd come so far hoping to see him and here he was, leaving. Tired, she gave in to the emotions overwhelming her.

She leaned forward in the car and slipped her hand down his cheek to cup his square jaw firmly, tilting it up toward her. She paused, looking at him closely. This face had driven her crazy for months, maybe years. It was just as angled and gorgeous as it always had been. The chiseled lips opened to speak. Instantly, she took advantage and lowered her head.

And kissed him. Thoroughly.

THERE SHE WAS.

He lifted his cell phone and snapped a picture.

Click. And again. *Click.*

Ian grinned so wide it damn near hurt his cheek muscles. He'd guessed that one right. After seeing them at the seminar and recognizing her, he knew she mattered to Brian. Damn right, she did. Now *that* was a kiss.

And that reminded him of Mary. And the last time he'd kissed her.

He loved Mary.

He missed her.

That she was continuing to keep him out of her life, hurt. And angered him.

He'd searched her sister's place. There was no sign of her. Where could she have gone? Her boss said she'd taken time off work. Then again, so had he.

He'd even finally broken down and called his mother-in-law. She'd hung up on him.

Bitch.

He stared at the other bitch – this one standing in his line of vision.

He'd called Karina several times, not to interfere, but to keep tabs on her whereabouts. Today he'd gotten an out-of-service message. If it was possible, he grinned even more widely. So maybe that meant she'd moved here. Closer to Brian.

He'd have to track down a new phone number for her,

but that wouldn't be too hard. He could only hope that she'd moved here permanently.

And given that kiss she'd just laid on him, the two of them were an item. Perfect.

Rejuvenated, with a new feeling of purpose in his life, Ian started up his car and backed out of the lot, careful to keep out of their sight and avoid attracting attention. He didn't want them to see him until he was ready to be seen.

Things had definitely changed. And in a good way.

Pay back was just around the corner… He owed Brian for siccing the police on him, for them hassling him. Thankfully he had an alibi to give them. For then. They didn't know about the other times. Now to stay focused.

And maximize the damage.

Chapter 8

S HE TOOK A step back from the Porsche and smiled coolly down at his astonished face. Now *that* she was proud of. Not to mention that the heat thrumming through her body had left a silly grin on the inside.

"Wow! Well that was quite a 'hello there,' Karina." Brian looked stunned as he killed the engine and snapped open the car door. His abrupt movement forced her back a step and put her off balance. He wasted no time; reaching out with both hands he pulled her into his arms. He pivoted smoothly, pinning her against the side of the car. He slid his thigh between hers, creating an intimate cage that did crazy things to her insides.

"Now it's my turn."

His kiss was hot. His mouth captured hers, consuming her and rendering her helpless with its heat. And she loved it.

Surrounding her physically, he overwhelmed her senses. Just like he had ten years ago. Sensuously, he took his time — and her breath. His lips played with hers, caressing them, teasing them and then delving deeply within. His legs trapped hers elegantly, like steel rods locking her in place.

Held within his arms, Karina was helpless against the erotic and passionate onslaught. A moan escaped her. She didn't care. Her blood pounded, her body heated and her breasts swelled. She twisted against him, desire rising from within. He kept her pinned, immobile, vulnerable...*as if she was his.*

Then she was free, at least from his arms, though her body was still captive to the sexual heat burning through her.

Then it was over. He gently set her away from him. She stood there, mute and still trembling.

"Welcome to Victoria, Karina." He dropped a gentler kiss on the tip of her nose. "I have to run, but I'm really glad you're finally here." With that, he climbed into his car and drove off.

It took several minutes for the other voice trying to get her attention, to pierce through the fog in her brain.

"Karina! Karina, come back to earth, please. You're crushing my ego. No girl has ever reacted to *my* kiss like that." Gently, Mark smoothed back her curls.

She turned to look up at the welcoming face. It was Mark – friendly, uncomplicated, giving, Mark. She walked straight into his comforting arms.

"Come inside. It's definitely coffee time. You look positively shattered."

They walked into the café, arms comfortably wrapped around each other. Karina felt emotionally and physically drained.

She let Mark lead her to a table and go for coffee while she composed herself. He returned, smiling with two extra large cups and many unspoken questions. He waited patiently while she took a few sips of the brew, then raised a questioning brow.

What to say? Finally she settled on honesty. "Mark, have you ever kissed someone and felt the world fall down around you? Been given a touch of heaven only to wake up the next morning and realize it was all a fantasy?" Her sense of balance was back, her feet firmly planted in the real world, yet the sense of wonder evoked by the amazing kiss was still with her. She hoped that feeling would remain forever.

"If I gauge my response by your reaction to *that* kiss, then I'd have to say no. Unfortunately." He added mockingly, "Brian has just set a new height for me to try to reach. Knock a woman senseless, with just one kiss. Next time we meet try greeting me the way you did Brian. Then we'll see."

"Cute, Mark," Karina shot him a look as she tried in vain to rebalance her world.

"He really means something to you, doesn't he?"

"Oh definitely, but the question is – what?" She flushed. She stared down at her cup and played with the handle. "I hated him for a long time, you know. Maybe hate isn't the right word, but…it's not far off the mark. I was definitely angry." She closed her eyes at the searing memory, before opening them to carry on. "But once I saw him again, it's like all those years of disappointment and pain disappeared. I just wish I knew what he wants from me now."

"It's hard to know how Brian is feeling at any given time."

"Really?" She smiled at him wanly. "I hope he's suffering – badly."

"Now, now. You're just mad that he scrambled your brains so easily." He smiled at her engagingly. "Really, maybe you should let me kiss you like that. Maybe it's island men and not just Brian."

She laughed in delight, her good humor restored. "I don't think so, but nice try." Karina took Mark's hand in hers and gave it a squeeze. "Thanks for being so great." She turned her attention to her purse, pulling out a pen and a notepad. "I've got to focus on other things now. Would you mind showing me the map?"

In fact, it was past time to get moving. She would be renting a basement suite from Susan's sister. Sandra was waiting for her at Susan's house. Then they'd carry on to Karina's new home.

Pulling into Susan's driveway later, Karina was still reflecting on the vagaries of fate. Why put a wonderful man like Mark in her life, but omit that spark of attraction then turn around and put a complex man like Brian in front of her, and load her hormones with gunpowder?

Thankfully, the afternoon was boisterous and lots of fun – a perfect distraction from the events of the morning. Sandra, a single parent of twin eight-year-old sons and the house, full with four adults and four children, provided little peace and quiet. However, no one noticed. Raised as a single child, Karina had no idea what normal families were all about. She was finding out, pretty darn fast.

Now that the men and children had disappeared from the room, Karina took advantage of the privacy. Quickly she shared the afternoon's parking lot scene with the sisters.

"I'm not going to run after him," Karina stated firmly. "At least not yet," she added with a grin.

All of the women laughed.

Paul, who'd just joined them, added, "You might need some help if you do catch him. He's twice your size."

"That's it; no short jokes, please. Besides I am not that small," she complained smacking her fist against the table and staring them down.

"Are you sure you want to live in our basement apartment?" Sandra asked. "My boys are going to drive you nuts."

"I'm going to love it," she replied honestly.

AND SHE DID. Every day she went home tired, but happy. Covered in paint or dust, always bruised and sore, but satisfied with her day's work. She texted about every stage of the shop's evolution to Serena and Cat, loving that they wanted to be kept in the loop about what was happening.

She was really comfortable in the brightly lit basement apartment that was part of Sandra's house. It was small, cozy and managed to get a lot of natural light. Best of all, it was within her budget. The twin boys were a built-in benefit. They adored the cats. She'd tried to warn them about cats being independent and snobbish, only to watch in amazement as the cats instantly adopted the boys. *Go figure.*

Misty and Mugs settled in with aplomb. After being stuck in an apartment all their lives, their first taste of freedom in the yard outside was mesmerizing. They'd tiptoed through the grass, mystified by the new world around them.

Most days she visited with either Sandra or Susan. Always, she found herself surrounded by the kids. Sandra's twins, in particular, seemed to think Karina was theirs.

"She lives in our house, so she's ours," they'd yell at Michael and Sara.

"She is not. She came here to be with us. So she's ours."

Their mothers just laughed. Karina found it wonderful and disconcerting at the same time. The children had taken to her immediately, even with her lack of experience. She loved it, but found their unconditional acceptance a little daunting. She didn't want to let them down.

Mark was standing outside the store when she arrived one morning. Dressed in jeans and an old t-shirt, he looked rough and masculine.

Karina fished out her keys. "Have you been waiting

long?"

"Not really; just a few minutes."

"The real question is, are you ready to work? I'm going to put all those big muscles to good use today. We want to finish putting up the rest of the shelves and change some of the lighting fixtures."

"I'm yours for the day, ma'am." He bowed with an old-fashioned flourish.

"Charming, sir; just charming." She fluttered her eyelashes back at him. "Now get your butt in here."

"Wow, this is huge." Mark wandered into the half-finished chaos, pausing in wonder.

"I know and supplies and merchandise are already arriving. We're storing most of it at Susan's and Sandra's until we get the interior finished."

"Let's get at it, then."

Susan arrived an hour later with coffee and fresh cinnamon buns.

"Boy, are we glad to see you," Karina said, grateful for the break and the treat.

"Karina, this looks so good."

"Do you think so? All I can see is how much more there is to do." Karina gratefully took a sip of her coffee while Susan gushed about the new products.

"You're going to love the huge teddy bears. I thought we could give one away on opening day. Maybe a draw or a door prize to give the 100th person to walk through the door. Something like that."

"That works." Karina smiled. "Maybe I should buy one for myself."

"Karina," Mark said with a grin, "you do that, and I'm going to tell Brian you sleep with a teddy bear because he's too slow to get his act together."

Mark easily dodged the wadded-up ball of napkins that flew his way, all the while guffawing with laughter.

"Don't get mouthy or I'll find lots more work for you," she threatened.

However, by the end of the day, having the extra pair of hands to help had made a tremendous dent in the workload. From the chaos a real store was emerging.

By noon the following day, Karina was putting the final touches on painting the nursery corner. Unicorns and teddy bears gamboled on a grassy hill beneath a brightly colored rainbow.

She was so engrossed in her work she barely heard the door open.

BRIAN STALLED IN the open doorway of Karina's new store. What a picture.

Karina probably wouldn't have appreciated his view, dressed as she was in shorts and a ratty old t-shirt, but he sure was. Her unconscious grace and wholesome beauty were stunning. Just then she leaned forward over the top of the ladder. Her shorts rode up just a bit more, tantalizingly close to giving him a view of her gently rounded cheeks. The muscles in her bare legs worked to hold her at the strained angles on tiptoe, and shifting to one leg… Perfect.

He swallowed. Hard.

Karina's t-shirt had fallen forward, moving with her swaying body hiding, then hinting at a taut belly. The material covering one shoulder had slipped down, the top too large and old to properly keep its shape, showing another bit of smooth skin and just a hint of pink straps.

Brian unbuttoned the top of his shirt, feeling an intense rush of heat.

Why had it taken him so long to get here? He couldn't find a reason as his simmering emotions flared up at the sight of her.

WITH AN INNER sixth sense suddenly kicking in, Karina realized she was no longer alone. She twisted around quickly, the ladder making an ominous creaking noise.

Brian.

"Careful." Brian raced to her side to hold the ladder for her.

Descending carefully, she tried to corral her thoughts. "Brian. What are you doing here?" She mentally kicked herself for sounding flustered. Even more agitated, she put her paintbrush down on the step and tried to clean her hands on the paint rag. She ended up smeared from elbow to fingertip.

"Here. Let me help." Brian reached out and held her hand firmly and proceeded to clean up the streaks on her skin.

She smiled her thanks.

"What are you doing here? Not that I'm not delighted to see you, of course." This time she got her voice right, cool and casually friendly.

"Mark told me he'd helped out yesterday. I just got out of a meeting and thought I'd come by and see for myself…maybe steal you away for lunch." He glanced down at his suit pants ruefully. "I didn't realize you were still painting or I could have brought a change of clothes. Maybe I could come by tomorrow?" He surveyed the bright interior with approval. "This is quite the store you have put together."

"Thanks for the offer but we're actually done with the bull work. I'm just adding touch ups." She returned to his invitation. "And I'd be delighted to have lunch with you."

She took him to meet Sandra on the way to the restaurant.

"So you're renting a basement suite from her?" he asked.

"Yes. So far it's working really well. The whole family is great."

Karina kept the lunch conversation light and friendly as they ordered meals and then ate. She told him about the opening day plans and the new computer system they were trying to get up and running. Brian shared that he'd be leaving town in a few days for another weekend seminar – his last for a while, as he was getting ready to sit down and write again.

"I'm going to be starting a weekly lecture series on Thursday nights. It'll run for six weeks, and then I'm taking a break."

"That sounds great. Maybe I'll take it and perhaps I can get Sandra and Susan to come along, too." Karina pulled out her day planner, a major necessity now and wrote down the dates. If nothing else, it would give her an excuse to see Brian again.

"I'm sorry to miss the grand opening. I'm going to be out of town."

"Don't worry about it. Stop by when you get back, if you can. The store will be up and running by then."

They walked out into the bright sunshine.

"I'll do that. By the way – how are the nightmares?"

She stopped walking and looked up at him, a little disconcerted by the caring question. A warm light in his chocolate eyes eased the tension of the question. Because of course, the nightmares were still bad.

A gentle masculine hand covered hers. "That bad, huh?" he asked.

Karina sighed. "I'm dealing with them. Hopefully, they'll go away soon." She brightened. "At least I'm not getting prank calls here."

He nodded. "Good. We haven't heard any more from Ian, so I imagine his marital issues have been dealt with and he's calmed down by now. Give it a little time. Your life has changed so much in the last few weeks that it's bound to carry into your dream state." He nodded toward the storefront. "Go back to your painting. I'll see you when I get back next week."

Uncertainly, Karina turned to go back inside the store. "Thanks for lunch."

Her mind was a whirl. Anticipation and letdown roiled into one emotion – confusion. That was it, no kiss, no invitation for another get together; just a casual friendly, 'I'll see you next week.' Well, what did she expect?

Then he did it.

"Oh by the way…" He turned back, tugged gently on her arm and wrapped her in his embrace.

His lips stroked and caressed, coaxing hers to open then dipped his tongue inside, igniting her passion. It was just like last time – but he'd initiated this searing kiss. And this time her body knew what to expect. Her lips trembled under the onslaught, answering his heat with intense flames of her own. Her body melted fully against him, yielding to his strength, surrendering to her passion. Liquid heat flowed through her, pooling, swelling and tormenting.

Karina barely heard the whistles or the catcalls from the

onlookers. The world existed just for the two of them.

Just as fast as the passion burned, Karina was left standing alone, watching him walk away.

"Damn it. Quit doing that," she yelled at his retreating back.

His laughing voice called back, "Quit doing what?"

"Scrambling my brains, then leaving!"

"Hold that thought until I get back." He glanced at her, the dark depths of his eyes piercing her heart, the heated promise in his gaze stealing her breath.

That louse, he knew she wouldn't be able to think of anything else now. She tried to come up with the perfect response.

Too late. He was gone. *Again.*

IN THE MURKY darkness of a deep Victoria night, anger and pain and hate filled Ian's mind.

Life had gone from bad to worse. Not only had his wife, Mary, decided that their separation was a good idea, but she'd gone one step further and had asked for a divorce.

Ian was going to lose it all.

He'd tried talking to her. He'd told her how much he needed her. Nothing had worked. Nothing he said had made a difference.

Then he tried threatening her. She'd hung up on him. Breaking his heart. Breaking him. After all this time. Now she'd disappeared again. And he had no idea where she was. And damn he'd tried. He'd checked out every spot he could think of. She'd disappeared. How she could afford time off work, he didn't know. She didn't have any money of her own. He'd made sure of that.

She'd never have done this before and she couldn't have done this on her own. Someone had to be helping her.

She'd changed.

And he knew who was to blame.

In the dead stillness of the night, he started making concrete plans to head in the only direction left open to him. Thank God Karina had moved here. Just in time and just for him.

He knew where she lived now. She also had cats.

Now he had multiple targets.

And multiple ways to inflict maximum pain on the two people who'd fucked up his life.

Second Chances

Book 2

Second Chances...at Love

Dale Mayer

Chapter 1

O PENING DAY WAS chaos. Fun. Exciting.
And absolutely nuts.

It started with a huge delivery of balloons and flowers from Brian with a card saying, *So proud of you. Wishing you all the best.* Talk about making her day. She grinned all morning.

Karina had never seen that many people in one place before. And never for something she'd worked so hard to set in place. Paul had taken on the challenge of their advertising and made it shine. Balloons floated out of the store with children attached. Mothers and fathers walked out carrying multiple bags, as full of happiness as their giddy children.

She and Susan answered endless questions and ran the till until they were both ready to collapse. Thank heavens Paul and Mark showed up to help. Sandra had also flitted in and out throughout the day.

It was a smashing success.

Closing time came and went, but the store was too full to notice. By the time the store had emptied and they'd finished cleaning up, the dinner hour was long past. Mark and Susan looked the way Karina felt – exhausted beyond belief.

"Well, I don't know about anyone else, but this is definitely a pizza day for me. How about you guys?"

Too tired to do anything but nod, adults and children agreed.

Susan turned to Mark. "Come and join us. You worked hard today. The kids are too tired to ruin the peace and quiet we all need."

Mark agreed.

Karina stayed behind to phone in the order. For all her bone-weary fatigue, she was smiling. They'd really done it!

The day's sales were a good start toward paying the bills. More than that, the incredible community response showed how happy everyone was to have a local toy store back.

The flashing light on the store's answering machine alerted her to phone calls they'd missed. Karina hit the play button, with pen and paper in hand.

Brian's warm voice filled the store. "Karina. I'm sorry I couldn't make it to the store today, but I wish you every success on this day. I'll call you at home later."

Tired but happy, she immediately dialed his number. "Hi Brian. I'm sorry I missed your call. And thank you so much for sending the flowers. It was a lovely way to start the day."

"Good. I'm glad to hear that. You aren't still at the store are you?" he asked in amazement.

She did her best to stifle a yawn. "Yes. We couldn't even close the doors until an hour after scheduled closing. Then we still had to clean up. I'm about to pick up pizzas and head to Susan's. We had a phenomenal day."

"Excellent. I'm sorry I missed it. You've been through a lot getting to today. You must be exhausted."

"Definitely an early night for me," she agreed. "I wanted to tell you that both Susan and I would be at the lecture Thursday. Sandra might come as well."

"Good. I'll see you then. Get your pizzas and get some rest."

"I will." Karina smiled into the phone. "Thanks for calling, Brian. It means a lot."

"I wanted you to know that I was thinking about you on your big day."

"Thank you." Karina grinned as she replaced the phone. Amazing how that simple connection could dispel the day's fatigue, at least for a few minutes.

BY THURSDAY, KARINA and Susan were finding their rhythm at the store. Business was steady, as dwindling inventory showed. They were already planning to reorder from several wholesalers. That evening, Karina dressed with extra care. This was the first of Brian's new seminars and boy, had she come a long way. And so had her relationship with Brian. They spoke on the phone every night. He'd stopped by several times and stolen her away for lunch. They hadn't taken it further than passionate kisses. That was good. She didn't want to start a relationship in bed. Not again. Of course, with the heat that flared every time he touched her that temptation became harder and harder to resist.

Susan and Karina were pleased with how smoothly things were going with their new business, though there'd been a few incidents that had them wondering if they'd upset someone in the neighborhood... Like graffiti on their store entrance, and the garbage dumped in front of their big display window – but those had been more irritating than scary. She'd mentioned them to Brian and he'd been concerned but not unduly worried at this point.

Tonight felt like another turning point in their relationship. It both terrified her and excited her. Could they now move forward? And if so, where would their journey take them?

The lecture hall was packed, as always. Mark was at the door handing out information sheets. Karina was so busy chatting with her friends Susan and Sandra, she didn't notice Brian approaching. A gentle fingertip stroked her cheek as he walked past, bringing bright red to her cheeks. She stared straight ahead, trying to ignore the curious looks from those seated around her. The caress lingered in her mind for a long, long time.

At coffee break, the group gathered in a corner.

"Good evening, ladies. How is everyone?" Brian asked as he approached.

Other people joined the group, leaving no opportunity for personal conversation. Yet threads of intimate energy continued to ebb and flow easily around them. Brian shifted closer to Karina and murmured in her ear. "How's the store doing? Are you happy with your decision to open the store?"

"Excellent." Karina beamed. "I was thinking just this afternoon about how far I've come since that weekend seminar. It's been wonderful."

"Good. That's the way it should be." He paused for a moment. "I was hoping you'd come for lunch at my place on Sunday. I can pick you up if you'd like. Come meet my daughter and spend a lazy afternoon at the beach with us." With that, he walked out of the room.

The two other women immediately closed ranks around Karina. "What was that all about?" Susan whispered.

Karina hugged her friend, bouncing with barely re-strained excitement. "He's invited me to his place on Sunday. I'll get to meet his daughter."

"Then he's serious," Sandra announced. Both women nodded knowingly at Karina.

"No one introduces a special friend to their children unless they're serious," Susan agreed gleefully. She hooked her arm through Karina's.

Karina was hopeful but didn't want to assume anything at this point. "But don't forget, Chelsea doesn't live with him, so maybe the scenario is different in this case."

"But you know that she's still a big part of his life. He'll be watching to see what you're like with her."

"Oh great. More pressure."

"Only if you let it. All of our kids love you, so you needn't worry about that."

"They also run right over me."

"You'll learn."

The Relationship Ownership seminar started again, keeping them all engrossed with Brian's message. Accepting ownership of one's issues in a relationship was something everyone could relate to.

And that gave Karina lots to think about.

"Glad to see you ladies here tonight." Brian walked up behind Karina, slipping his arm around her waist.

She smiled up at him, enjoying the naturalness of the moment. "The lecture was excellent. Lots to think about."

He grinned. "This one always pushes buttons for people."

"I'd forgotten how busy you always are with these affairs. I'm glad we caught up with you tonight."

"Me too," he murmured quietly. "I'm just sorry you're leaving so soon."

She smiled. "There are many people waiting to speak with you. Besides, I'll drive over on Sunday for a visit."

"Counting on it." He dropped a kiss on her cheek, smiled at the others and walked back to the crowd waiting for him.

On the way home, the discussion among the women returned to parenting and blended families.

"The issue seems even bigger when there are twins in the picture. Most men are just fine with one child, but a pair of rambunctious boys? Not a chance," Sandra said.

"But the twins are terrific," Karina replied, feeling a stab of loyalty toward the kids. Sandra didn't have an easy time raising the twins on her own. Karina didn't know how long Sandra had been divorced but long enough that the kids hadn't once mentioned a father to Karina.

Sandra looked over at her and smiled. "The boys are still no angels. They're mine and I love them dearly, however, I know what they're like. Look at you. You're always ready to take on the world. Your heart's just a big marshmallow. Look at the dog that the boys convinced you to keep. Your cats are still walking around with their noses out of joint."

Karina smiled sheepishly at the reminder.

"Brian would be very lucky to have you. You'd be loyal forever and probably give him a half a dozen children in the process."

Karina chuckled. "Half a dozen kids? There's no way. Two sounds good though."

IAN PARKED THE car at the far end of the strip mall where Karina's store was. It was early. And the lot empty. But that didn't mean someone wasn't watching. He wanted to get in and out of there fast.

He pulled on his gloves and carefully removed the envelope from his folder. He exited and locked his car, then casually walked around the back of the mall up the delivery lane. At the far side he turned to study the still-empty lot.

Good he was alone.

With the envelope in his hand, he walked to Karina's store and casually slid his package through the mail slot.

Then without looking around, he returned the way he'd come.

By the time he was back in his car and pulling out of the lot, there was more traffic on the road. But it was unlikely anyone would be paying attention to the gray car leaving the parking lot.

And he was done.

For now.

THE NEXT MORNING Karina awoke out of sorts for the first time since moving to Victoria. Many mornings she enjoyed the walk to the store, but not today. She was also tired after a restless night. A shower and coffee hadn't improved her mood any, either. She hoped spending time in the store, talking with customers and arranging displays would do that.

She was the first to arrive so unlocked the door and headed into the dark interior. She didn't notice the letters inside the drop-off box until the lights were on. She tossed the bundle on the desk as she headed straight for the coffee maker.

Susan came in a few minutes later. "Good morning. Did you have a good night?"

Karina smiled at her bubbly friend, feeling better already. Susan invariably managed to kick Karina back on track. "It was okay." She shrugged. "But I was restless."

"I forgot to tell you last night but I need to help out at the school this afternoon, just for an hour or two. Is that all right? I'll call Sandra at the clothing store in a bit and see if she can help if you're swamped. She's working today and she has another girl that comes in on Fridays."

"I'll be fine. Fridays can be busy but I should be okay. Especially if it's just for a couple of hours."

"What's in the mail? Anything interesting?" Susan sorted through the stack Karina had tossed onto the desk.

"I don't know. I haven't looked." Karina shrugged dismissively.

"Hmmm." The odd tone in Susan's voice brought Karina over to her side. Susan held an unstamped, ordinary manila business envelope with Karina's name written in bold black lettering on the front.

"This was tucked inside a handful of other envelopes."

"Weird. Let me see." Not giving Susan a chance to refuse, Karina reached over and snatched it out of Susan's hands. She opened it and pulled out a single sheet of unlined paper. One line of text was scribbled in the center of the page.

Now I know where you *are, too.*

"Oh, God. This has to be from Ian. There's no way it isn't." She checked the back of the page. It was blank. There was still something in the envelope, though. Pictures.

Pictures of her and Brian at the seminar. Of her and Brian kissing in the parking lot. Here at the new store.

Oh, God.

Karina held up the pictures. "He's been stalking me." A wave of panic bubbled up inside her chest.

Susan gasped. "Oh no. That's a little creepy."

"A little?" Karina cried. "It's a *lot* creepy."

Waving her hand at the pictures, Susan said, "Somehow he found out you moved here – but how?" Then she snapped her fingers. "We advertised about opening day, everywhere. Newspapers, the store website, even the posters had our pictures and our names on them."

"Not to mention listing the store's address," Karina added holding up the envelope. "He probably came by, made sure it was me, then came back with this."

"But why?" cried Susan. "And what do we do about it?"

"First things first. Let's open the store," Karina said. "Afterwards, I'm going to call Brian. And then the police."

Only it didn't help. She turned to Susan a few minutes later. "Brian's line is busy. I even tried Mark but he isn't answering his cell phone, so I left a message. I'd really rather speak to the same cop that Brian is already dealing with over Ian." She blew the steam away from the hot cup of coffee clutched in her cold hands. Inside, tension wove itself into a tighter and tighter knot.

By noon, Karina still hadn't managed to get in touch with either Mark or Brian. Susan had left for the school. Sandra had stopped in several times to check on her, but business had been slow each time, so Karina sent her on her way. With all the customers, and friends coming in and out, Karina should have felt better or at least been too busy to worry. However, it didn't work that way. And neither did her uneasiness change.

She tried Brian for what felt like the seventy-fourth time. "Hello."

She almost dropped the phone in relief.

"Brian, this is Karina. I've been trying to reach you all day."

"What's wrong?" he said, alarm in his voice.

"A letter was inside the store when I arrived this morning." She took a deep breath, trying to steady her voice. "Just put it through the door slot sometime between closing last night and opening today. No return address, and it's not stamped. There's no way to identify the sender, but my name is on the front of it. It has photos of me in it. Of us. From the lecture. From here. Brian, I think it's from Ian."

She grabbed the single sheet and read off the ominous message.

Stark silence lasted several long seconds.

"We don't know that it's from Ian," Brian responded cautiously, obviously choosing his words carefully. "We haven't heard from him since that weekend. None of us have."

"Until now," Karina pointed out. "Brian, I'm scared. I need to call the police but I wanted to talk to you first."

"When are you done for the day?"

"It's Friday, so we don't close until six. Susan's gone for another hour at least. No customers here so it's pretty quiet."

"You're all alone?" he asked, tension in his voice coming through the line.

"Yes. But it's only for a couple of hours, max." Her voice rose with apprehension. She walked over to the window and peered out at the parking lot, but nothing seemed unusual or out of place. "Do you think I'm in danger? What about Susan? Is she? Brian, you're scaring me!"

"Look, I just want you to be careful. I don't think Ian is dangerous. He's upset over his wife, that's all. He didn't murder her, or anything. Calm down. Besides we don't know for sure that it's from Ian."

"*I* know it's from him."

"I'll call the police. This way the information goes directly to the same officer I dealt with before. I'll call you back in a few minutes."

Karina hung up the phone, her hands trembling, and settled in to wait. *Brian, please be fast.*

IAN SAT IN his small gray car in the middle of the strip mall's small parking lot outside the toy store. He smiled as he realized just how easy it was to be invisible. His sedan was nondescript and blended in with the surroundings so effectively, no one noticed it. And if anyone who passed by had actually noticed him, they'd given no outward sign.

His location gave him the perfect view of the store. Earlier, he'd even gone in and taken a walk through the place. Just to push it. Not when she'd been there, though. He loved knowing that she had no idea he was so close by.

He was actually looking forward to Karina spotting him. But not just yet. He wanted her to worry, to get paranoid and start to panic. The first step had been the letter. He'd turn up the heat on his campaign soon enough.

He wished he'd seen her reaction when she opened the letter and saw the pictures.

He was happy when, every few minutes, Karina peered nervously out through the window or door, her body language full of fear and anxiety. As if looking for someone. Was she searching for him?

He loved the idea. Or could she be waiting for Brian to show up? Because that would be perfect. So far, this had been too easy. He liked his games to be a bit more challenging.

Now that he knew she was working at her store, he saw the perfect opportunity to check out her apartment. He'd driven by several times. Seen the kids and the huge dog. He liked dogs and for some reason they usually liked him. He glanced at his watch. And the kids would be at school for a few more hours. Perfect.

Feeling almost giddy with anticipation, Ian turned the key in the ignition. He couldn't wait until they found out about the rest of his plans. He glanced down at his cell phone and the photo currently on his display. He smiled. Damn, but Karina looked good. Maybe he'd find a way to fix that too…

Chapter 2

T HE NEXT HOUR felt like an eternity to Karina. Brian still hadn't called back, and she was working her way through yet another pot of coffee, hugging her cup to her chest for comfort as she paced around the empty store. She walked to the window for the millionth time and stared out into the lot until it occurred to her that putting herself on display made her even more vulnerable. And once *that* thought entered, she couldn't make it go away. Then she remembered the receiving door at the back. Could someone sneak in that way? How long before she'd notice them? She raced to the storeroom to make sure that door was locked.

Taking a deep breath, she realized how skittish she had become. She was letting Ian get to her. It wasn't fair. She'd been settling nicely into her new life, looking forward to a new future and now this.

Susan came in just then, breathless from hurrying.

"I'm back. Were you swamped Karina? Was it okay? Nothing else weird happened, did it?"

Karina just looked at her darkly. "The store's been dead most of the afternoon. I wish it had been busy, though. Then maybe I wouldn't have worked myself into such a state."

Susan frowned. "Didn't you get a hold of Mark or Brian?"

"Yes; Brian. He wasn't happy. He was going to call the police and then call me back, and I still haven't heard from him. He also sounded alarmed when he heard I was here alone so that that really set me off." Suddenly remembering why Susan had left in the first place, Karina asked, "How did the rehearsal go?"

"It was so much fun! Everything went wonderfully. The kids looked so cute in their costumes. Too bad you couldn't see them. They were so funny."

"I could use that right now."

"Did Brian say when he'd call back?"

"No. He just said that he'd talk to me after he spoke with the police. But he should've done that by now."

"I did, but I came here instead of calling." A deep voice came from the open doorway. "And of course, you two ladies were so busy talking you didn't notice me."

"Brian, I'm so glad you came," Karina gasped. Without a thought, she raced around the counter and flung herself into his open arms, feeling instantly comforted.

"Is this more serious with Ian than we thought?" asked Susan.

"No, but Officer Markham wanted to see the note and speak with you both."

He squeezed Karina hard then released her, but not before placing a fleeting kiss on her lips. "Worried yourself sick, haven't you?"

She threw up her hands in exasperation. "What did you expect? First you say I shouldn't be alone. Then you promised to call me right back, only you didn't. I've been storming around here like a madwoman, waiting for news or for something to happen."

Brian smiled down at her then introduced the women to

the police officer who'd just entered the store. "He's helping us deal with the Ian stuff. If it is indeed Ian." He held up his hand. "We'll give the letter to the officer and let the police decide, okay?"

Karina retrieved the letter from the counter and handed it over to the officer.

He examined it carefully and asked several questions, jotting down a few things in a small notebook. "I'm going to take this and see what we come up with. Do you have any idea why he'd be upset with you?" he asked Karina, his gaze intent but thoughtful.

"No. I've spent all day thinking about that. My friendship with Brian is the only connection I can think of." She searched Brian's face. "And of course, we all went to university together."

The officer watched her as she watched Brian. "University together?" He jotted something down and asked, "How long ago?"

"Close on ten years. And I barely knew Ian in university at all." Brian looked at Karina. "You knew him only slightly better."

"And I didn't like what I did know," she said seriously. "He often had uncontrollable outbursts in classes, he would yell then go really quiet and glare at the person he was arguing with. Not just for a moment or two but for the whole class. He was really creepy that way."

"I'm not sure how he thinks yet," Officer Markham said, "but if in his mind he can trace a lost relationship back to you, he may be targeting your relationship as payback."

Susan gasped at that, her face paling quickly. "Karina's not really in danger, is she?"

To reassure her friend, Karina put her arm around Susan

and gave a squeeze. "It's all right, Susan. This is probably nothing." She cast a worried glance at Brian, who gave his head an almost imperceptible nod.

"Maybe, and maybe not," the officer said, putting his notebook away, and the note and photographs back into the envelope. "In the meantime, if anything else happens, call me right away." A call to an accident came through to him. He quickly handed his business cards to Karina and Susan and left the store.

"Brian? What do you think?" Karina looked to him for reassurance.

"Maybe he just wants to scare you away." He wrapped a gentle arm around her shoulders and hugged her.

Soothed by the touch, Karina leaned into his warmth, grateful that he was here to talk to.

"That's true in a twisted way," added Susan thoughtfully. "Think about it. At the seminar, Ian tried to warn everyone not to listen to Brian. Maybe this is a similar thing. Maybe he's trying to scare you away from Brian."

"Maybe. But then Ian clearly wasn't thinking in a calm, rational manner. Stalking Karina and taking photos would indicate that he's spent a lot of time and effort obsessing about her. About us," Brian said.

Dismayed, Karina looked at Brian. "If his hate is still motivating him after all this time, he wants a whole lot more from us. The question is what?"

"We can only wait for his next move. That and be smart. Don't walk to work for the next while. Arrange not to be alone for long periods of time, if you can." Brian was in protective-male mode once again.

"Do you think Susan, Sandra or the kids are in danger?"

"No, because I don't agree that you're in danger. He's

clearly angry, and this is a nuisance, but I don't think he's so deranged as to really hurt anyone. If he was, I believe I'd be his target. Not you."

"I'm going to warn Sandra and Paul, regardless," said Susan. "If he knows where you work, he likely knows where you live by now. And I think he's right, Karina. You should take extra precautions." Susan turned back to Brian. "Why haven't the police tried to talk to Ian?"

"They're trying. They're still working on tracking him down. Apparently he quit his job and left his townhome around the same time his wife walked out."

"Then we should keep an eye out for him," Karina suggested, her heart thumping nervously in her chest. "He could be anywhere. He might even be hanging around the neighborhood, or be outside the store."

"If you see him, call the police immediately," Brian warned.

That was only sensible. She turned and walked over to the front counter, guilt weighing heavily on her shoulders. She felt responsible for putting everyone in danger.

As if reading her mind, Susan wrapped an arm around Karina's shoulders. "You're not to blame for this," she said firmly. "We're all in this together and together we can deal with it."

Brian stepped in. "I'm the one he's angry at. However laying blame is not going to help us at all now. We need the police to convince Ian to leave us alone."

Karina smiled at the two people rallying around her. They'd come to mean so much to her in such a short time.

"Listen, Karina, why don't you go home early today? This has been a difficult day for you. I can close the store up tonight. Paul is going to pick me up at closing time and take me out for dinner." She shrugged. "Maybe he can come an hour early and stay until I close."

Karina was torn with indecision as she looked at her friend. She desperately wanted to retreat to the safety of her apartment, but she didn't want to leave Susan alone at the store either.

Brian took the decision away from her.

"Go home. I'll stay here until Paul arrives, then I'll pick up Chinese and bring it over to your place. You have my number on your cell phone so call me if anything comes up or if you're worried at all."

Susan agreed wholeheartedly with Brian's suggestions.

The next thing she knew, Karina found herself standing in the open door, saying good-bye to them both.

"I'll be there about half an hour after Susan leaves and I'll come over with dinner, okay?" Brian asked. "Have a nap. It would be good for you.

"That's not likely, the twins are at home with the babysitter. You'll be lucky to get five minutes of peace at all," said Susan with a laugh. "Go home; but no more coffee for you. You'll never sleep tonight at this rate."

Susan was right. The twins were waiting for her. They exploded from the house as soon as she pulled into the driveway.

"Hi Karina! Did you get any new toys at the store to-day?" Daniel asked.

David piped up with, "Do you want to play Nintendo with me?"

"Can Max come out and play with us in the yard?" Daniel bounced at her side.

"Hi, guys! To answer your questions in order, no we didn't, I'd love to play, but it will have to be tomorrow, and yes, you can take him out for a bit." Finally escaping the rambunctious pair, she let Max out to play with the boys then cuddled the cats for a few minutes. She wandered into her bedroom, refusing to look at her comfy and inviting bed. If she lay down, she'd be out in no time. She walked to her closet to hang up her sweater instead. She felt unsettled. That's when it hit her.

The room looked…different. *But how?* She turned in a slow circle, nerves dancing along her spine. No, it had to be her imagination. She might have left her nightie on top of the comforter, instead of tucking it under her pillow like she usually did. Karina tilted her head, considering. She *had* been rushed this morning.

That had to be the answer for finding it laid out on the bed as it was. She'd probably been preoccupied with Ian, and his crap was throwing her off balance and making her see boogeymen where there weren't any.

Which was probably exactly what Ian wanted. Taking a deep, calming breath, she pulled herself together and headed out to the kitchen to do a quick tidy. She'd just finished wiping down the counter when there was a knock at the door, accompanied by the delicious, unmistakable aroma of Chinese food wafting in the open window.

She smiled in greeting. "Hi there. I thought we'd eat outside, if that's okay with you?" She grabbed the plates and cutlery she'd set aside and led the way to the backyard.

Brian nodded. "That works. It's nice here. You have a huge lawn and lots of privacy."

"The apartment is on the small side, but that doesn't really matter. There's lots of space outside, yes. Privacy…" She laughed. "Not so much. The twins have become a large part of my life. They have a babysitter at home for after-school, but they're usually waiting for me when I get here. Then they come feed the cats and play with Max. So there's not much privacy – at least until the kids have gone to bed."

"Kids, cats and a dog. Well, it certainly didn't take you long to get settled in, did it?"

She looked around at the green trees and flowering shrubs. "It felt like home right from the beginning. It's a nice feeling."

She started to unload the Styrofoam containers from the bags and placed them on the patio table.

"My goodness, how much did you bring?"

"A lot. I didn't know what you liked, and I wasn't sure if the twins were going to be joining us for dinner."

"If I'd told them you were bringing Chinese food, then they probably wouldn't have given us a choice. However, I kept that bit of information to myself."

They smiled conspiratorially at each other.

"We can always share," suggested Brian.

With her mouth full of succulent chicken, Karina shook her head emphatically. When she could, she replied, "Later. If there's any left."

Indeed, it was much later that they dropped off the leftovers to Sandra and the boys and headed to the park to walk off dinner. Karina looked around in appreciation. "This was a wonderful idea. I hadn't realized how beautiful it is here. The smell is fresh, not heavy like in the middle of summer, but green and new."

"Are you still happy that you came?"

"Definitely," she answered instantly. "Already, I feel more at home than I ever did in Vancouver. It was a nice enough place, but my best friends and I were all making big life changes. I might have ended up without them anyway, if

I'd stayed there. Here I feel like part of some big family. And speaking of friends and family, I called Mark today but haven't heard back."

"Mark's brother was in a car accident and he's flown to New York to be with him and his brother's pregnant wife. Sorry, I should have mentioned that earlier."

She stopped in her tracks, stunned. "Oh no! How terrible. Here I am, so worried about a silly note and Mark is in the middle of a family crisis. I'll send him an email in the morning."

Brian wrapped an arm around her shoulders, urging her to continue walking. "I'm sure he'd appreciate that."

"I hope his brother will be okay. It must be difficult for him. I feel so involved with everyone here. After the weekend seminar, it was hard to go home. And once there, I wanted to change…everything."

"Which of course, you did." He grinned at her. "In a big way."

This whole scene – the sunset, the walking together, being in his arms, the peaceful setting – could have come out of any romantic movie.

Her steps slowed.

Brian stopped and tugged her around into the circle of his arms, to stare down at her thoughtful face.

"What's the matter?" His lips teased gently across her temple. "Tell me." He tilted her chin, sliding his lips across her cheeks, stopping for a moment to caress the tip of her nose before gently heading off to explore the other side of her face. "You can talk to me." His whisper fluttered down her spine.

Then he lowered his head and dropped a loving kiss on her forehead, the tip of her nose then a soft gentle kiss on her lips.

Pleasure washed through her. With her eyes closed against the tender onslaught, she leaned into him. His arms tightened, holding her gently against him. Breaking the kiss, Brian gazed back at her, as if searching for answers in her eyes. His darkened, responding to whatever confused signal she was putting out.

Never able to lie verbally, she hadn't a hope of hiding her feelings, especially now.

A fire ignited in his eyes. He lowered his head, stealing her breath and promising so much more in exchange.

Children's laughter burst from the green space on the other side of the trees, shattering their passionate bubble. Brian lifted his head and pulled her close.

Karina buried her face against Brian's broad chest and snuggled deeper in his warmth.

Now *that* was a kiss.

BRIAN STARED DOWN at his desk and the stack of papers he needed to go over.

"Karina should be here soon, shouldn't she?" Mark asked, snapping open the clasp on his briefcase.

The two had been working all morning, prepping for the next seminar, and now everything was set. They'd been friends for a long time and had been colleagues for long enough that they'd established a casual, yet efficient rhythm that allowed them to make these preparations in record time.

"Yes." Brian glanced outside the bay window, for what had to be the twentieth time in the last hour. Seemed like he'd been waiting for her forever.

"Good." Mark straightened and sent a knowing look at

Brian. "You need to make this relationship move along."

What the hell did that mean? Brian stared at his friend. "And how do you suggest I do that? I'm a little out of practice, remember." And how. He didn't want to rush her. Not this time. His own insecurities were still getting in the way. He hadn't dated much since his divorce. Hadn't wanted to. He felt rough and out of practice. Now when the results counted, he wished he could be more confident.

Mark busied himself closing up his briefcase. "I don't know. But you have to do something." He turned around to face the front door. "That girl is special."

From the sound of Mark's voice, it appeared there was more than a little interest on his part. And that wasn't good. He frowned at Mark, then said cautiously, "Meaning?"

"Treat her right or I'll step in and give her a choice," Mark said bluntly. "So far, I've left the field wide open to you. But if you ever hurt her, then she's fair game."

No way in hell that was going to happen. Brian's hackles rose. "In all the years we've been friends we've never once fought over a woman. Don't start now." He stood up slowly. This was not the time to back down. "Know this my friend, in truth she's already mine and has been for a long time. She just doesn't know it. We could have spent these years together, but I was too big a fool to do anything about it before." His gaze hardened. "I'm not now."

In the true fashion that had preserved their long friendship, Mark laughed uproariously. His face turned red and he collapsed back down on the chair. Finally he gasped out, "Oh that's great." He chuckled a little more. "Glad to know it. Body language doesn't lie. Right from the first weekend, her body said she was yours. But I wanted to make sure that you knew where *you* belonged."

IAN WATCHED AS Karina pulled out of her driveway and disappeared down the street. The upstairs occupants had left earlier. Churchgoers, he thought. Perfect. That would give him at least an hour to do what he wanted to do.

He waited another few minutes, in case she'd forgotten something and turned back, then got out of his car and walked casually to Karina's side-door entrance. He'd already copied the spare key she'd hidden under the flowerpot. Such a ridiculous hiding place. Even if the point was to let the boys get at the dog, the flower pot location was obvious and stupid. He shrugged. Stupid or not, it made his job easier.

He slipped inside and bent to greet the dog. He'd come by several times already to get to know him. They'd made friends very quickly. "Hey, Max. How's it going, buddy?"

Max had a great personality. Lousy watchdog but from what he'd seen the dog was a good friend for the twins. Should be the twins' pet, actually. All boys needed a dog. And Karina left the poor thing alone all day.

Not good for the animal. With that thought in mind, Ian opened the door and let the dog out. "Go, Max. Enjoy some time outside."

The dog could use a good run.

Grinning as Max raced over to scatter the flock of sparrows on the lawn, Ian turned his attention to the rest of Karina's apartment. By now he knew it well. He liked being here, except for the damn cats. He hated those things. But they must have sensed his dislike because after his first visit they'd stayed out of sight. *What's with that?*

They must know.

He'd never hurt the dog but if he got his hands on the cats…now that would be a different story.

As though he'd summoned one, a flash of fur tore across Karina's living room floor. Ian smirked. Yep, that was one pain-in-the-ass pet to take care of. "Here kitty, kitty, kitty."

Chapter 3

E ARLY SUNDAY MORNING, Chelsea was the one to open the door as Karina arrived. Brian stood to one side, mouth open as Chelsea raced forward arms open.

Karina bent to pick her up, smiling at the blue inquisitive eyes. "Well, hello. Aren't you a sweetheart! How are you?"

"Good. K'rina's here, Daddy!" Chelsea turned to her father. "Look, K'rina!"

"I see that," Brian answered with a chuckle.

In a moment of true Karina abandon, she tickled the little girl. Chelsea loved it. Chortling and giggling, the two of them didn't even acknowledge Brian's presence.

Brian watched as the two important females in his life bonded. Her response to his little girl gave him insight into another side to Karina he hadn't seen. He loved watching the two of them.

Later, when Brian carried fresh coffee outside to the deck, he found his precious daughter sleeping, carefully protected in Karina's arms. His heart's defenses crumbled. How could he not care about such a woman?

Quietly, he placed the coffee beside Karina.

"Karina, is your arm sore?" he whispered. "Do you want me to take her and lay her down inside?"

No response. Perhaps he spoke too softly. He leaned

closer to repeat his words when her even breathing caught his attention.

Both his angels were sleeping.

Brian stepped inside to pick up a cotton throw from the sofa in the living room and brought it outside to drape over the sleeping beauties. He settled back in his chair and sipped his coffee, content to watch over them… *Forever.* He realized then that he wanted Karina desperately and on so many levels. He wanted her in his life and in his bed. He'd grown up a lot since university. Matured, loved, married, become a father and divorced.

Friday had been an eye opener about how easy it could be to lose it all. He didn't know how dangerous Ian was, but he didn't want to take the chance Karina was in danger.

He'd love to have her move in here with him. But it was likely too far, too fast for her. Still it was the perfect answer regarding Ian. And maybe that was okay too.

With an incredible feeling of rightness to his world, he settled back in his chair, enjoying the sunshine and warm breeze.

Marly arrived to collect Chelsea soon after.

"Your relationship is serious, isn't it?"

Marly's question surprised him, but it shouldn't have. She'd always understood him. "Yes, it is." He grinned sheepishly. "At least, I hope it is."

"Good. It's time." She led the way to the car.

He stared after her. The simplicity of her statement struck him. It was time. He'd been alone for several years now. Was healed from his divorce and ready to move on. Feeling more settled than he could remember in a long time, Brian carried the still-sleeping child to her car seat. He'd just finished a second cup of coffee when Karina stirred.

"Good afternoon, beautiful," he said softly. "How was your nap?"

Karina smiled and stretched, pushing the blanket off her legs. "It felt wonderful, thanks."

"Where's Chelsea…?"

"Her mom picked her up a little while ago."

"Oh."

Brian shifted his chair closer to hers and reached out to take her hand. "You were wonderful with her, you know. And she adores you."

Karina's answering smile was warm and caring. "She's easy to adore."

"I was thinking about something while you were sleeping."

Her gaze turned wary. "What?"

"I'm thinking about the Ian mess. The danger to you. To Sandra and the boys." He thought about Mark's promise and took a deep breath. "What if you moved in here, with me – until this blows over at least?"

Shocked silence filled the air.

An array of emotions flickered over Karina's face before she hopped up from her chair.

"No. I can't. I'm sorry. But it's…no, it wouldn't work," she mumbled. She looked her watch, then grabbed her purse and keys and headed inside. "I have to go. Thanks for lunch and for introducing me to your daughter. She really is a sweetheart."

He opened his mouth to protest her trying to rush away but before he could get the words out of his mouth, she was gone.

Just like that.

"SO WHAT IF I ran?" she muttered to herself. It didn't matter…

But it did matter. She knew that. Brian's suggestion had scared her. She hadn't seen it coming. Not from him. *She'd* thought of it, dreamt of it. But if she moved in with him, she wanted it to be as the next step in their relationship – not because he felt protective.

Talk about pushing her buttons. She hadn't just run, she'd panicked.

Confused, Karina turned the last corner to Sandra's house. Relief filled her at the sight of the cozy, familiar home.

She pulled in beside Sandra, who was just climbing into her car. The twins came racing over to see her, their cheerful greetings brightening her mood. Max danced in circles around them, barking playfully. She frowned at the dog. *What was Max doing out?* "Hi, guys."

"Hi Karina. You left Max out! But that's okay, 'cause we're looking after him. We're going to soccer practice now. Can we take him with us?"

No, Karina hadn't left Max out. She knew that for sure. She was always careful that way. Both cats and the dog had been inside when she left. She took a deep breath and looked at her door. Nothing looked out of place.

"Sure. No problem, as long as it's okay with your mom."

The boys grinned and dashed over to their car, shouting, "Great! Come on, Max. Let's go."

Karina waved good-bye as the car pulled away, a careful smile pasted on her lips. Once they were out of sight, she walked slowly up to her door. She wanted to call Brian but considering how she'd left…. Then again, she'd bolted because of his suggestion and right now, staring down at the closed door and worried what she'd find behind it, she just might jump at the chance to move in with him.

Should she even enter? Of course. There was a small chance that she really had left the dog out. Who could be sure? She'd been so excited for her date that it was possible… Maybe, but not likely.

Reaching a hesitant hand out, she turned the knob and watched in disbelief as the door opened. It was unlocked.

Her hand dove into her pocket for her cell phone. "Brian," she started without preamble, "my door is unlocked and Max was outside. I know I left him in and locked the door on my way to your place."

"Don't go in. I'm on my way."

When she didn't answer, his voice snapped through the phone lines. "Karina! Are you listening?"

She stared at her open door, dread building deep in her belly. "Yes. I'm walking back to my car. I'm scared it might be Ian." She turned and ran back to her car, got in and locked all the doors.

"Good. I'll be there in a few minutes."

She desperately wanted to make sure her cats were okay…but a big part of her dreaded what she might find.

Brian had to have broken every speed limit because he came ripping around the corner in record time. "Oh, thank God," she whispered. She opened her door and ran over to him.

He hugged her fiercely. "Let me take a look, if there is something wrong, I'll call Markham."

"I want to go in."

"I'm going in first." He set her back slightly to look down into her face. "If it's fine, then you can come in. If it's not, then call Markham. Okay?"

She firmed up her lower lip and nodded. "It's Misty and Mugs I'm worried about."

He gave a curt nod. "I'll go check."

He strode toward her door and she followed a few steps behind. She chewed on her bottom lip when he pushed the door open with his foot and disappeared inside. "Oh, please let the cats be fine," she murmured.

Brian came to the door and waved her in. "There doesn't appear to be anything wrong, but there's no sign of the cats."

"Oh no." she ran inside. "Misty! Mugsy? Where are you?" She walked toward her bedroom. "They hate strangers."

"Hating strangers is probably a good thing. If Ian was here, then they'd have hid from him."

She ran to her bedroom closet and pushed the door open. "Misty, baby? Are you in here?"

A tiny plaintive mewl came from the back. "Oh, thank God. Come here, baby." Karina reached up and tugged the cat down from the closet shelf, cooing to her all the while. "Where's your sister, huh, baby?"

Just then, Mugsy appeared from the bottom of the closet and twisted around Karina's ankles. "Oh here she is." Karina smiled with relief. Ignoring the cat's complaints she scooped the second one into her arms and carried them both to the kitchen where she opened up a can of food for them. Once they were eating, she looked over at Brian. "So…he didn't break in?"

"We need to look around and see." Brian closed the door so the cats wouldn't go out. "Let's do a tour and see if anything is missing. It might have been the twins too, you know."

"No." Karina immediately shook her head. "It wouldn't

have been. I have rules and they respect them."

"You still need to take a look around," Brian replied.

The kitchen looked normal and so did the living room. The suite was small enough that it didn't take long to go over every inch. Once back in the living room, she turned to Brian, feeling very puzzled. "I don't see anything wrong."

"Good. Then we don't need Markham to stop by."

She shrugged. "I guess not. It's very odd, though. And disconcerting." She hated the sense of violation mixed with her fear that she'd brought this on herself. What if she'd been in such a rush she had forgotten to lock the door, maybe she hadn't even shut it properly. Max was a smart dog. If it had opened even a crack, he'd have snuck out.

She turned around to see Brian testing the couch. He stretched out full length, his feet dangling over the arm. Karina stared at him uncertainly. "You're too big for that couch."

He chuckled quietly. "Maybe, but if I'm staying here, I need a place to sleep. Unless you have another suggestion?" He raised a questioning brow.

"No, I don't." Her cheeks tingled and felt hot, and she knew they were bright red. "You're staying here?" She was both delighted and confused.

Brian stood and walked toward her. He pulled her stiff body into his arms. With his chin resting on top of her head, he said, "I'm not trying to upset you. I'm trying to keep you safe. My place is bigger but if you want to stay here then I'm staying with you."

"You aren't sure that Ian wasn't here, are you?"

"No one can be sure if he was or wasn't." He squeezed her a little bit tighter, letting the implications soak in. "I just want to keep you safe.

Finally, very quietly, she whispered, "All right."

But what would this step mean?

"Your place or mine?" Brian asked quietly.

"If we're doing this to minimize the danger, then we should be as far away from Sandra and the twins as possible," Karina suggested carefully. "I couldn't live with myself if anything happened to them. Ian hasn't targeted them but if he comes here, the twins could cross his path and who knows what he might do."

"Then my place it is."

Karina headed into her bedroom to pack enough clothes for a few days. She forced herself to do the job at hand and not think too far ahead. She hauled the large suitcase out onto her bed, then returned to her dresser and pulled open the top drawer.

And jumped back. *Oh God.*

"Brian!"

He came running.

She pointed to the mangled rose on top of her intimate clothing. And the picture taken inside of her store.

AN HOUR LATER, Brian honked the horn and waved at the boys before driving down the road. Thankfully Sandra and the kids had returned not long ago. Karina sniffled. "You're not saying good-bye forever, you know," he said.

Karina smiled, albeit a little tearfully. "I know that. It's just that they've come to mean so much so quickly. I'll miss them. And Max." Sandra had agreed to keep the dog. In truth he belonged to the twins already. The cats were in their cage in the back seat. Instead of their usual howling, they'd gone completely silent. Maybe they were as anxious to get out of that place as she was.

And even if she wanted to, she wasn't allowed in until Markham had investigated anyway. A good enough reason to move in with Brian – at least for a few days.

"We can invite them over for a BBQ on the weekend." He smiled. "They could bring Max, too. Besides, the twins will have lots of fun on the beach."

Karina jumped at that possibility. "That's a wonderful idea. Could we invite Paul and Susan and their kids, too? Chelsea will love them too." She paused. "As an afterthought, maybe we should invite Susan and her family on a different day. It might be easier on Chelsea if there aren't so many strangers at once."

"Did I mention inviting Chelsea?"

"No, but even if I am living in your space I get to do some of the things that I want to do," she added with a smile. "That means visiting with Chelsea again."

"She can be quite a handful."

"She's adorable and all kids can be a handful." Karina flushed, belatedly remembering that she had far less experience with children than he did.

"We'll take it slow and see how it goes," Brian suggested. "There's time."

There were major advantages to this new arrangement; living in Brian's house was one of them. On waterfront property, located just outside the city, the spacious home had stone fireplaces, high ceilings and skylights that lit the hallways during the day. And she loved the luxury of having her own balcony.

Later that night, Karina watched from her patio doors as Brian walked out along the beach. He could go out the backyard right onto the sandy shore. What was he thinking about? In truth, he looked satisfied, happy even. Then again, why shouldn't he be happy? He'd gotten everything to go his way. Well, maybe not everything. She was here in the spare room, not the master bedroom.

A fact that Cat had laughed at and Serena understood. They both approved of Karina's new living arrangements – especially considering the recent nasty events.

She wished she knew where she stood with him – and where she was going. Did he know where they were headed? If not – why the hell not? Someone in this relationship needed to know and it sure as hell wasn't her.

It was stupid to wish that this relationship could progress normally – instead of being confused and accelerated because of danger, misguided guilt or his protective instinct. She sighed in disgust. Who was she kidding? Since when had this relationship ever been normal? Certainly not in the beginning, when she'd jumped into bed with him right away, all too willing to help him forget his ex-girlfriend. Still, time healed many things and maybe they needed to focus on what they did have.

Yet, living together was convenient. But was it too convenient? And although she didn't want to be casual lovers, once passion flared, she knew she'd take him any way she could.

THE NEXT MORNING, Brian drove Karina to the store, where a surprised-looking Susan watched from behind the front display window.

"Sandra called me last night and told me what had happened," Susan whispered loudly, glancing at the pair of customers browsing nearby. "Did you spend the night with him?"

"Good morning to you, too." Karina grinned. "Yes, actually, I did. But not in the way you think." Quickly, she explained the events of the last twenty-four hours. "I explained the situation briefly to Sandra last night. However, Brian was waiting so there wasn't much time. I thought maybe I'd have coffee with her, today."

"Give her a call now and set it up," Susan suggested.

The morning passed quickly. Karina finally looked up from her current task and saw Sandra enter the store looking for her.

"Hi. Sorry, it's been crazy in here. I forgot about the time."

"Not a problem. You ready to go?"

It didn't take long to get to one of Karina's newfound favorite coffee spots. Once they bought coffee and took their cups to a table, Sandra pinned her with the inquisitive eye. "So. Where did you sleep last night?"

"I slept in the spare room, of course." Karina laughed. "Just because I'm in his house, doesn't mean I'll move into his bed just yet."

Sandra gave her a bemused smile. "Sure you do. But you don't want to seem too eager."

Karina started as the truth flooded through her. "I want it all," she announced simply. "I want to marry him, have his children and grow old together. It scares me to death." Karina stared at her bright-red fingernails intently, but they weren't giving her any answers to her problems. "Maybe I'm asking for too much."

"Never." Sandra shook her head, her voice gentle but firm. "If that's what you want then don't let yourself be shortchanged."

"I know he cares, but I'm not sure to what extent."

"Maybe it's time to find out." Sandra nodded toward the doorway. Brian walked through the glass doors and headed toward them.

Karina beamed at him. "What a nice surprise."

Brian dropped a kiss on her cheek. "Ladies. I stopped by the store and Susan told me where you were. Do you mind if I join you?"

He reached for a spare chair from a neighboring table, but Sandra jumped up and offered hers.

"I have to get back anyway as I'm running late." She gave Karina a meaningful look. "Remember what I said." With a smile for Brian, Sandra was gone.

Brian offered to pick up a snack for her but when she declined, he ordered a coffee but stayed quiet.

"Brian? What's wrong?" Karina asked studying the pre-occupied look on his face. "You're too quiet."

He glanced up, a small smile playing at the corner of his lips. "Do you know me that well already?"

"Yes, I think so. So what's up?"

"I spoke to Officer Markham this morning." He gazed at her steadily.

Dread knotted in her stomach. "And?" she asked, careful to keep her voice calm.

"They found out where Ian's been staying. Unfortunately, there's no sign that he's been there in the last few days."

She frowned. "What're they doing about it?"

"They're still looking for him. However, the police say he's getting better at covering his tracks. Crooks, if they don't get caught early on, end up building on their skills to evade capture."

"It's a horrible thought, isn't it?" She stared down at her

own coffee cup, unable to hold back the shiver rippling down her spine. Horrible to consider Ian getting better at this scary stuff. He was too damn good now.

"Yes. Markham also said you can go back to your apartment but he recommends you stay at my place until they locate Ian."

Karina propped her elbows on the table, staring at him across the way. Damn, the man was gorgeous. And damn her for being an idiot for particularly noticing it at a time like this. She forced her brain away from studying his serious face and back to the questions at hand. "I'm fine with that. But I do have to wonder when our lives will get back to normal?"

"What's normal?" he asked, his face lightening slightly with humor. "Think about our relationship so far. There's no normal in there."

She shook her and snorted. "Quit joking. You know you don't mean that. The longer we're caught up in this drama the less normal our own situation becomes."

"Our relationship will be what we make it." Brian reached across the table to cradle her hand in his much larger one. He traced the outline of her fingers with his roughened ones. Shivers slipped over her spine as she watched him touching her, mesmerized.

"Let's give *us* a chance, Karina. To see what might be."

She listened intently, searching for hidden meanings, wanting to understand the emotion behind the words.

He tried again. "I know I can't change the past. But we aren't the same people we were back then." He looked closer at her, his half smile vanishing as his forehead creased. "You still aren't sure, are you?"

"It's hard. I want… I need more than last time." She bowed her head and stared at their clasped hands.

"Look at me, sweetheart."

She raised her head and stared into his eyes, searching. Confusion melted away as understanding rushed in. Flames of barely-controlled desire danced in his dark eyes. He'd loosened the reins just enough to show her the need riding his soul.

Karina was entranced. "Brian?" Her voice trembled in response to the heat and desire emanating from the splendid male across from her.

"Now do you believe?" His voice was gritty with barely restrained desire. Steel threaded his voice as he reinforced his message. "This is real. As real as it gets. But it's up to us to take it to the next level."

She had no desire to argue that point. It was true.

"Why are you waiting then?" Her voice was barely above a whisper.

"I want you to want me just as badly. To come to me knowing that you can't wait another moment to be in my arms. There's a country and western song that says something like, I don't want someone just to live with me; I want someone who can't live without me." He lowered his voice so deep, it resonated up and down her spine. "I need this to be your decision. To trust that I will be there in the morning. That I will be there for you."

"And if I said that I was ready now?" Yet, she dropped her eyes.

"Then you'd burn as badly as I am. But you're still a little scared. Uncertain. I don't want you to take that step until you're ready – not a moment before."

He lifted her hand. Gently carrying it to his lips, he tenderly dropped kisses on her knuckles. "I don't want you in my bed for one night or two, I want everything that you have to give, for *always*."

His words echoed in her mind for the rest of the after-noon. They took on a life of their own, warming her thoughts, tugging at her heart and steaming through her body. A part of her was furious at him and at herself. Damn it, why wasn't she ready? And how had their roles suddenly reversed. Earlier, she'd been the one holding back from jumping into bed with *him*. Now he was holding back and waiting for her.

Susan just laughed at her when she told her about the conversation she'd had with Brian.

"Am I glad Paul and I are well past that stage. Why don't you just crawl into his bed and seduce him? I'm sure he wouldn't object."

Karina just scoffed. "Like any man is going to object. My life has changed so quickly in so many areas. I'm still reeling and need a little time to adjust. Foolish maybe, but I don't want to make a mistake. This thing between us is too big." In most aspects of her life she was like Max the puppy, leaping in with abandon and joy. But in relationship area she was more like her cats, hiding in the closet.

"I can understand that." Susan smiled contentedly.

"So, Susan, why don't you go home tonight and seduce Paul yourself? Meet him at the doorway in a negligee – or even less – and make love to him there in the hallway, before dinner," Karina challenged. "You could have the kids go to Sandra's and give Paul a treat."

Susan immediately blushed, but looked intrigued at the thought. Finally, she shook her head. "No. Paul would be shocked."

"So?" Karina countered. "Shake him up a bit." A mis-chievous grin curved her lips upward. "You never know, you might like the playfulness."

Susan laughed softly and shook her head. "We'll see, but I make no promises."

It was late when Brian finally arrived to pick Karina up. She was exhausted and irritable. All she wanted was to go home and put her feet up for the rest of the evening. Damn, but she was tired. She slouched farther into the cushioned seat and closed her eyes. "I want to drive myself. I want my independence."

"I don't want you travelling alone. Let's just play it safe a little longer." Brian punched a button on the dash. Soothing jazz filled the car.

Karina slept the whole way home only waking as the car rolled to a stop.

Still sleepy, she shifted and stretched, easing her back into a more normal curve. She moaned in pleasure as her muscles loosened up. Slowly, she let her head gently loll from side to side, finally letting it drop back peacefully against the headrest. She sighed contentedly.

Stark silence filled the car.

She opened her eyes to look at Brian. The shadows in the car played over his face, highlighting the sexual tension radiating off him. Glittering black eyes stared at her. His nostrils flared and he looked like he'd lost most of his control.

God, she loved that. She uncrossed her legs slowly, letting her knees fall apart. His eyes followed perfectly. Wonderful. She was just in the mood to push him. She smoothed one red nail slowly against his thigh, then a little higher, stopping briefly at his belt. His breath caught and then started again as she kept moving.

He closed his eyes, his jaw tight with tension. His voice

hoarse, he asked, "Where does this woman come from? She hides and then pops up at the oddest times."

"She's part of me. Today some magical combination teased her into coming out. Maybe it was finding out that she's really wanted."

"So you need to be exhausted from work, worried about Ian and waking from a nap…?"

"You missed the most important point. I need to wake up hungry."

"Christ!"

Karina laughed and slid out of the car. Had she pushed him enough for now? She was having so much fun playing, it was hard to stop. "I'm going to go in and have a long hot soak in a bubble bath. Maybe you should have a cold shower, yourself."

As they walked up the front steps, he paused for a moment, then said calmly, "As much as I love seeing this part of you, the next time she pops up, I'll make sure she's not all talk."

Karina contemplated his words for a moment. That was fair. She was almost ready to take the next step in their relationship, but not totally. This teasing was fun, but it wasn't fair unless they both found it enjoyable.

"Thanks for the warning. The next time it happens, recognize the invitation."

"I'll be waiting. Let your sensuality out, let your passion ripen and when you can't stand it anymore, come to me and we'll both go up in flames." His eyes darkened with promise.

Fiery images caused Karina to shudder with need. The meaning behind his words only awakened and heightened the images that already lived in her mind. Their passion would burn them, consume them and unite them. God, she couldn't wait.

THE DAYS PASSED in one continuous span of time, virtually unnoticed by Ian.

He waited patiently, letting Brian and Karina live their lives, innocently unaware of his constant presence, of his watching their every move. He'd followed them home from the store to Brian's lovely house on the beach where they cozied up nice and safe. Or thought they were safe.

They never noticed the car that always sat in the small lot beside Karina's store or even him as he strolled past several times a day. They never connected him to the gray vehicle that shadowed their every trip, no matter how short or insignificant.

Now Brian had moved her into his house. How convenient for Brian.

How convenient for Ian.

Every day Brian drove Karina to work. Every evening he picked her up. Sometimes she was alone at work, but not very often and not for very long. And she was never alone at his house, unless Brian went for a walk. Interesting.

And so simple.

<h1 style="text-align:center">Chapter 4</h1>

THE NEXT FEW days fell into an easy pattern.

Even though they'd picked up her car, Brian continued to drive Karina back and forth to work, not wanting her to be alone at any time. For the balance of the time, they worked on building their relationship.

By the weekend, with no further sign of Ian, Karina wondered if they'd blown the situation out of proportion. She still woke nightly, only Ian was no longer the reason. She felt safe with Brian. But other issues rose. Like her feelings for Brian. Their relationship remained platonic. Friendly, caring even but definitely hands off.

And that was her fault.

She knew exactly what she could do about it, but fear stopped her from taking that next step. And that was just stupid.

The phone rang when she was at home making lunch. "Hello?"

No answer. Spotting the notification that they'd missed another call, she clicked through to listen to the message, but there was nothing more than a dial tone. She shrugged and returned to the salad preparation, promptly forgetting about it.

Until it happened again.

Brian delivered fresh coffee outside later that afternoon.

"The phone just rang but there was only a dial tone. Must have been a wrong number."

Uh oh. "That happened earlier. Twice, in fact." she said. "I missed a call when cleaning and there was only a dial tone." She looked at him sharply, prodded on by the threat constantly hanging over their heads. "Do you think it could be Ian?"

"Anything is possible. But chances are it wasn't him." Brian shifted closer to her and pulled her into his arms. "We'll stay vigilant though, and hope it had nothing to do with him."

Sounded good…in theory. She wondered how much of this mess he'd shared with Mark. "When is Mark back?"

"On Wednesday, I believe. Why?"

"With him being gone these last couple of weeks, he doesn't know I live here with you."

"Yes, he does. I sent him an email updating him." Brian squeezed her warmly then released her again.

Karina looked at him sheepishly. "Good. I've been here a week but I'm caught in limbo. I want my life back to normal."

"We don't have many options at this point. Maybe the goal now is to make peace with our new 'normal.'"

"I know…" She broke off the thought, unnerved when the phone rang. She stared at Brian.

"I'll answer it." Brian headed into the kitchen.

Karina held her breath until she heard Brian's voice, then relaxed back into her chair. She turned her attention to the meal she'd offered to cook the next day. Sandra and the twins were coming over for a barbecue. No amount of control could keep her mind on preparing dinner, though. Instead it returned repeatedly to appetites of a carnal nature – namely hers.

Sexual tension was always just under her skin these days. Oddly enough, one of the worst times for her was when Brian was in the shower. God, she wanted the freedom to join him.

Reality rudely disrupted her sensual musings.

"That was Officer Markham on the phone." Brian ran his fingers through his short hair, irritation radiating from his body, before sliding his palm down his face. He slumped into his chair, facing her.

"Problems?"

"There was no one on the phone when I answered. I tried dialing *69, but couldn't get a number. So I called Markham."

Karina winced. She was glad that he'd called the officer but hated the thought that Ian might be behind this latest trouble. "What did Markham say?"

"He didn't say much. He reminded us to be careful and to keep tabs on these calls." Brian took her hand and tugged her gently forward and onto his lap. Karina buried her face in his shoulder and snuggled in close against his chest.

She breathed deeply, trying to let the tension inside of her go. Held close in Brian's arms, it was easier to believe that everything would work out fine.

THE TWINS HAD a blast on Sunday. They brought Max, and between the dog and the beach, they wore themselves out. Sandra teased Karina and Brian most of the afternoon. Karina cooked hot dogs for the twins and steaks for the adults. Later, they collapsed on the patio chairs, savoring their wine. Full of food and the added treat of ice cream and soda, the boys reacted differently – they revved into high gear, running along the beach with Max and kicking a soccer ball where the adults could see them.

That game turned into exploring the driftwood and checking out what the ocean had washed ashore. Excited voices grew louder over some find in the clump of bushes behind the neighbor's shed.

Karina laughed, enjoying the boys' adventure – until the boys raced over with their find – a stainless steel coffee mug.

"Hey, Mom. Look what we found. Can we keep it?"

"Where did you find it?" Brian asked.

"Over there." They pointed toward a thick patch of scrub brush not far from the house. "Someone must have been sitting there for a long time. The whole place is packed down."

"Yeah, maybe they were hiding in the bushes, spying. That's so cool. We should go spy on someone, too." Daniel spun around as if to find a close enough neighbor to practice their espionage skills on.

"Can we keep it, Mom?"

"*Please?*" Sandra said.

"First off, no spying. That's not cool. And as for the mug, I think it should be Brian's. It's his place and we don't need one of those. Besides, it's more fun for you guys to just keep hunting," Sandra said. "So why don't you go look and see what else you can find, and leave that mug here."

Excited about the possibility of finding more treasure, the boys took off in a different direction.

Karina hadn't said a word. She stared suspiciously at the mug while a yawning black pit opened in her stomach. She looked over at Brian. He seemed relaxed, unconcerned. Of course, it was a public beach. People were allowed to walk or sit wherever they wanted. But then, why was the mug there, next to Brian's house, in the bushes?

None of the adults referred to the cup again. The next time Brian rose to go into the kitchen, he casually took it with him. He returned with the bottle of wine and filled Karina's glass.

Sandra refused more. "I'd love some, but," she said, standing, "it's time to head home. David, Daniel, it's time to go, guys. You have school tomorrow."

Loud groans echoed over the sand.

"Mom, why did you have to say that? We were having so much fun until you wrecked it." This last came from David, the oldest by one hour and the self-appointed leader.

"Yeah, Mom, like, why remind us?"

Karina shook her head at the pair. They were too cute to resist so she got up from her comfortable seat to hug them both.

"There's still some fruit custard left. Do you want to take home the leftovers?"

"Could we finish it now?" David asked.

"No, you can't." Sandra stepped in. "Tomorrow, when you get home from school you can both share it, but no more food tonight. It's late. Say thanks and let's go."

After they left, Karina felt loneliness close in on her. She'd enjoyed their visit. She only wished that Chelsea could have joined them, but Marly had already made plans for the two of them. Her brain cycled back to the mug.

"Brian. That mug the boys found in the bushes…?"

He slipped an arm around her shoulder, steering her toward the roses. The scent was strong in the evening, but the heavy sweetness was tempered by the tang of ocean air. "Yes, I think it's probably Ian's. But we don't know that for sure."

She hated this uncertainty. Frustrated anger coiled deep in her belly. "Will you call Markham? There could be prints or DNA on it."

"I will, but I doubt he can do much with it." Brian ran his hand through his hair. "There aren't likely to be any useable fingerprints left on it at this point, especially considering most of us handled it after the boys found it, but that will be up to him to determine."

Frustrated and depressed, Karina stepped away and started back toward the front stairs. "I hate thinking that he might be watching us." Faint tremors edged into her voice despite every attempt to stay in control. "I'm going to bed. I just hope I can sleep."

"You can always come into my bed if you get scared," he said, his voice deepening, his eyes darkening with heat.

Shivers slid down her spine. And this time Ian had nothing to do with them.

Spinning around, she looked up at him.

Slowly, as if giving her time to run, he reached for her, searing her with the heat of his kiss. Fear, confusion, loneliness and intense need tangled together. Warm fingers slid under the hem of her t-shirt, caressing her breasts. He squeezed and rolled the tight buds of her nipples, before finally palming each breast.

His tongue slowly explored her mouth, stroking her bottom teeth, caressing her and suggesting so much more pleasure. Tenderly, he dined on the sweetness, showering his loving attention on first her bottom lip and then on the upper one. Her senses melted with the heavy scent of roses, ocean air and man. She didn't know where one started and where one stopped. She didn't care. She burned.

Her mind tumbled with sexual images, of being filled by him, loved by him, of being his. Of him being hers.

Images. Pictures. Movies. Watching…

Ian

Ice cooled the molten lava, as her mind wrenched her back to reality. Revulsion burned in her gut. She whispered hoarsely, "What if he's here – watching us right now?"

He squeezed her against him, his heavy breaths warm against her hair.

"He isn't."

"But we don't know that, Brian. I can't stand this," she cried. Unnerved, she bolted into the relative safety of the house, and her bedroom. But the suffocating darkness followed.

A storm threatened long into the night. The air was electric, crackling with the fury fighting to break free. When it finally did, Karina awoke; tense and rigid with stress. The room was full of shadows. The darkness of the room mirrored the darkness of her thoughts. There was no way she could surrender to the comfort of sleep. She knew nightmares would dominate tonight. She huddled deeper under the covers.

God, this was so stupid. If she were in her own home, she'd just get up and make a cup of herbal tea. Maybe put on the television or listen to soothing music for a while. And while those things sounded perfectly reasonable, what she really wanted to do was crawl into Brian's bed to be held and to feel safe. But after tonight's scene, that would be seriously stupid.

Wouldn't it?

Why was she resisting? None of her reasons seemed logical at this point. Was she ready for the next step?

Definitely.

Satisfied that she'd finally made the right decision, she slipped out of bed and into the hallway. The skylights offered a glimpse into the fury raging outside. She wore only her sheer, silky negligee and shivered in the chill air as she headed in the direction of his room.

She frowned. Brian's bedroom door was open. She peered inside to stare disappointedly at the empty, rumpled bed. That figured. She finally bolstered the courage to take this step and he wasn't even here. Sighing softly, she turned to head back to her own room and noticed a pale glow of light coming from downstairs. Curious, she made her way to the main level.

A small fire crackled in the fireplace, throwing out the soft flickering light she'd seen from upstairs. Brian reclined on the leather couch, his feet propped up on a nearby ottoman. There was a brandy snifter, with just a hint of amber left inside, on the coffee table beside him. He was fast asleep.

She smiled tenderly down at him. She carefully covered him up with one of the mohair throws he kept over the couches, and dropped a gentle kiss on his forehead. There were still a few pieces of wood sitting off to one side. Quietly, she added another one to the fire. The flames danced to their own tune, unaffected by the pounding of the storm outside – as she should be. Brian was here; she wasn't alone. She really had no reason to let fear dominate.

She tossed back the remaining cognac from his glass and with one last loving look, she returned to her own bed.

Alone.

Brian woke with a sore back and a pounding head. He struggled to sit up and groaned at the tight muscles. A blanket lay over his legs. *Karina.* He tossed it off to the side and stood up checking out his watch. Well past midnight. He glanced around his study. That's right. He'd stayed downstairs for an extra finger of brandy tonight and must have fallen asleep. Having Karina so close, yet not nearly close enough was a slow, twisting torture.

As he shuffled down the hallway he wanted nothing more than to open her bedroom door and crawl in beside her. Then he heard her cry out. His footsteps slowed as he approached her door. Though the sound soft was muffled, her obvious pain and fear tiptoed into his heart.

He reached out and turned the knob, slowly pushing her bedroom door open. From the doorway, he could see her twist in her sleep, the covers rippling with her unrest.

Hesitantly, he walked forward, not wanting to shock her awake but wishing he could help. She cried out again, huddling deeper under the blankets.

"Karina," he whispered softly, reaching down to stroke her shoulder and back hoping she'd calm down without having to wake her up.

It took several minutes for her to relax. But eventually the tightness in her face eased and her body loosened as she slipped into a deeper sleep.

He couldn't help but notice the sheer, silky negligee she wore, one with loose shoulder straps that kept slipping off. Twice he successfully tugged them back into position but on the third time, he had to fight to keep his hand from lingering. To explore the tempting expanse of her smooth bare skin. Beads of sweat broke out on his forehead as he remembered the details of their night together so many years ago. A hint of her familiar perfume teased his senses, and he shuddered with the effort to control himself.

She was so precious to him. So caring and so honest in her emotions. He needed her in his life.

He was desperate to take their relationship to the next level, but he wanted there to be a natural building a real relationship together. He didn't want her to come to him out of fear, or because she felt it was expected.

And she seemed close. But he didn't think she was close enough.

KARINA AWOKE EARLY the next morning to find police in Brian's kitchen.

It had been another night of almost no sleep. The hot shower hadn't relieved the groggy heaviness, but maybe coffee would.

She mustered a smile for Officer Markham while reaching for the cup that Brian offered her.

"Are you okay, honey?"

She just shrugged in response. "Is there anything new or are we still in the dark?" She didn't bother looking up. It was easier to stare into the depths of her black cup.

"No, there's nothing new. Except this mug – if it's his. If this proves he's been on this property it adds to the evidence we have of harassment, stalking even. Even so, he hasn't done anything dangerous."

She frowned. "So you might get him on a smaller charge, but he'd be out in no time and possibly he'd be even angrier."

"If he even goes in. If he's given bail or gets home arrest...and he continues on this path with menacing phone calls and this sort of thing—" The officer indicated the mug. "That would show he's not letting the issue go. And if his behavior escalates, obviously, our concern would go up proportionally."

Karina had to be satisfied with that.

"I'm afraid that's it for now." Markham shrugged his massive shoulders at them. "Thanks for the coffee. And just be sensible."

He shook hands with them both and walked out.

Karina stepped out onto the front porch to watch the police car drive off. One question burned in her mind. What would bring the police back the next time?

Chapter 5

AFTER MARKHAM LEFT, Karina hugged her coffee cup and pondered the relationship she and Brian had. She'd made her decision the night before, but how could she bring up this topic of conversation with him?

The answer came sooner than she thought.

Brian walked into the kitchen. Sheepishly, he said, "I presume you came downstairs last night. Thanks for the blanket."

She smiled gently at him. "You looked comfortable, so I left you."

"I woke up after midnight and made it back to my own bed." He massaged the back of his neck. "My neck is still stiff, though." He walked over to the coffee pot and refilled his cup.

"Couldn't sleep last night?" Karina asked casually, her eyes on him.

He raked his fingers through his still-damp hair and stood silently for a moment. Then, as if making some monumental decision he turned and said, "Not a chance. I kept trying to remember all the reasons why I said I'd wait for you to come to me. But somewhere along the way, I fell asleep dreaming of you." He watched her intently.

Stunned by his admission, Karina didn't know what to say.

"Don't tell me you're surprised," he asked.

"No," she said quietly. "That's what took me downstairs to look for you."

In two strides, he was next to her, staring down at her in disbelief. "You came to me last night and I was asleep?" His voice rose in astonishment. Disbelief and chagrin shone in his magnetic eyes.

"I was scared."

"Oh." Any remnants of hope in his expression faded quickly from his face. "Then I realized something important." She took a deep breath. "I was only fooling myself, while cheating us both."

"Cheating us both? In what way?" He asked carefully. Slowly, he picked up her hand to hold between his own.

"I finally admitted that I really do want to be with you." Her voice dropped to barely above a whisper.

"Because you were scared?" he asked. "Because you wanted comfort and being with me was the way to get it?"

"Because I wanted to be in your arms." Her voice rose slightly. "Do you really think that I would have sex with you just so you would keep me safe?"

"No." He shook his head. "But I don't want you going to bed with me because you mistake wanting comfort for wanting me." There was bleakness in his voice.

She'd never heard that tone before. Her heart squeezed as she realized he was as unsure about her as she was about him. She took a deep breath and blurted out, "It's you I want."

His eyes warmed several degrees and even twinkled a little. "Are you ready to give me another chance?"

Warmth and a sense of surety, of rightness built inside her. She smiled. "Absolutely."

"Then maybe the conclusion I came to last night won't be out of line." He lifted her hand, turning it over to drop a kiss on her palm, awakening nerve endings deep inside. Quietly, he said, "I thought that maybe we should get out of town for the weekend. Go to my cabin on Salt Spring Island and spend some time alone." His velvet voice slid over her as he asked, "Would you come away with me this weekend?"

A second kiss brushed across her knuckles, the third and the fourth he placed gently on the inside of her wrist.

Shivers raced over her, warming her heart deep inside. There was a hidden question in his words. She knew that. This was no time to hide what she wanted.

Her barely audible voice breathed the answer they both wanted. "Yes."

He drew her into gently into his arms. From the comforting reassurance of his embrace, she listened to his plans.

"We'll leave Friday, after you're finished work. We can catch the ferry over and be at the cabin by seven. Have dinner and a walk on the beach before the evening settles. Pack lightly and only tell Susan and Sandra. This weekend is for us. We'll return on Sunday evening. How does that sound?"

She nodded, not trusting herself to speak.

It wasn't until she prepared for bed that night that she realized something else. Having agreed to take the relationship one step further, she needed to go and see a doctor about birth control. Something she hadn't fully considered before. Hell, she'd come close to lying down in the grass with him last night without giving any thought to the consequences.

The coming weekend haunted her every thought, and decade-old, remembered passion made her shiver with anticipation. Wants and needs mingled constantly. Just feeling this way was a new experience. She began to wonder if she'd even make it to Friday night, at this rate.

By Wednesday morning, she was excited but had her nerves more or less under control. Added to the excitement was Mark's return. She'd missed him. And when he breezed into the store at lunchtime with his arms wide open she'd run into them, laughing with joy. He was a special friend – one who knew her too well, it seemed.

"So how's life with Brian?"

"Fine." She grinned up at him. She knew he wouldn't leave it at that and waited for his next question.

"So how's Brian's bed? Comfy?" His wicked glint went straight to her heart.

"How would I know?" she countered, delighted with the teasing byplay.

"That's it! If you don't know by now, it's time to haul you into my bed." He pulled her close and hugged her again.

"If I ever give up on him, I'll come to you." She patted his chest affectionately. "Come and say hi to Susan."

Susan laughed at the sight of the two of them. "We missed you, Mark. It just wasn't the same around here without you." Susan gave him a big hug, planting a kiss on his cheek.

Mark chuckled loudly. Standing there, with an arm around each of them he added, "I'll have to go away again, if I get to come back to all this attention."

"How is your brother doing?" Karina asked, remembering the reason for Mark's absence.

"He's going to be fine. His recovery is a little slow, but he's at home now, surrounded by his loving family." Mark grinned lopsidedly. "Now enough about me and mine.

Anything new? What's going on with Ian?"

Karina's happiness deflated. *Ouch.* Mark's question certainly took the levity out of the day.

She answered his question somberly. "We think he's been watching the house and there've been several prank phone calls. Of course you already know about the break-in at my place. But even though we're sure it's Ian, we don't have any actual proof that he's behind these events."

She walked into the back room to get Mark a coffee, and he followed.

"That's frustrating. And there's nothing the police can do?"

Karina shook her head. "Not really. They're still looking for him, but there's not enough evidence to charge him yet. They are working on it though."

Mark squeezed her hand. "You know that if you need my help with anything, all you need to do is ask."

She nodded, her affection for Mark filling her chest. What had she done before she met all of these wonderful people? She tamped down a wave of emotion that threatened.

Thankfully, Mark knew enough to change the subject. He glanced around the store.

"You know, this place looks incredible. Unbelievable what you two have done here." He turned around, his arms wide. "Are you happy, Karina?"

She stopped and thought about it. "Yes I am. About everything but Ian."

"That's understandable. Now you have me here to keep an eye out for you, too." He grinned. "Let's go for lunch, we'll bring something back for Susan, if she doesn't mind letting you go for an hour. Then this afternoon, I'm yours to put to work."

The women weren't going to turn that down. After lunch they made the most of the extra pair of hands, crossing several items off their To-Do list. Mark drove her home at the end of the day. When they arrived, Marly, Brian's ex was just bringing Chelsea up from the beach.

Mark joined the ranks of the forgotten as Karina headed toward the cherub before her. Chelsea squealed and raced up the beach as fast as her chubby legs would let her. Karina covered the distance much faster and tossed the little girl high in the air.

Marly stood off to one side in amazement.

At her sideways look, Mark nodded. "They are quite something together."

"How about we go get dinner started, huh?" Karina placed Chelsea on her shoulders and marched toward the kitchen.

Once in the kitchen, though, Chelsea was more concerned with trying to catch the sunbeams drifting through the room than helping. So instead, Karina put Chelsea down at a sink full of soapy water before she set about cooking.

"Chelsea! Watch the water, sweetheart. Don't put it on the floor!" Brian's voice came from the doorway. Karina waved him off.

"It's only soap and water, Brian. She's happy, so who cares?" Karina grinned. Mark laughed from behind Brian. Marly who'd been invited to stay for dinner, smiled at the picture.

Chelsea was the center of attention at dinner, with Mark and Karina on one side of the table, and Marly and Brian on the other. This was Karina's first chance to observe the relationship between Brian and his ex-wife. Unfortunately, it wasn't very enlightening. Brian seemed to treat Marly the same as he treated Karina – with affectionate friendliness. Marly was still a big part of Brian's life, due in part to Chelsea, and Karina reminded herself that it was good for Brian and Marly to have a decent, grown-up relationship rather than being adversaries.

But Karina wanted to be so much more. And she would be after this weekend. In two days time. Uncomfortably, she realized belatedly that Mark was doing the same thing – but he was observing her relationship with Brian. He only offered 'interesting,' as a final good-bye comment.

Thursday morning during a lull in store business, she went into the back to call Mark to find out what that comment had meant.

Mark's laughter rang through the line. "What are you two waiting for? The uncertainty is destroying you both. Get it out of your systems, and then you might actually become aware of the rest of the world."

"I am not obsessed with him," she said. Her irritation loosened her tongue, and she unintentionally let their plans slip. "After this weekend we'll have it sorted out!"

Masculine laughter reached her ears. "Oh, Karina," he purred, "what exactly are you planning?"

"Nothing and it's none of your business!" Damn her unruly mouth.

Her words did nothing to dispel Mark's amusement. "Brian mentioned something about not being here this weekend. Are you two planning to go away?"

"We're going to his cabin for the weekend."

"Now, that's a smart move. Get away from all the problems. Then you can both relax and have time just for each other." His voice softened. "I'm envious of you both. You have something special. Nurture it, Karina. It can too quickly be lost."

Her own voice quieted in sympathy and understanding. "I will, Mark."

"Remember, if it doesn't work out, I'm always here."

"Thanks," she said, his words bringing a small smile to her lips.

"The room actually crackles with passion when the two of you are together," Mark said. "That's worth building on."

Three cups of coffee later, she was still thinking about it. Because of course, he was right. She was an idiot. Once again satisfied with her world, Karina went back to work.

Content that is, until that evening's seminar started, and Ian made another appearance.

THE THREE MUSKETEERS, as Karina had started to think of Susan, Sandra and herself, stood off to one side of the auditorium, waiting for the men to join them at coffee break.

The feeling of anticipation and excitement vanished, however, when she spotted Mark heading in their direction. His expression was angry, and tension radiated in almost tangible waves from his body. Karina felt herself going still inside, her head beginning to pound. Mark gestured to the three of them to follow him, and he led them off to a corner, away from the rest of the seminar crowd.

"We think Ian is hanging around."

Susan gasped. "What? How? Where?"

"The hotel staff saw him by the elevators," Mark clarified.

Sandra whispered, "Oh, no."

A knot of fear clogged Karina's throat.

"The police have been called and the hotel security has been notified."

Sandra and Susan both moved to stand protectively on either side of Karina. Their support was strong and instantaneous, and immediately Karina felt safer.

"Brian is talking to Officer Markham right now," Mark explained. "This harassment needs to stop. It's the last thing we need here tonight. Not only does he need to leave the two of you the hell enough alone, we don't want future seminar participants staying away because we have a reputation for making people angry."

Brian appeared, slipping his arm around Karina's shoulders. "The police are on their way. Security has been briefed and are watching all the entrances and exits." He glanced around the crowded room that hummed with conversation. "So far, it seems like nobody else has noticed anything out of the ordinary, which is good." He dropped a kiss on Karina's temple. "It's time to get started again. Keep your eyes open everyone."

Oddly enough, Karina's headache lessened as the next hour passed. There was no sign of Ian, and her headache disappeared completely by the time they made it to the pub. For the next few hours, beer and laughter flowed freely. Brian and Mark were confident that Ian had been stopped. That was their theory.

Not Karina's.

It didn't feel right. She sensed Ian was not out of the picture. In fact, he was probably planning his next move right now.

IAN GAVE A friendly smile to the two policemen that

approached him. He'd taken a seat in the lounge, a coffee at his side, in full view of the two hotel security men. He'd only caught a glimpse of Brian and Karina tonight before being spotted by both security and staff. It was so predictable of them to call in the police. Predictable and disappointing.

It was a quirk of twisted humor that made Ian sit in the lobby in full view of everyone. He wasn't going to hide. If they wanted him, they could come and get him. What a perfect way to set the police at ease over the whole thing all the while buying himself some extra time to carry on.

"Good evening officers," he said by way of greeting. "It's a nice night out, isn't it?"

The second officer eyed him cautiously. As if he were a bomb about to go off. Ian laughed inside.

"Mr. Blackburn." The first officer nodded to him. "We have a few questions we'd like to ask you." The one officer narrowed his eyes at him. "Downtown."

Ian raised a brow. "Of course, if that's really necessary. I came here hoping to gain admittance to the lecture tonight. He's a great speaker and has helped me understand much in my life." He lifted his cup and took a sip of the hot brew. He laughed inside again. "Unfortunately, my interruption many weeks ago has made me unpopular." He leaned forward. In as sincere a voice as he could manage, he said, "I really feel bad about that. I certainly don't normally act that way."

He leaned back and sighed theatrically. "I was a little… overwrought… over my wife's decision to leave me."

The two men looked at each other uncertainly.

"Please, understand. I regret my previous behavior. I'd hoped to attend the lecture tonight and learn more myself."

The first officer pulled out his phone and walked a few feet away. The second sat beside Ian with a notebook in hand. "We need to verify your address."

Ian immediately gave him the address of his last place. He'd just moved yesterday but not even his old landlord knew that yet. Then in the most cooperative manner he could manage, explained he had a new cell phone as well and proceeded to rattle off the numbers. These answers were easy to give. He'd had lots of time to come up with reasonable explanations.

Besides, he hadn't done anything wrong. Not really.

Not yet.

Chapter 6

ODDLY ENOUGH, IAN didn't prey on Karina's mind the next day. Mostly because she was too busy making herself sick over the coming weekend. Nerves and excitement had hit hard.

Brian was picking her up early from the store so they could make the five o'clock ferry.

She had packed this morning before coming in to open. Thankfully, business was steady throughout the afternoon, keeping her well occupied. That was a blessing as far as Karina was concerned.

Hearing the door yet again, she looked up with a bright smile to welcome the next customer. Instead, her face tingled warmly with embarrassment as she watched Brian walk in. Nervousness took over and she didn't know what to say.

Susan looked over at her, her expression curious. "Hi Brian. Is it time to pick Karina up already?"

"I'm a little early," he replied easily.

Karina found her voice with effort. "I'm not quite done. I'll be a few minutes yet. Do you want to come back or…?"

"I'll wait. I don't have many chances to visit with Susan, so you go ahead and finish off."

He was as good as his word. He headed toward the back of the store where Susan had gone to give them a few moments together.

Karina stared at his receding back in frustration. How could he be so calm and unconcerned? He'd obviously not gone through a day of paralyzing nerves like she had. Damn him anyway.

Her temper simmered as she returned to the unpacking. She tore into the top box in the shipment, ripping off the cardboard and tossing the packing foam on the floor. *Calm and cool was he?* Fine, she could be the same way. She was done in record time.

"Brian, I'm ready!" She reached for her purse and went into the back to talk to Susan.

"We're leaving now. See you on Monday," she said to her friend.

"Have a wonderfully sexy weekend." Susan grinned mischievously.

Karina's cheeks warmed. She pinned Brian in place with her accusing glare.

He widened his eyes, a glint of amusement shining deep inside as he said, "What's wrong with telling Susan where we're going?"

She knew when she couldn't win. Reaching out, she gave Susan a quick hug, and then brushed past Brian.

She could hear his deep laughter as he followed her out of the store.

"Second thoughts?" His voice was gentle, kind.

"No, I don't have second thoughts." She was quiet for a few minutes. "I just wanted this time to be private, ours alone."

They'd reached his parked car. Gently, Brian pulled her into his arms for a tender moment. "And it will be," he whispered in her ear while stroking her back. The comforting motion reassured her.

Curled tight against him, Karina realized that she really was hiding. She leaned back to study this man who held her as if she were precious and irreplaceable. His face was so beautiful. Strength and confidence flowed from the crags and dips. The late afternoon had brought a shadow of bristles to his lower jaw. Slowly, she stroked the planes of his face. With every caress, the light in his eyes deepened and darkened. He tilted his head into her hand, a regal greyhound asking to be stroked. Content in who he was, capable of surrendering to his own needs, willing to bend for hers. She could learn much from this man.

Lost in the moment, she felt a wave of love overwhelm her. She reached up to cup his face with her hands. Slowly, oh, so slowly she lifted her face to his and placed an angel's kiss on his devilish lips.

With a Madonna smile, she pulled back to look at the flabbergasted man in front of her. "We'd better go or we might miss our ferry."

With a pat on the cheek, she turned and slid onto the front seat of his car. This time she was the one to walk away. This time he was the one left standing still in one spot, stunned.

Perfect.

IAN FOLLOWED THE Porsche as it wove through the traffic from the store back to Brian's house. He pulled over a couple of hundred feet away from the building and sat, considering his options. It was a Friday. And for whatever reason, Brian had picked her from the store early today. Why?

Even as he watched, Brian and Karina came back out carrying overnight bags. They stored the bags in the back before getting back in the car. Interesting. They appeared to be going away for the weekend. The question was – where?

He let them get a fair distance down the road before he pulled out behind them. He wasn't too worried about losing sight of them – Porsches weren't exactly common on the streets. He watched as they headed into the ferry lanes leading to the terminals. He pulled off to the side, keeping his car on the shoulder. Thankfully this terminal was smaller. At the big ones, once you went down the access road you'd end up right on the ferry without any way out.

From where he sat he could watch Brian pull into the Salt Spring Island ferry line up.

He grinned when he realized that meant they'd be gone overnight for sure and possibly for the whole weekend.

Perfect.

Now he had time to case Brian's house. And find the perfect hiding spot.

Chapter 7

THE CLEAN, FRESH breeze from the ocean washed away the heaviness of the hot afternoon.

The view from the ferry was glorious. Greedily, Karina wallowed in the experience. This island trip was aggravatingly short – just under an hour – and not nearly long enough to absorb the spectacular ocean scenery. Watercraft danced over the waves – everything from different-sized motorized craft to catamarans to unbelievable luxury yachts. She shook her head in disbelief at some of them. Regardless, it took her only minutes to fall in love with the islands.

"Brian, this is fantastic." She turned to beam up at him.

"It is, isn't it?" He inhaled the sea air. "I've been coming here since I was a child but I never get blasé about this view. Too bad the trip is so short."

She turned to him in surprise. "That's what I was just thinking."

With the islands rapidly approaching, she could see small cabins dotting the landscape. Karina was entranced.

"This would be a wonderful place to live," she told him, overwhelmed by the coastal scenery.

"My family used to come here several times a month to just get away. Some summers, we'd just move here."

The late-afternoon sun magnified the beauty of their surroundings. They stood lost in their private enjoyment until it was time to disembark.

On the road to the cabin, Karina absorbed what she could but there was too much. Why hadn't she realized sooner how much the water meant to her? They drove through miles of woods where the sun twinkled between the branches. They passed one house, then several more.

Brian laughed at her inability to sit still, twisting and turning in her seat. "We'll go sightseeing tomorrow." He pulled the car to a stop in front of a beautiful rustic building. She gasped, her jaw dropping. "This is a cabin?"

"We've done some renovations over the past twenty years, but compared to the new modern homes in the area, yes, this is a cabin."

"I had visions of no running water and no electricity," she admitted, feeling sheepish.

Brian laughed. "I assure you, hot showers and electric stove *are* part of the deal." There was a lightheartedness to his step as he unloaded their bags. "I always feel ten years younger when I get here," he added. "I have such happy memories of this place."

"With your line of work, you could live here, at least for summers." Karina suggested.

"I've thought about it. Maybe down the road I will. I don't know." He shrugged. "Marly only wanted to visit the odd time and never would have entertained the idea of living here full time."

"Yet, it's an ideal place to raise Chelsea." Looking around, Karina couldn't imagine *not* wanting to spend summers.

"Chelsea loves it here but she loves it at home too. Both places right on the water but with very different settings. This one is wilder, whereas that one is a groomed beach.

Here there's almost no one, in Victoria, the beach is open to the public. There are plusses to both. After Marly and I split, even though it was an amicable split, I ran here for comfort. The isolation called to me, helped me heal."

Karina could understand that. It hurt her to think of him needing to heal from another relationship. He'd been married to Marly – of course, the breakup would be difficult. It wouldn't matter if it were a friendly mutual decision. There was an emotional letting go required. If she'd had such a place to go to during her tough times, who knows what changes she'd have made years ago.

"Let's head into town for dinner. Salt Spring Island offers several wonderful restaurants." He hoisted the bags up the stairs to the main bedroom overlooking the bay.

Karina wandered through the beautiful house. There were huge windows covering the back wall, allowing for an uninterrupted view of the rocky coast. A fireplace took up an entire wall, with wood already laid. The upstairs, sparsely furnished yet more profound for all that, included a huge, king-sized, four-poster bed.

"Magnificent," she said, trying not to stare at the bed. Images burned her through her consciousness. She flushed, realizing he was looking at her as she stared at the bed.

"Do you like it?" he asked, watching her intently.

The heat in her cheeks burned more hotly. "It's gorgeous. The whole house is wonderful."

"Good." He nodded in satisfaction.

"Are you hungry?"

She looked at him carefully. They were standing in a bedroom with an oversized bed between them. The glint in his eye suggested so much more.

Her eyes narrowed, she stared back at him before answering smoothly. "Seafood sounds good."

A knowing grin broke over his face. But all he said was, "Dinner it is. Let's go."

Karina pivoted sharply and headed quickly back down to the car, anything to get rid of the sharp edginess deep inside. Easier to say than do as Brian climbed into the Porsche. She fought her instincts to head right back into the bedroom. She closed her eyes to block out the beautiful sight of lean, muscled thighs and strong, wide shoulders so close to hers. With nothing visual for her eyes to feast on, the rest of her senses took over. His cologne seeped through the interior of the car, the faint musk gently teasing her senses.

They drove the short distance into town. Brian parked the Porsche close to the boardwalk and he turned to look at her.

"Shall we?" he asked.

"Oh yes!" She couldn't wait. She wanted to experience everything this place had to offer.

Slowly, they walked through the more tourist-oriented spots then on down to one of the many wharves. A local artist stood on one end painting the setting sun. The summer evening found kids and families involved in everything from swimming to baseball. Peaceful, serene, beautiful, it was a perfect place to visit. Friendliness bubbled over from everyone they met.

It wasn't too long before Karina's stomach complained loudly at the delay of getting food. Brian just laughed before tucking her arm in his and heading in a different direction. The restaurant was set back a little from the hustle and bustle of the town's main street.

"Dinnertime."

The restaurant was small and simple. It was an upscale

dining experience for such a small town, obviously catering to a more select clientele. Karina wasn't too concerned about the décor or the customers. Too discomforted to eat throughout the day, she'd existed on coffee. Not the smartest thing to do.

Now her system was screaming for food, especially when the menu consisted of crab, scallops, bouillabaisse and many other mouthwatering delicacies.

"Is there anything here you don't like?" he asked.

"Raw oysters," came her prompt reply. She grinned at the flash of disappointment that crossed his face.

"Too bad."

"No, it's not – we don't need them."

His eyes gleamed at her knowingly, and his lethal grin snaked out, catching her unawares. Mesmerized, her body froze with instant awareness. Lightning coursed through her. The world around them faded away and she could hear nothing, except for the drum beat of her blood pulsing through her veins. Her temperature spiked ever higher and her breasts felt full and swollen.

"I'm very glad to hear it." His voice was gentle, yet, oh, so hot at the same time. The waitress arrived to take their order, reminding them of their surroundings and bringing them back to the present.

She tried to shield herself against that dangerous voice, but it just poured over her, bathing her in molten lava. She knew she shouldn't play with fire, but all she could think of was wanting to burn up in his flames. Her restraints had slipped loose, releasing the waves of her own sexual heat. She was sitting in a restaurant full of strangers and all she could think about was climbing onto his lap and taking those firm lips for her own.

His control appeared firmly in place, but she knew she could crack that steel wall. But not here – no, not in public. Mentally grabbing hold with both hands, Karina pulled the unwilling remains of her restraint together.

With tenuous control, she lifted her eyelids slowly and gave him a slow, sexy smile. The corners of her mouth hitched a little higher at the glazed look in his eyes, the ruddy flush that stained his high cheekbones.

"We could ask for takeout?" he suggested, his voice raw, hoarse. He closed his eyes briefly. "Christ," he whispered roughly. "You do pick your times, don't you?"

"Do I?" she teased him mercilessly. "Or should I say – I do?" She batted her eyelashes at him, bringing a reluctant grin back onto his face.

The waiter delivering their food interrupted his response. Food that Karina couldn't remember him ordering. With the devil still riding her hard, she picked up a large prawn and licked off the butter in tiny kitten-like laps.

"Jesus, you'll pay for this," he promised, his voice still gritty.

"I can hardly wait!" she whispered huskily in response.

"Shit!"

Brian dropped his head into his hands, his attention firmly on the ice cubes in their water glasses.

Her knowing laugh rippled through the air.

He raised his head to look at her. "Witch. You are so in trouble."

"What's the matter?" She leaned closer, bathing him with a heated look. "Aren't you hungry?"

He held his hands up in surrender. "Mercy!"

"Never."

With a glint in his eyes, he hopped up, reached into his

wallet and tucked several large bills into the waiter's hand. The two men spoke quietly for a moment before the waiter hurried off into the kitchen with their plates. He was back with a large paper bag by the time Brian had hauled her to her feet and tossed her sweater over her shoulders.

Karina didn't look once at the scenery on this return journey. She kept her heavy-lidded eyes on the magical man beside her. She felt like a seductive, sexy feline, sure of her own attraction and the reaction from her man.

She loved it.

The Porsche skidded over the gravel in the driveway before coming to a spitting stop.

He hastened around to her side, their dinner bag in one hand. Reaching down with the other, he offered her his assistance to slide out.

She accepted his hand, the epitome of a lady. However, it was a pure seductress who slipped past him, brushing her breasts slowly against him on her way.

"Are you *coming*?" She tossed the question over her shoulder as she walked into the living room. Her husky laugh underlined the double entendre clearly.

"I have high hopes," he muttered beneath his breath.

Brian strode into the living room, heading directly for the fireplace. Squatting down, he held a lit match to the wood. As the fire caught, he blew gently on it, coaxing the flames to burn brighter.

Watching him, Karina empathized with the flames. He'd taken embers buried deep within her and coaxed them into the raging fire that now burned within her.

CROUCHED IN FRONT of the fire, Brian struggled to slow

the heavy pounding of his blood.

For all her sexy-kitten act, he knew it would take just one wrong move to make her run. And that was the last thing he wanted to do. God, he wanted her. Expectancy coursed through him, shaking his control once again. A groan was desperately trying to escape, but he held it back.

He was still reeling from the depths of emotion he felt with Karina, extremes that he'd never thought would exist for him. Being in new territory was an unnerving experience, though. If she only knew that when it came to this relationship, he was just as unsure as she was.

That was partly why he had a hard time telling her how he felt. He could barely verbalize his emotions to himself…telling her in any coherent manner was out of the question. And he didn't want her to feel pressured to respond in kind. To tell him the words he wanted to hear just because she thought it might be expected. He wanted her to mean them.

And she wasn't there yet.

But she might be after this weekend.

Chapter 8

KARINA WATCHED BRIAN give the fire one last poke before he stood up and turned to face her.

"Wine?" he asked.

She didn't know if this was a delaying tactic or a stoking of the fires pulsating between them, she didn't need the latter and wanted no part of the former.

"Why don't we share a glass?" she suggested, as a tiny smile played at the corners of her lips.

With complete understanding, he pulled out the bottle of white wine that he'd put in the fridge to chill. Karina leaned against the counter watching as he triumphantly pulled a brandy snifter out of the cupboard and turned to show her.

"A sacrilege for any connoisseur," he said. "But it serves our purpose beautifully." He poured several inches into the glass then carried the glass into the living room.

"Come and sit down." Brian patted the couch beside him.

Karina curled up next to him, snuggling warmly against his chest. He held the balloon glass to her lips, inadvertently dribbling cool droplets onto her chin and on down to her silk top.

"Wait," he said, forestalling her attempts to wipe off the drips. Cupping her chin, he kissed the spot where the droplets touched.

Her breath caught. Her heart raced at the touch of his lips.

Gently, so gently, he completed his ministrations. Then he bent and kissed her. When she'd have deepened the kiss, he pulled back slightly and with tiny licks and delicate kisses meandering teasingly over her jaw and cheek. At her ear, he traced the delicate pink shell with his tongue. Karina leaned into his tormenting caress, shivers of pleasure wracking her frame.

His hands cradled her head, holding her captive while he journeyed where he wanted. His exploration whispered across to her eyes, stopping for a moment to bathe her lashes in warm air, then carrying on again down the bridge of her nose for a quick kiss.

Willingly enslaved between his need and her own, Karina was suspended, caught, desired and revered. And so far, he'd only kissed her. She didn't remember this heat, this building need, the last time. Then the ability to think at all slipped away and the ability to feel stepped up to center stage. And her need to touch. She reached for his shirt.

His shirt buttons slipped free easily and Karina could only stare in wonder at his muscular chest gleaming in the half-light. She smoothed her hands up his chest to slide the shirt as far down his arms as she could. He was so beautiful to her.

As Brian struggled to free himself, Karina placed a gentle kiss just below his nipple, watching in wonder as lean muscles clenched and rippled in response. She stroked his skin at the belt line, a tiny smile on her lips as her touch sent a tremor through his long frame. Teasingly she slid one finger just inside the heavy denim and slid it from one hipbone to the other.

His answering groan, combined with the startled catch of breath was infinitely satisfying. He threw off his shirt then reached for the bottom of hers and flicked it over her head. Startled, Karina found herself lifted and shifted to one side, with her arms still trapped in her shirt above her head.

"Two can play this game."

He unclipped the front closure of her bra, but left her flimsy material in place, leaving the valley of skin open to his touch. Karina lay frozen, caught, trembling with anticipation. Brian lowered his head and took a pouting nipple into his mouth. She cried out and arched upward.

He raised his head and looked at her.

"I have never seen a woman so glorious in her passion as you are right now." His voice was dark and colored with midnight dreams.

"I've never felt like this before," she admitted softly. She smiled up at him tenderly.

Swiftly he removed her shirt and her bra. She stood up and stepped smoothly out of her slacks. Somehow, the socks went at the same time. She stood proudly before him in nothing but a lavender thong and a devilish smile. Deliberately, she bent down to the fireplace and tossed another log on the fire, exposing her firmly curved buttocks with a shadow of lace between.

"The fire could do with another log," she said.

"My fire doesn't need any more fuel," he muttered hoarsely. Following her actions he unbuttoned his jeans, preparing to take them off.

"Let me," she murmured walking over to him and laying her hands on his.

"I'm too combustible for that," he said.

She ignored him. Swiftly pulling the zipper down, she slipped her hands inside his jeans and shorts and smoothed them over his hips. His erection caught under the soft material of his shorts, and Karina gently released him.

"Damn. I'm not going to survive this."

Her husky laugh rolled free as she dispatched the rest of his clothing.

"You're the one overdressed now," he said.

"You mean this?" She gestured to the tiny triangle of material still shielding the last of her. "Well, that's easily taken care of." With one swift movement, she stood before him naked.

"You are so gorgeous," he murmured. He opened his arms wide. Taking the first step toward him, Karina took on her new self, as though she were shedding a skin that no longer fit. The next step she took for herself, for Brian and for what they could become together.

This time there was no slowing down. Their bodies melded in the firelight as he lowered her to the thick rug, watching the flames reflect off her skin. "God, I need you," he whispered shakily, kneeling between her parted knees. He slipped a hand up her ribs to cup her breasts, then leaned over to tug first one nipple then the other into his mouth. Stroking her silky skin, he slowly and surely fed the flames. She arched beneath him and cried out for more.

Finally, stretched out fully above her, he balanced his weight on his forearms, resting at her entrance, asking an unspoken question.

With a glorious smile, she wrapped her legs around his calves and tilted her hips upward, giving him her answer. He lowered his head and gave her a deep drugging kiss while he slowly, carefully and reverently, sank deep inside. Finally coming home.

She gasped and shifted slightly beneath him. He raised his head and looked at her in question. "Are you all right?"

"Perfect," she murmured. She gave a little wiggle and smiled teasingly.

He groaned and dropped his forehead onto hers. "Witch."

Karina laughed and stroked the heavily muscled buttocks, caressing upwards to his back. She loved the feel of him. So strong. So careful. So gentle.

And she wanted so much more. Without warning, she dug in her nails.

He gasped and arched, his hips plunging deep. Brian lowered his lips and kissed her hard and deep and so, so hot. She melted beneath him. He started to move, his tongue plunging deep in tandem with his hips as he took the lead in their intimate dance. Deep and then deeper, strong and then stronger, fast and then faster yet again, Karina writhed beneath him.

The faint sheen of sweat made Brian's skin gleam in the flickering light. Overwhelmed, Karina quivered at the brink of heaven. She shivered in his arms.

Groaning slightly, Brian leaned down and pulled her pebble-hard nipple deep into his mouth. And sent Karina over the edge. Explosions wracked her soul and tremors wracked her body, until finally Karina sagged beneath him.

One last thrust sent Brian over the edge to join her. With lungs heaving and arms trembling from the effort, he collapsed on top of her.

Karina smiled through the silent tears running down her face, and held him close.

This was as it should be, where heaven met earth, where

man met woman, where Brian became hers. Not borrowed, not temporarily – but hers.

For the first time in a long while her world was perfect – and the night endless.

Brian found a blanket to wrap around Karina, tucking her up on the couch. He pulled on his shorts then went in search of the wine bottle to fill their communal glass.

Karina cuddled under the blanket, watching the dancing flames in the fireplace. She was exhausted yet exhilarated. Closing her eyes, she leaned into the cushions and rested.

An appetizing aroma wafted her way, tantalizing her. With a start, she realized it was after nine and the world outside was fading into darkness. And outside of the teasing bites of dinner at the restaurant she hadn't eaten anything since breakfast. With one appetite appeased, her stomach grumbled on cue.

"I heard that."

She twisted around as Brian came from the kitchen, carrying a platter with wonderful aromas. "Just what magic did you perform while I was dozing?"

"I reheated our dinner," he answered smugly.

"Boy, this waiter is the best yet."

Karina eyed Brian's muscular bare chest before her gaze dropped to his bulging thighs covered by snug jockey shorts. He noticed and a pink flush swept over his cheekbones.

"No comments on the house uniform, please," he said, smiling.

"Oh, no! I approve! I insist that this uniform be worn all the time this weekend," she said with a leer.

However, as her eyes swept over his frame and lingered on the most interesting spots, the material began to move.

"Stay down!" he commanded his shorts.

Karina erupted in laughter. "At least stay leashed while I satisfy a different appetite," she managed to say between fits of giggles.

Brian grinned. He pulled the coffee table closer and placed the food in front of her.

Hungrily she eyed the plates of seafood.

She reached for the largest prawn on her plate before leaning back in her seat. "Better eat quickly, if you want your share!"

With a shout of laughter, he bent down and plucked her up, blanket, prawn and all. He turned, stretching out over most of couch with her now on his lap. Smiling down from her now-superior position, she offered him the second bite of her delicacy.

Brian pulled her in for a tight, close hug, tucking her head against his chest and resting his head on hers. He squeezed her hard before letting her go. "I'm starved!"

They grinned at each other and set out to fill their stomachs.

TO SAY IT was a fantasy weekend come true would be correct. And Karina loved it. The days and nights were filled with hot loving and long talks, and long walks with hot conversation. The weekend was for the two of them, and the two of them alone, and Karina took full advantage of it.

They shared coffee from the same cup and shared water from the same shower. They argued, empathized and sympathized, sharing story after story. They laughed, they cried, but most of all, they made love.

Over and over again, they learned each other's bodies — sometimes hard and fast and sometimes slow and languid.

And eventually they even made it to the king-sized bed upstairs.

The sun shone hot Sunday afternoon making the water twinkle and shine. Karina walked the beach holding hands with Brian.

"What's bothering you?" he asked during a break in the conversation.

She glanced at him. "Is it that obvious that something's upsetting me?"

"Now that I know you – how you think, how you feel, how you come apart beneath me – yes!"

She blushed at the warmth of his voice, but no longer at his words. With a tug she lifted their clasped hands and placed a kiss on his knuckles.

"It's not a big thing."

"All the more reason to tell me." Slowing to a stop, he pulled her into his arms and looked down at her.

"It's just…"

"What?" he prompted gently.

"I don't want this weekend to end." The words came out in a rush, half muffled against his chest.

He hugged her more tightly, whispering against her curls, "Neither do I. Neither do I."

THERE THEY WERE.

Parked several houses down, under the shade of a large tree, Ian watched as Brian's Porsche turned into the driveway.

He smiled, proud of himself for having made the right decision. He'd been certain they'd only be gone for the weekend. And now that they were back and lost in their idyllic world, he could set the stage for his big plans. It'd been a snap to get inside the house, and he'd taken his time, exploring. He'd checked out the layout, found a few places to hide. A big place like that, he could hide out for days and the two of them would never know.

Malice churned inside Ian as he watched the two people he despised more than anyone else, get out of the car and stroll inside. They were so lost in each other they had no clue about anything going on around them. It was dark enough he could follow their progression through the house by following the lights that turned on and off. He laughed grimly as the path ran straight to the bedroom.

Good. Lovers would be much easier to surprise. Maybe next weekend would be the perfect time. A special weekend for them all – in more ways than one.

As he drove away, the rain started to fall and he giggled. His tire tracks would be washed away and no one would ever know that he'd even been there.

Perfect.

Chapter 9

T HE NEXT MORNING, Karina lay in bed listening to the birds chattering outside the window. She should be getting up; it was her turn to open the store. Yet, her mind couldn't get her body to respond. Of course, part of that was because of the muscular, male thigh thrown across hers.

This morning, however, she lay in a state of contented joy.

Waking up with him beside her would never get old.

Now it was Monday morning and time to face reality. That included the store, Susan and possibly, even Ian.

As gently as she could, she slipped out of bed and into a hot shower.

The coffee had almost finished dripping and the toast was almost done when Brian walked into the kitchen. Neither of those two things seemed to matter to him, though, as he strode straight toward her, plucked her up off her feet and kissed her soundly.

"Good morning." He dropped a kiss on top of her head and released her. "I saw you sneak out of bed. That wasn't nice."

"Maybe not, but it was definitely time to get moving." She smiled regretfully, turning back to the toast. "I'm supposed to open the store this morning. Are you still planning on chauffeuring me back and forth?"

He sighed. "I'd love to keep you here in bed with me but as you need to go, I'll definitely be driving you."

SEVERAL HOURS LATER at the store Karina was preoccupied with work when Susan arrived. She glanced up with a smile. "Good morning."

"Well? How was it?"

"How was what?" Karina replied, hiding her grin. She glanced out the window, her attention snagging on a lone gray car parked at the far end of the lot. She frowned as the car jogged something in her memory. *It had been there before, hadn't it?* She shrugged. *So what?* There were dozens of people who worked in the shops along this strip mall – the car could belong to any one of them.

"Your weekend. *Duh!*" Susan exclaimed, pulling Karina's attention back to the conversation at hand.

Forcing herself to keep her expression calm, Karina looked over at her friend and decided to take pity on her.

"We had…" She paused to find the right words. "We had a wonderful time, full of spectacular lovemaking and very enlightening conversations."

Relief swept across Susan's face. "Well, thank God for that. With that out of your system, you'll both be easier to live with."

Sandra walked in later that morning. Her grin warned Karina that the conversation was about to become embarrassing again. She waited with dread for the other woman to say something.

"Don't you look well loved!" Sandra's voice was tinged with envy. "I'm jealous."

For the second time that day, Karina's face colored

bright red. "Go ahead and tease. The fact of the matter is I *am* well loved." She couldn't resist adding, "You should try it yourself."

Sandra shrugged. "Not likely, the twins would be hell on a boyfriend. Was everything okay when you returned home?"

The question encompassed all manner of things. However, Karina knew exactly what they were asking. "There was no sign of anyone nor was anything disturbed." She shrugged. "Brian's going to call the police and see if there were any new developments while we were gone."

Susan veered the subject back to a safe topic.

"Well, in the meantime we have a busy week to get through. The new girl, Janice, worked out well on Saturday, by the way. I suggest we hire her to work every Saturday and one or two afternoons a week. What do you think?"

"Sounds good to me. We could both do with a lightening of the load." She immediately thought of what she could do with a few extra hours and Brian.

After that, the day flew by. The bell rang for the millionth time, and Karina looked up to see Brian walking toward her. Astonished, she glanced at the clock. It was already closing time.

"Are you ready to go home, sweetheart?"

"I will be in a few minutes. I thought I still had over an hour yet. It's been so busy, time ran away on me." Karina raced to close the store. She took a moment to look outside, realizing that most of the cars and shoppers were gone. It was definitely time to go home.

"Strange," she commented. "That gray car's still there."

"Which one?"

She pointed to the back of the lot. The same nondescript gray sedan was sitting off in an out of the way corner. "That one. It's been there all day. And I think I've seen it before."

"Maybe it's someone who works in the mall."

"Maybe. But I don't think it's normally parked all day like that."

"It might be broken down."

"I hope not, for their sake. Let's go home." Karina locked the door and they walked to the Porsche, dismissing the strange car.

Walking in the front door, Karina wondered what was bugging Brian. He'd been quiet all the way home. She tossed her purse and coat down on the table by the door.

Before she had a chance to turn away, Brian came up behind her, sliding his hands under her skirt to stroke all the way up her thighs.

"Sorry, love. I can't wait." His voice was husky with arousal.

He drove one hand inside her panties and palmed her tender flesh. She moaned at the instant flash of fire his touch sparked. His large fingers teased her, sliding across the outside of the plump folds. Karina shifted to give him more access, bumping against him. He was rigid, pressing and pulsing against her. His fingers dipped, spreading her, making her ready for his entry. With his tongue he stroked along her neck, taking tiny bites down her shoulders. The flames shot higher.

Impatiently she pushed back against him, rubbing her buttocks against his erection.

Brian ripped her panties down, giving her only time enough to step one leg out, before bending her forward over the table.

"Brian," she cried as he entered her in one thrust.

Then she couldn't talk at all as need stole her breath…and her voice. He pumped and pounded into her with a force that bounced the table against the wall. In one quick motion, he reached over, shoving the table back squarely. With the table secured, he braced his arms above hers to hold it steady, then exploded in motion, hammering into her uncontrollably. Karina was on the edge, crying out. She was already so close. Pulling back slightly, he slipped a hand down over her belly and stroked her swollen nub. She reared back and climaxed – hard. With one last jackknife, he surged into her and groaned, before collapsing against her.

Karina recovered before Brian did. She could feel his chest heaving against her back. It was such a perfect moment to tease him, she couldn't resist.

"Welcome home, dear. Did you have a nice day? Would you like a cup of tea, honey? Are you tired? Maybe you'd like to go to bed for a while." She giggled as he squeezed his arms around her in retaliation.

"Witch." Brian loosened his arms, but only to adjust himself and close his pants. With her still chortling, he grabbed her and tossed her over his shoulder.

"What are you doing?" Karina was laughing so hard she hardly felt the light slap he delivered to her bottom.

"You just said you needed a nap, I'll help you get one." With that, he hauled her up the stairs, whistling with very step.

Around ten o'clock, they finally managed soup and toast. Karina wouldn't have changed anything about the evening.

On Wednesday morning, she decided that she wanted to do something playful. She considered a seduction scene, complete with a certain negligee she'd been hiding for years.

It had flowers in all the right places and not much else. Yes, Brian would like that. Chances are she wouldn't be wearing it for long anyway. She set the date for Friday night.

For the next two days Karina kept her plans close, telling no one – except Cat and Serena, who'd quickly become her co-conspirators. Before long, she had an entire evening of fun planned.

She considered the fact that she and Brian had spent the weekend loving, but not telling each other of their love. She was just as much to blame as he was. Too overwhelmed before the weekend to mention how she felt, she didn't want the words just to be connected with sex. Their relationship was so much more than that. She was also hesitant to say it again. She'd done that once. And he'd run away.

The other thing that still bothered Karina was the fact that she had a few items left at Sandra's that she wanted to collect. The two of them had discussed making the trip to get the last of her belongings but hadn't made the time. Straddling two places made living with Brian feel temporary. So along with her other plans, she wanted to be completely "moved in" before he got home from work that night.

Most importantly, this Friday night was to be the setting for telling Brian how she really felt. To that end, she'd written an erotic letter titled, "Fantasy Man." It was essentially her story about how and why she'd come looking for him this time. And how different her future had turned out than expected.

Friday morning she fairly tingled with excitement. Mentally, she ticked off the items on her list for the evening. She had strawberries, wine, steak and chocolate. The strawberries had been Cat's idea. Sandra was going to pick up Karina and drop her and the last of her belongings off at Brian's house. She told Brian that Sandra needed her help for a short while after work so Sandra would drop her off after. Even better, he was going to Mark's for the afternoon to work, so he wouldn't be anywhere near home.

Karina left the store when Sandra arrived. It took a half hour to get her belongings unloaded at Brian's and safely stowed out of sight. The cats were in hiding again, likely thanks to all the commotion of moving in bags and boxes. She called them several times but they refused to come out.

Typical.

A half hour later, Karina was soaking in hot scented bathwater. Multiple candles burned in the steamy room, contributing their delicious scent. After her bath, she smoothed on body lotion, adding a tiny dab of perfume to several sensitive places. She finished with a special conditioning treatment for her curls. There was still work to do in the kitchen, so she dressed casually and headed back to the kitchen.

Brian said he wouldn't be home for an hour yet, but she'd soaked most of that hour away. Efficiently, she pulled out the marinating steaks and chopped, diced and tossed a fresh green salad. All she had left to do now was the garlic bread and the strawberries.

The strawberries were luscious: red, plump and uniformly sized. She laid them, freshly washed, on a towel to dry. The chocolate was almost ready for dipping. Now, was there anything else?

Oh, the letter! She must have rewritten it a dozen times. Based on her own sensual longings, it came from the deepest part of her heart. Just the thought of giving it to him made her stomach curl with nerves. She took another sip of wine. The letter was explicit and would add another erotic touch to the evening. *Would it offend him? Excite him? Would he even understand what she was trying to say?*

Everything was ready now – except for her. Now she needed another ten minutes to get dressed and do her makeup. She ran a hand over her hair. The curls had almost completely dried into manageable ringlets. Just a quick combing and they'd be fine.

The doorbell rang.

Damn it, whoever it was had lousy timing.

Karina raced down to answer the door. She just needed another couple minutes.

There was no one there. *How odd.* She walked out onto the front porch and looked around. There was no vehicle in the yard, or any sign that there had been one. *Had she imagined the doorbell rang?* No, the multiple bells, playing a musical chord would be hard to mistake.

Sudden shivers raced up and down her spine. This didn't feel right.

She hurried inside. The click of the door shutting behind her echoed in the high vaulted hallway. The hollow sound emphasized the emptiness of the house. She shivered. Maybe what she needed was a soothing cup of tea.

The kitchen was bright and welcoming, and being there took the edge off her nerves. Some of the houseplants from her apartment at Sandra's would look good in here. She headed over to the counter where the kettle sat and plugged it in. A sudden chill filled the air. Something was wrong.

She turned.

The glass doors were wide open. The ocean breeze blew fear and a dark, cold ugliness through the kitchen. Frantically, her gaze scanned the rest of the room.

And there he was. Ian sat at the kitchen table, staring at her. In front of him, lay the knife that she'd used to chop the salad vegetables.

Chapter 10

"OH, GOD," SHE whispered, her heart sinking. She needed Brian. The one time she was actually alone here in the house and Ian showed himself. That couldn't be a coincidence. He had to have been watching…and waiting. Just the thought of Ian keeping such a close watch on her, to time this so perfectly, brought her close to the edge of panic.

"Hello, Karina. Did you ever wonder why a criminal would bother to bring weapons of his own?" His smile was slow, cold and…empty. "When there are always so many available, no matter where you go?"

"No, I can't say that I ever thought about it. What are you doing here, Ian? It's been years." She kept her voice cool and unconcerned. But her gaze shifted constantly between the knife and his face before zipping to the open glass doors behind him. Could she make a run for it?

"I didn't get a chance to say hi on Thursday night. Too bad. However, I did get to have a nice chat with the police instead."

He looked anything but happy at that reminder. In fact – Ian *was* pissed. A menacing, dark evil lived in those eyes, a malevolent essence that had been growing inside for who knows how long. It was obvious, Ian had crossed over the fine line of sanity into madness.

And she had no idea what to do.

The teakettle whistled sharply behind Karina. Shaking inside, she forced herself to make a pot of tea in as relaxed a manner possible – as if finding a crazy man inside her house was an everyday occurrence. So what if her hand shook so badly that she spilled most of the water. Not knowing what else to do, she carried the pot over to the table before going back to the cupboard and pulling out two cups.

Through every movement she felt the intensity of his gaze burning into her, but he never said a word.

The open glass doors seemed to represent freedom. What would he do if she made a run for it? His eyes stalked her, like a tiger crouched and waiting for her to make a move. Feeling very much like Ian's prey, she wasn't sure where her best chance lay. *Bolt or stay?* So, she did nothing.

"Do you want milk and sugar in your tea?" She carried on, treating him like she would a visiting neighbor. Operating on nerves alone, she opened the fridge and automatically brought out milk for her own tea. Not that she'd be able to get a sip of it down her throat.

"I don't want any tea." There was no inflection in his voice. There was no hint of the bright anger burning in his eyes. Unfortunately, there was also no sign of sanity, either.

"I'll call Brian and see when he'll be home." She grabbed at the first excuse that came to mind. And hoped to at least make contact with Brian before being stopped. She punched one number. Two. Three. Four—

"Put down the phone." His voice was low, deadly. Her hand stalled in midair.

He didn't touch her. He didn't have to. He'd picked up the knife instead.

The receiver dropped from her numb fingers. Karina closed her eyes, fighting the overwhelming urge to run. *Run where?* He was a big, fit man. He'd overtake her in no time. If she went down to the beach, there was a chance that she might find someone to help her there. However, the beach could be empty in this wind, and there was just as good a chance that she wouldn't make it that far.

The front door was too far away to reach. It also wouldn't help much. There were no neighbors close enough to hear her scream.

So what was she going to do? She turned to face him.

"What do you want from me?" Surely, that wasn't her voice that sounded so calm, so normal.

"I want my life back."

"And you expect *me* to give it back to you?" she questioned him in disbelief.

"You and Brian. Yes." He nodded agreeably.

She lifted her hands toward him "How?"

"That's for you to figure out." He leaned back comfortably in the kitchen chair. His hand continued to play with the knife handle, belying his apparent lack of interest.

"What you really want is your wife back, isn't it?" Karina could understand that. He'd lost something important to him.

"I want my old life back – the way it was before my wife went to Brian's seminar."

"And what if she doesn't want you back? Then what?" Karina was starting to get irritated. Okay, it wasn't the most sensible way to deal with someone so obviously out of control. Then again, she wasn't feeling very sensible at this exact moment. Fury over the fact that he'd threatened and terrified her over the last few months burned away some of the fear that lodged in her belly.

She couldn't possibly help him. He was marching to a

tune that only he could hear and follow.

"You're nuts," she sputtered. *Nope, definitely not a well-thought-out response.*

"I'm not fucking crazy!" As though a switch had been flipped, fury roared in, instantly replacing Ian's complacency. He jumped up from his chair, knocking it over in the process. His wrath spurred him into action and he kicked the hapless chair across the room. "Don't call me crazy!" He grabbed up the knife and stabbed it into the table beside her hand.

"I'm sorry. I'm sorry. Please, calm down. I'm sorry, I didn't mean it." She cringed at the hell she'd unleashed. *Oh, please, Brian, where are you?* Tears flooded her eyes. What could she do? Ian *was* crazy. She sat motionless in her chair, desperately trying to hold back her sobs.

"Just shut the fuck up. God, I hate crying women." He paced the kitchen. "Don't you have anything to eat here? Wussy strawberries with chocolate. Namby-pamby salad. Is that the kind of shit you feed your man? How long do you expect him to be happy with that gourmet healthy crap? Where's the fucking meat? Cheese! Peanut butter! Where are the goddamned basics?"

He slammed the cupboards closed, storming through the kitchen like a tornado. Anything that was in his way, he dumped. Anything he didn't like he threw to the floor in disgust. Items he wanted he tossed onto the table.

With every loud bang and crash, Karina jumped. Ian terrified her. His large, burly, frame rambled through her kitchen, leaving a path of destruction as he went.

By accident, he happened upon the breadbox. Until now, she'd thought the red toadstool was a cute, whimsical addition to Brian's kitchen.

Ian ripped open the bread bag and dumped out the contents. He reached for the knife and casually made himself a sandwich.

Karina just stared at him in horror. This relaxed, calm manner frightened her even more than the violent outburst. The uncertainty of not knowing what would set him off next terrified her. A creeping numbness was slowly overtaking her muscles. How could she reach Brian? How could she reach anyone? There was no way to make a phone call, and she didn't dare try to run – although that option nagged at her.

If Ian would ever get away from the door long enough she'd make a break for it.

What if she made her move when she heard Brian's car? Could she get to him before he exited, allowing them both to get away? Brian would have his cell phone, and he could call for help.

Part of her didn't want Brian to come home. No, God, that wasn't true. She wanted him home desperately, but didn't want him walking into this dangerous situation.

Ian returned to the table with his mess of sandwiches. He'd already eaten the better part of the first one, but now several more were stacked up on the table. He rummaged in the fridge, still grumbling about the apparent lack of decent food.

"You don't even keep any beer in this place. What's with this skim milk shit?" Disgust oozed out of him. Obviously, he wasn't a believer in the current recommended healthy, low-fat lifestyle. Ian pulled over another chair and sat down at the table with his stolen goods.

Karina stared across the room. The knife was on the other side of the kitchen.

She glanced back at Ian. He was busy inhaling his food.

She couldn't even tell if he was chewing, the food went down in Doberman-sized bites at an alarming rate. If she was going to make a move, it needed to be now.

There was a noise from the driveway.

Ian froze and then cocked his head to listen. Finally shoving back from the table, he walked over to the patio doors to listen.

No doubt about it, a car was pulling into the front driveway.

Karina slid off her perch as soundlessly as possible and edged over to the kitchen entrance leading to the front door. Ian's attention was focused outside, toward the side of the house. He'd see any cars turning toward their place from the main road. Yet, if the car had already turned in, his line of sight would be blocked.

Without giving herself a chance to second-guess her actions, she raced to the front door. A yell erupted behind her as she pulled it open, her fingers fumbling with the handle. Finally outside, she jumped down the steps and raced on wobbly legs toward the car. It was Brian. *Thank God.*

She waved her arms at him in panic.

"Ian's here! We have to get out. Keep the car running!" she screamed.

Unfortunately, he misunderstood her. Brian shut off the car, climbing out of the vehicle and running out toward her.

"Karina, what's wrong?" He grabbed her arms, trying to hold her still.

"No! Go! In the car! *Ian's here.* He's crazy. Hurry we have to run!" She tried to pull him toward the Porsche. "Come on, he's got a knife! We've got to get out of here!" Karina sobbed, her uncooperative mouth stumbling over the words in her panic.

"Get into the car. We'll call Markham on the cell."

She almost made it.

Until Ian stepped out from the darkness blocking her path.

Karina shrieked in fear and surprise and stumbled backward into Brian's arms.

"Ian, what are you doing? My God. What do you want?" Brian's voice was strong and forceful, and a tiny feather of relief whispered over her. Gasping for breath, Karina worked hard to regain control. Brian was here now. Between the two of them, they might just be able to get out of this unharmed. But she needed to get it together and be strong.

Ian just stood there, a macabre grin on his face. He didn't say a word. Slowly he lifted his right hand. The kitchen knife gleamed with sinister intent in the dusky, late-afternoon light.

Karina felt Brian's breath catch as the truth hit home. Now he, too, saw just how insane Ian was.

"When I say so, I want you to run to the Sorenson's place. Okay?" Brian whispered against her ear.

She nodded, her eyes fixed on the nightmare beside the car, but her mind tuned to Brian. Her muscles tensed, awaiting the word.

"Now!" He passed her his phone and gave her a slight push in the right direction.

Karina jack-rabbitted to freedom only to realize as she reached the marginal safety of the trees that she was alone. Brian wasn't with her. Frantically, she searched in the fading light. The clouds sweeping in from the ocean added a gray dinginess to the air.

"Oh God!" she whispered. "No, Brian, no!"

Two shadows struggling behind her in the dark left no

doubt as to Brian's whereabouts. He was trying to subdue Ian and give her a chance to get away. Karina watched helplessly as the figures slammed to the ground, one trying to fight off the other. Was that Brian or Ian down? If it was Brian, she had to help him. Ian's madness made him strong. She crept closer, wincing at the grunts and sounds of physical contact echoing in the shadows. There was no way to tell one from the other. In the darkness, they blended, formed and reformed, both unidentifiable in combat. One thick, muscled arm rose and slammed down against the opposing body with an audible thud. Silence followed.

Slowly, the aggressor struggled to his feet. The other body lay crumpled on the ground, motionless. The man stood, shakily gasping for breath and staring directly at her in the gloom. *Could he see her?* Was it Brian?

Karina stood perfectly still, unsure, and too afraid she'd reveal her position to the wrong man. The figure took a few steps in her direction. Karina broke out of her frozen stance and raced toward the safety of the nearest neighbor's home. Running was all she could think about. Just as she broke through the dense tree line, the shouts coming from behind her finally registered.

"Karina! Karina! Stop! It's me, Brian."

With her chest heaving and her breathing ragged, she stumbled to a stop. Turning around she could barely make out Brian crashing through the trees behind her.

"Brian! Oh, thank God." Her body shook so violently she could hardly breathe, and her heart slammed against her ribs, urging her to keep running. Brian's arms wrapped protectively around her, and they stood locked together for a couple of minutes. To Karina, it felt closer to an eternity. Just as she thought she might be able to stand on her own,

Brian pulled back to look down at her.

"We need to call Markham. He can get someone out here to look after Ian."

"Is he dead?" she asked as they started back in the direction of Brian's house.

"No. I just hope I hit him hard enough to keep him out until they get here."

"Are you hurt?" Frantically, she ran her hands over him, looking for any injuries. Ian could have killed him. As she checked him over, Brian contacted the police.

Officer Markham answered on the first ring. Brian, his voice still ragged from the running, brusquely told him what had happened, and that they needed him and any cruiser that might be close by.

"He's out cold, but I don't know how long he'll stay that way. I don't want to try to subdue him again. His strength is unbelievable. I can't help but think I got lucky."

"Head out to the main road just in case Ian does come to." Karina could hear Markham's side of the conversation through the cell. "You'll have a better chance if there are more people around. We're on our way. And do not go back there."

Karina's relief that help was on the way warred with her fear about Ian. "Do you think we should go back, grab the car and make sure he's still out?"

Brian frowned. "Markham said not to go back, but I don't want him to wake up and take off. Damn. I should have tied him up right away."

"I need to know that he can't come after us again." Karina shivered at the thought. "Let's go do it now before he wakes up."

Quickly but carefully, they retraced their steps in the

dim evening light. The overcast sky made the journey more difficult without the help of moonlight. Now that the adrenaline was beginning to leave her system, Karina's feet were in agony. She hadn't had time to grab shoes before running out the door. She knew the rough twigs and rocks had cut them up. When they got closer to the house, she felt Brian's body tense.

"Brian? What's the matter?"

"Ian's gone! Damn it!" Brian pivoted, searching their surroundings. "Turn around. We're getting out of here now!"

He tugged on her arm, pulling her toward the main road.

"Oh, my God. He's here somewhere. Maybe he's still watching us." She couldn't stop swiveling her head in all directions, searching the darkness. She hated the feeling he was out there, somewhere, watching them.

Brian angled farther over to take them to the main road. "Can you run, Karina?"

Though her feet were sore, she broke into a run instead of wasting energy answering. Fear had already consumed the bulk of her fuel stores. Adrenaline could only carry her so far before exhaustion would take over. The realization made her steps falter.

"Come on, honey. You can do it. Just a little bit farther."

Karina forced her exhausted body up onto the main road. It was deserted.

"Now where?" Karina pressed her hand against her screaming lungs and stumbled to keep moving on. It was easier now that they were on the paved road but the bottoms of her feet were swollen and agonizingly sore. At least there was still no sign of Ian. Thank God.

"We'll head up to the crossroads. There's sure to be someone there. Come on." Brian's steps faltered and he slowed to look at her. "Damn, I'm sorry, Karina. I didn't realize you were barefoot."

She shrugged, unable to pull in enough air to answer. Instead, she grasped Brian's arm and gave it a squeeze. Groaning, she dug a little deeper for the last shreds of strength she could gather and then she pushed on.

Headlights appeared at the crossroads, accompanied by flashing lights and barely discernible sound of sirens.

With the promise of safety ahead, Karina collapsed on the grass at the side of the road, sprawling out to give her lungs a chance to recuperate. She was finished. And all she cared about was the fact that, as far as she knew, Ian wasn't anywhere nearby. And even if he were still around, with any luck, the sirens and lights would chase him off. She inhaled the smell of warm grass, fumes and fear – what a combination.

Brian sank down beside her. "There's no sign of him. I don't want to assume he's left the area, though." He continued to search the surrounding gloom from the grassy spot beside Karina. As the patrol cars approached, he waved them down and they came to a screeching stop.

Karina was beyond talking. Brian was doing a bang-up job giving the explanations. The two officers were immediately on the radio, calling for backup and paramedics. Minutes later, Markham and his partner arrived. He initiated an immediate search of the area, barking orders to the other officers.

"Are you two okay? Do you need medical attention?" Markham asked, crouching low to the ground beside Karina.

"No." Karina shook her head. "I'm just scared and very

tired. My feet hurt a bit. I don't have my shoes." She managed to sit up with Brian's help, and saw the obvious relief on the men's faces.

"Can you tell us what happened, Karina?" Officer Markham asked, wrapping a rough wool emergency blanket around her shoulders.

"I don't really want to, but I guess I don't have a choice," she replied wearily. Brian pulled her into his arms, silently giving her his support.

Karina leaned against Brian, taking strength from him. Closing her eyes, she related everything that happened since the moment she'd turned around in the kitchen to find Ian sitting there with her knife. Shutting the world out to relive her memories was a hidden blessing. When she finished her account and opened her eyes, she saw the blood had leached out of Brian's face and pain creased his features. He hugged her tightly.

"I can't believe he got up after that last punch," Brian added, his voice raw. "It should have been enough to keep him out. He has to be gone by now, right?"

"Oh, no. He's still here," Karina said bitterly. "He's here and he's watching us. He isn't sane anymore. He wants us and he's not going to let this go."

"Did you see any other weapons besides the knife?" Markham asked.

Karina paused to consider. "No. But I can't be sure that he didn't have more hidden on him." Shivers raced up and down her arms. Just the thought of Ian with other weapons was enough to destroy her fragile newfound security.

Brian pulled her closer into his embrace.

Markham stepped away to put a call in to the department, leaving the two of them sitting on the grass.

Wordlessly, they held each other, savoring their lives and the connection between them after coming so close to losing everything.

But icy fingers of fear wrapped themselves around Karina's spine. She knew there'd be no rest as long as Ian remained free.

Chapter 11

THE NIGHT HAD darkened to a deadening flat black. Angry clouds built and thickened overhead. Again, rain threatened.

More police cruisers arrived to help and there were at least six officers combing the area for Ian, maybe even more. It was hard for Karina to tell in the chaos. There had been some shouting earlier, and a spike in activity. Karina had desperately wanted it to mean that Ian had been caught, but that wasn't the case.

Markham trudged over to them and said two officers had spotted someone among the trees, and they figured the individual had to be Ian, but the person vanished into the darkness and they'd lost him.

The paramedics arrived soon after. Karina had been checked over, her feet bandaged. They suggested she go to Emergency for further treatment but she refused. Brian had been checked over but was fine. Though the officers and Brian wanted her to go the station and wait, she refused. She wanted to see Ian caught – with her own eyes. She *needed* to know that their ordeal was over. Without that, she couldn't imagine moving forward with her life.

Two officers had gone back into Brian's house. Another had gone over to the Sorenson's house. The older couple had been on their way to their daughter's house for dinner and once they heard the news, they decided to make it an overnight stay.

Officer Markham had kindly shared his thermos of coffee with Karina while she rested inside the cruiser. She continued to turn down offers to take her to the station, even when they included the promise of food.

The mention of dinner had sent her into a depressed slump. Dinner should have been fresh barbequed steaks followed by luscious, chocolate-dipped strawberries for dessert. God, she didn't think she'd ever be able to look at a strawberry again without hearing Ian's voice criticizing the 'wussy' fruit.

So much for her big plans for tonight.

Another yawn escaped. Karina realized she was going to have to move and soon. She sat up and peered out into the night. Flashlights flickered in the distance, like a group of large fireflies, and the sound of barking dogs filled her ears, but there were no people nearby.

"Brian, I'm really going to have to find a bathroom soon." She considered the bushes close to the car. The police had thrashed them thoroughly, so they should be safe. She really didn't want to go back into the house and no one was around to drive her anywhere where there might be a washroom.

Brian opened the door and helped her out.

"I'll go in the bushes here? Do you think they're okay?" By now, she was getting desperate to find a place to go.

Brian nodded and walked around the car with her.

"Just be quick."

"I will. Please, stay here. *Right* here." She waited for his promise before hobbling around behind the bushes. She was done in a matter of minutes, and she stood up, ready to head back to the car, when she heard a noise. Fear spun her around, and she frantically searched the dark. She couldn't see anything, but the hairs on the back on her neck stood up.

"Brian?"

There was no answer. She hurried back to the car. Brian was slumped, unmoving on the ground.

"Brian!" Panicked, Karina ran her hands over him. His chest rose and fell, which meant he was still alive. *Thank God.* It was too dark to see much else, so she couldn't be sure of the extent of his injuries. He let out a horrible groan.

"Shh. It's okay. Just lie there quietly for a minute." She stood up, looking for flashlight beacons in the dark. There were several small groups of lights, but they were all off in the distance.

"Hello! Officer Markham! Can you hear me?" she yelled. "Anyone? Help!"

There was no response – at least not one from him, or any of the other officers.

"I can hear you, Karina."

Karina spun around and froze in shock and horror. Ian stood behind her.

In the moonlight, he looked positively horrifying. His battered face was swollen from Brian's repeated blows. Blood had dripped down his face from a cut on his forehead. Scratches covered one cheek. His eyes were the worst – cold, empty pits, echoing the madness within, glared at her.

She trembled. *Dear God, this can't be happening.*

"What did you do to Brian?" she demanded.

He gave her a twisted smile. He'd obviously been scrambling through the brush at some point, because leaves and dirt clung to him and his hair was filthy. Karina's heart thumped in her chest. Only moments ago, she'd been content, knowing that soon Ian would be caught and her nightmare would be over. Instead, she now stood protectively over Brian and faced her biggest nightmare.

The police were close but not close enough.

Summoning her wits and every remaining ounce of strength she possessed, she tried for reason. "Ian. Let me get help for Brian, please?"

"If I wanted him well, I wouldn't have hit him in the first place." He snorted in disgust. "Besides, that was just a start. I still owe him a few." He gave a mocking laugh that chilled her.

Karina couldn't leave Brian, and neither could she fight Ian off.

Had the police heard her yell? Not likely, as they would have investigated by now. *Dogs!* The police might not have heard her but what about the dogs? Should she shriek for them? She could probably get one good scream out before he was on her. Alternatively, she could whistle, not too well, but enough to get the dogs' attention. It was a skill the twins had delighted in teaching her.

Turns out, she didn't get the chance.

While she stood there trying to come up with a plan, Ian jumped her. He wrenched her arm backward. painfully twisting her facedown over the front hood of the car.

"Stupid bitch!" he spat. "The cops are too far away to help you. So shut the hell up."

Broken whimpers escaped her throat as he twisted her arm higher, pressing her face against the cold metal.

The hold loosened slightly as he leaned around her.

Karina knew it was now or never. While he was still bent over, she twisted to the side and lashed out with her right foot, catching him in the temple. Panicked, she barely registered the pain. The barefoot kick wasn't hard enough to knock him down, but it was enough that he loosened his grip.

Instantly she bolted, racing toward the men searching the night, screaming as loudly as she could. She ran on, deaf to the men yelling and the dogs barking, and unaware of the night sky brightening with moonlight. She ran, blind, until her world exploded in a flash of pain. The ground raced up to meet her just as something heavy plowed into her back.

Her body writhed in agony as pain overtook her world. She screamed once, a sound full of fury and disbelief.

Barely aware of her surroundings, the loud crack of gunfire echoed in her ears, followed by men's shouts.

Then she couldn't hear anything.

BRIAN STOOD BY, watching helplessly as the paramedics loaded Karina into the ambulance. She'd roused briefly, confused by the cacophony of sounds, sirens. He'd tried to calm her down, tried to explain what was happening to her, but she merely stared at him, her eyes full of confusion, before blacking out once again. He needed to be with her, to make sure he was there when she woke again.

But first, he had to walk through his house with Officer Markham. His head was pounding but that did nothing to dull the anger ripping through him.

After the ambulance pulled away, he led the way back to the house. The house told its own story. Half-finished sandwiches sat haphazardly on the table with cold, half-full cups of tea. Puddles of yet more tea pooled on the tabletop. Dishes, food, cutlery and many other broken and smashed items littered the floor. In stark contrast, a full gleaming tray of chocolate-dipped strawberries sat untouched on the counter.

"Wasn't Karina crying something about strawberries?" Brian asked Markham.

"That and letters, I think. It was hard to make any sense out of it. You can ask her about that when she wakes up."

Brian's face turned stony at the stark reminder that Karina was unconscious and headed for surgery. Ian had stabbed her twice, but thankfully only one stab wound required an operation. Yet any injury was too much.

The longer Brian stared at the chaos in his kitchen, the more he was reminded that Karina had been caught in the middle of this nightmare.

His fist slammed into the table. Frustration and anger rolled off his shoulders. Dear God, why hadn't he been there? She'd been in danger and he hadn't been there to save her. The need to smash something vied with the need to hold her close. But neither was a reasonable option right now.

Even outside, when they thought they were safe tonight, he hadn't helped her. She'd had to fight off Ian a second time. All he remembered was standing guard near the bushes, waiting for her to relieve herself. After that, there was only pain and bright lights that were quickly followed by blackness. Her screams had snapped him back to consciousness.

Fear and horror had consumed him as he'd watched the knife lift, the moonlight gleaming on the long blade. Only he'd been too far away to stop it. Just close enough to watch, terrified and helpless, as the woman he loved collapsed.

Gunshots had finally dropped Ian right beside Karina. And the shots hadn't killed Ian. They'd only wounded him in the shoulder and the leg and not enough to even cripple the man.

As Brian stared around his kitchen at the damage Ian inflicted, he was damn sorry the police hadn't finished the job. Maybe in a few years when the pain and the memory dimmed, he'd find the grace to be grateful that Ian's life was spared. But right now, he wanted to kill the man himself.

It was late, he was tired and his kitchen could remain the way it was until the police were done. He needed to get back to the hospital. Back to Karina.

He left the police to do what they needed to do.

His arrival at the hospital coincided with an orderly wheeling Karina down the hallway.

Brian was horrified to see her beautiful face lying slack, leached of all color.

Panicked, he looked around for someone to ask. "Nurse? Nurse!" he called out blindly. He spotted a woman in pale-green scrubs walking down the hall toward him and raced over to her. "What's wrong with Karina? What's happened to her? She doesn't look normal."

Gently, the nurse laid a hand on his arm. "Karina is fine. They're taking her into surgery. She did regain consciousness, at least long enough to answer a few questions."

The nurse led him quietly down the hall. Before he realized it, he was sitting down in the emergency room.

"She's going to be fine, but I want someone to take a look at your head. Can you tell me your name?"

"My head's fine. Ouch!" He turned to glare at the nurse as she poked and prodded close to his injury. "And it's Brian. Brian Saunders."

"Well, Brian, you might need stitches. Wait here and I'll bring the doctor over."

Brian scowled furiously.

The nurse ignored him, not even attempting to hide her wide smile.

There was no way Brian was going to sit here in the ER. He hopped up determined to go find Karina but he wasn't fast enough.

"Just where do you think you're going, sir?" asked a young male doctor walking toward him. "Just sit back down and let's take care of your head."

"It's Karina that needs looking after – not me," Brian answered, exasperated.

The doctor grinned at him cheerfully. "Then think about her. How's she going to feel when she wakes up and sees you covered in blood like this?"

Hell, the doctor was right. Brian sat back down.

The same nurse came back over to clean up his head. She smiled, giving him a pat on the cheek. "I knew if he mentioned your girlfriend we'd get your cooperation."

His frown held no heat; she was right after all. He would do anything to avoid upsetting Karina.

"Your face is going to upset her already without adding any more shocks."

Startled, he looked up at her. "What do you mean?"

She picked up a small mirror and held it up in front of him. "That's what I mean."

Surely that wasn't him? Dear God, he was the stuff nightmares were made of, with puffy, swollen cheeks and black eyes all liberally dotted with flecks of dried blood.

"Just think, I've already washed most of it off. Let's finish this then go see how your Karina is doing."

Unfortunately, by the time they were done, Karina still wasn't out of surgery so the nurse had to take him down to the OR waiting room instead.

She said, "Now, get a cup of coffee and let the doctors do their job." The nurse returned to her station.

He chose to call Mark first, who promised to be at the hospital in moments, and then Brian called Susan. Susan burst into tears when she heard the news and handed the phone over to Paul. Brian quickly sketched out the evening's events and Paul promised he'd bring Susan to see Karina in the morning.

By the time he put the phone away Brian was emotionally and physically exhausted.

Mark arrived shortly after that, bringing coffee and fresh sandwiches, figuring correctly that Brian hadn't eaten.

"You look horrible. Don't argue! Just get it into your stomach! You can't look after Karina if you collapse."

Once again, there was no arguing with that logic and Brian began eating his food. Afterwards, he almost felt human again. Silence reigned between the two friends as unspoken words hung in the air.

The first words to come out of Brian's mouth surprised them both.

"I love her, you know. God. I wish I'd told her first."

"Tell her when she wakes up."

"She'll think I'm just saying that because she's hurt. She believes some of the damnedest things."

"If she does, it's because she's uncertain. After your weekend together, she shouldn't feel that way at all," Mark reassured.

"I know that. It's just we didn't get around to open declarations of love. We were so close and loving the entire weekend that words didn't seem necessary – and now I see they were even more necessary than I thought." Brian buried his head in his hands. "God, I'm a fool."

Mark eyed him sympathetically. "Karina's been through a lot. She needs to know that you're there for her in all ways and forever. She needs the emotional security of that." He leaned forward, adding, "Just as much as you need it, too."

Brian somberly contemplated that bit of wisdom. So often, honesty at that level was missing in relationships. He didn't want that. He wanted to know that Karina was his, heart, body, mind and soul. He needed to know that. Just as she needed to know that he was hers. If she still wanted him, that is.

They hadn't exactly had a clear path so far. However, Ian was well and truly out of the way now. And although he was currently being treated in the same hospital, he'd require psychiatric care and most likely live out the rest of his life in a padded cell.

Karina and Brian were free to resume their lives – whatever that meant. He refused to think about Karina moving back into her old place even though Ian wasn't a problem anymore. That wasn't even an option.

A grimace crossed his face. Would she even want to return to his home – where she'd been terrorized? It was still a mess. He mentioned the problem to Mark.

As usual, Mark's practical nature rose to the situation. "When the police let you, get a cleaning crew in. Bring in lots of fresh flowers. If you're serious about this relationship, offer to let her redecorate the place or whatever she needs to do to make her want to live there again. The house is beautiful. It wouldn't do to let Ian ruin that for you both as well. He's caused enough problems."

"True." Brian hesitated. The next words stuck in his throat. He needed to tell someone.

Mark was looking at him, his expression curious. Brian

took a deep breath, finally blurting out, "The guilt is killing me. I should've have been able to save her from all this. Jesus, Mark, what good was I? Knocked out cold by the bastard I was trying to protect her from."

Mark shook his head. "You did what you could, Brian. You're not a super hero, you're a human being. You remember that, right?"

Brian hesitated and then nodded.

"Gentlemen?" A tired voice interrupted them gently.

Turning, Brian recognized Karina's surgeon. He jumped to his feet anxiously. "Doctor. How's Karina? Did everything go okay?"

The doctor smiled reassuringly at them. "Karina's going to be fine. With physiotherapy, she should have the full use of her shoulder again. They're settling her in for the night right now. Depending on how she feels, she might be able to leave in a couple days. Now, if you'll excuse me, I'm going home to bed." The doctor listened to their thanks, shook hands with them and walked away.

Surprised, Brian looked at his watch. Good Lord, it was almost two in the morning. He looked over at Mark. "Did I get you out of bed? I just realized what time it is."

Mark laughed at him. "That's what friends are for. Let's take a quick look at her then you'd better come back to my place for the night. You can't help her now. She needs to rest and so do you."

Later on, lying on Mark's couch, Brian worried about Karina. He'd wanted to stay there with her, but the nurses had said she'd sleep for at least six hours now. He'd be back by then. She wasn't going to wake up alone.

If he had his way, she'd never be alone again.

IAN WATCHED THE guard constantly. He lay inside the prep room beside the surgical doors. He'd be going in next.

Inside anger burned deep. Almost burning through the pain. He deserved the pain. He deserved more than that. He'd failed. And failure was not an option. His injuries were minor. They had to be. He was still here. The pain pills they'd given had dulled the agony, but not his anger. *Two bullets.*

The damn cops actually shot him twice. But neither bullet did him in.

Nothing else they did to him would, either.

Alive, and not behind bars, meant a second chance.

It hurt to move, so he did so deliberately. His insides squeezed tight, bitterness burned the back of his throat. He could not let this stop him.

Brian couldn't be allowed to win.

He had to pay for the pain he'd inflicted.

So pay he would. Determined, Ian watched the guard laugh into his cell phone. *Good. Enjoy your conversation. Keep your attention elsewhere. You'll never see me coming.*

Until it's too late.

Chapter 12

K ARINA SLEPT FITFULLY, surfacing off and on before finally waking at six am, alone.

The hospital smells were unmistakable. Nightmares had tormented her sleep, but waking to this reality was worse. Tears rolled down her face and she was helpless to stop them. Chilled to the bone and feeling like she'd never get warm again, she tried to pull the blankets up higher, but her arm wouldn't work properly. The IV needle in her arm was awkward and frustrated her attempts to get comfortable. She wanted it gone and not being able to do anything about it was suddenly the last straw. Hot tears rolled down her cheeks in earnest. She didn't want to be there. She wanted to be back in Brian's house, with everything the way it was before Ian's rampage.

That thought stopped her cold. That's what Ian had wished, to turn time back and have things return to the way they were before. Only that option wasn't available – for any of them. Just as Ian had to live with change, so, too, did she. The past twenty-four hours were now a permanent part of her experience.

Where was Brian? Was he okay? What about Ian? Had the police killed him? Please, tell me they have caught him. The alternative would be too awful to think about.

Tired, confused and uncomfortable with pain, the tears

rolled faster and faster until she was sobbing uncontrollably.

"There, there. Take it easy, dearie. I know you're hurting. It's time for your shot. I'm going to quickly check you over and make sure everything's okay first." The nurse bustled about and Karina lay acquiescent under her ministrations. "You feel rotten don't you? Well, here's your medication. Just lie back and rest now. Soon, it'll all go away."

It was already going away. The nurse's voice floated in and out of Karina's mind, before finally disappearing completely. Karina drifted back to sleep on drug-induced wings.

THE NEXT MORNING, Brian was firmly ensconced in the chair at Karina's bedside when the doctor walked in. He placed a firm hand on Brian's shoulder and pointed to Karina, deep in slumber.

"She's sleeping and will for most of the day." He studied Brian's face. "You on the other hand don't appear to have gotten much rest." He looked down at his tablet and made several clicks. "Try to grab some more rest. She won't wake up for hours. And you're no good to her like this."

Damn. Brian nodded and straightened. "Fine. I'll come back in a couple of hours."

"Do that. I need to tell you that her attacker is coming out of surgery now. He'll survive to pay for his actions."

"Thanks for letting me know." It was both good news and bad. "I'm torn between wanting him to be worse off and sorry that it was necessary for him to be hurt at all."

"That's understandable. Don't feel guilty about it. Just go home and rest, and maybe do something constructive to distract yourself. You've got at least four hours before she wakes up again." With that last bit of advice, the doctor left the room.

Brian wasn't happy about leaving Karina. Nevertheless, it was an opportunity to start removing all traces of Ian's visit to their home, which would help her recover faster. There was no way he was going to let her return to Sandra's house.

With that in mind, he headed to his house to clean up. He'd spend a few hours doing that, then he'd come back to the hospital to watch over her again.

OPENING HER EYES, Karina lay still, taking inventory of just where she was and why. Pale-colored light peeked around faded yellow curtains that hung in the window. The quality of the sunshine made her think it had to be early morning, maybe even dawn. Memories flooded back, and Karina closed her eyes against the unbelievable rush of pain and vestiges of panic. Shivers wracked her system until the realization settled in that it was finally all over.

A distinctly odd sound came from the other side of the room. Slowly, carefully, she shifted to look.

Brian lay stretched out, slumped half off the visitor's chair, fast asleep. Karina grimaced. He was going to be brutally sore when he woke up, not only from his position but also from the blows he took to his poor face. Just look at it. Her heart went out to him.

He made a snuffling noise in his sleep. One of his hands came up and rubbed his nose before falling back to the arm of the chair.

Even battered and bruised as he was now, she found him beautiful. When the nurse came in, Karina was lying quiet in the morning light, her gaze locked on Brian. She watched as the grinning nurse tiptoed around Brian's long legs.

The nurse smiled down at Karina. "That's quite a watchdog you have there, young lady," she whispered conspiratorially.

"Isn't he though?"

"Let's have a look at you." The nurse bustled around, checking Karina's bandages and her blood pressure, taking her temperature and adjusting her new IV. "I'll bring you some fresh water. Are you ready for a glass of juice?"

"Yes, please. Any chance of a coffee?"

"I'll see. Be back in a minute." She tiptoed out of the room.

Karina couldn't help it, she giggled. What kind of watchdog was he anyway?

"I heard that," came a raspy voice from the chair. "I have to admit, it's one of my favorite sounds."

"What is?" she asked.

Slowly he opened his eyes. That deep, magnetic gaze sought hers and smiled.

"Listening to you laugh – that is, if I can't listen to the sounds you make when I touch you." His voice deepened even further.

Heat climbed Karina's throat and warmed her cheeks.

"And I love the fact that I can make you blush." Amused satisfaction tinged his voice as her skin burned even more hotly.

He pulled his large frame up and out of the small chair, and stretched. With a stifled groan, he worked the kinks out of his back and neck before taking the two steps to her bedside. "I'd scoop you up for a big hug but I don't want to hurt you."

She reached her good arm up slowly to accept whatever version of an embrace he'd give. He dropped the bed's side rail and gently lay down beside her, cuddling her close. His kiss warmed her heart and his smile warmed her soul. But his face brought tears to her eyes.

"How are you feeling?"

"*Shh.* I'm fine."

She stroked his bruised face, her fingertips brushing across the bruised colored splotches. "Your poor face! He hurt you." Gently, she reached out with her free arm to stroke the split lip and swollen jaw.

Brian covered her hand with his. "I'm fine. How are *you?*"

She tried to smile, but knew it was a bit wobbly. "I'm a little stiff, a little sore, but I'm okay," she said. "Did anyone say when I could go home?"

"It's up to the doctor, but I'm hoping he'll let you come home today."

"Home sounds good." Her smile faltered as she remembered what had happened in his home. No, home didn't actually sound so appealing. She anxiously pleated the sheets with unsteady fingers as she muttered, "I want to go back to Sandra's basement suite."

"Out of the question. First, you need to rest and to heal. And someone needs to be there to look after you. That's my job. Second, I think it's important for you to go back and face the bad memories at the house so we can put them to rest." He took a deep breath. "You are what's important here. I'm so sorry you were hurt. Even more sorry I couldn't stop him in time. But I want a future with you and if you can't live in the house then we'll look at moving."

Tears came to her eyes. He'd stopped short of saying he

loved her but he'd come damned close. Maybe that was enough for now. "I don't want to move. I love that house." Unfortunately, he was also right – she had to go back to the house in order to move forward.

But that was later, not right now. Right now she could enjoy being safe in his arms. And try to forget all the parts of her body that were hurting. And there were so many.

"Now isn't that cute. You should have told me and I would've brought two cups of coffee." The nurse was standing behind them, holding a coffee and a glass of juice.

"You've been tripping over me all night, so it's not like you didn't know I was here." Brian smiled at the pleasant-faced woman. "Besides, that's probably not much of a coffee if it came from the cafeteria."

"I'll have you know this came specially from the nurses' station and is exceptional coffee. How was I to know that you were awake? You've growled at anyone coming in to look at this poor girl all night, as it is. We were all relieved when you finally fell asleep."

She carefully set the drinks down on the little movable table and swung it closer to Karina. "Are you sure you want to be so close to this bear, Karina? He looks like he needs a couple of pots of coffee before he'll be safe to live with."

Karina just smiled at the two of them.

"It's all right. I know what he's like to wake up to. Of course, he's usually much more fun than this," she said with a grin.

The tables turned with that comment. Brian flushed a ruddy color, right on cue. Karina chuckled, and ignored his glare.

"When can she go home?" he asked.

"Not until the doctor says so. He won't be here for his

rounds until ten, so both of you relax. It will still be a little while yet."

She walked out, promising to return with more coffee.

Karina wasn't feeling quite so good anymore. Aches and pains were surfacing everywhere, especially in her swollen feet. They burned as though they were on fire. She moved her legs restlessly, trying to get comfortable.

She thought of the beach outside of Brian's house. Sitting on the sand, smelling the fresh ocean air, watching the waves roll in – that would be perfect. What she wouldn't give to be able to soak her feet in the cool water. And there were so many other good things about Brian's place. She'd just need a day or two to get over recent events. Put it all behind her. As she healed physically, she could work on her emotional healing as well.

"Are you all right for a few minutes? I want to make a quick trip down the hall."

"I'm fine. You go ahead."

The nurse walked in with a steaming paper cup just as Brian walked out.

"You mean he actually left you alone? Wow." The nurse smiled down at Karina with envy.

"He does leave me alone occasionally," Karina smiled. "But it's nice having him around."

"It's a wonderful thing to have someone like that in your life, for sure. Now, do you want to wash up a little? We can't let you have a shower but I can bring some warm water and help you freshen up."

"Thank you. That would be great." Karina smiled happily at the suggestion.

The nurse bustled about, making her preparations. "We're all talking about your man down at the nurses' station." She looked over at Karina. "We're all jealous, you know. None of us has a partner willing to sit protectively over us like that. It's very romantic."

"He also feels very guilty," Karina said dryly, accepting the bowl and washcloth.

Not long after, she felt renewed and refreshed. Thankfully, Brian had brought her a change of clothes including her yoga pants and a sleeveless blouse that wouldn't interfere with her bandages.

"Isn't it amazing what a little feminine armor can do for you?" The nurse chuckled. "Now you look better. All ready for his return. The clothes will help. The ones you arrived in aren't fit to wear any longer."

The nurse helped her get dressed, taking advantage of Karina's upright position to check out her wounds. "You look great. You'll definitely be sore for a while but if you don't try to wrestle with anyone else, these should heal fine."

Karina grimaced. "I'll be happy to never wrestle again, especially not with a nutcase."

Brian's hard voice arrived before he did. "You'll never have to deal with him again." He appeared around the closed curtain just as Karina finished dressing. At the mention of Ian, his face was twisted in anger. "Ian is under heavy guard and is not in any physical shape to attack anyone."

Karina shifted in her bed until she was next to him. A wave of gentleness softened his features and wiped away the anger.

"I trust you. I know you will keep me safe," she whispered, reaching out her hand to grasp his. She looked directly into his eyes. "I love you."

He gazed deep into her eyes, then bent down, carefully wrapping his arms around her, and hugged her. When she whimpered, he immediately loosened his hold. "Sorry," he murmured. "And…I love you too."

Her smile blossomed. She wondered if he'd ever say it. Held carefully within his embrace, Karina thought she'd never been closer to anyone in her life. Her heart swelled, because for the first time, she knew what it was to be connected like this to another human being. To be so close in heart, mind and soul, to know how the other thought, when they were hurting and when they needed to be loved.

She could feel Brian swallowing, obviously choked with emotion. She knew exactly how he felt.

The doctor's arrival shattered the moment.

"Well, it's nice to see you awake, young lady. Sit up on the bed and let me check my handiwork."

Several painful minutes later, the doctor said, "You're a lucky lady, this could have been much worse. The shoulder is going to ache for weeks to come. Under no circumstances are you to rip these stitches. Take it easy for a while. Start using the arm a little bit when it feels better. Other than that, be gentle with yourself. You need time to heal."

He handed her a prescription, saying to Brian, "Take her to her doctor next week or earlier if you're concerned. A nurse will show you how to change the dressing and clean the wounds, which you'll need to do every day. Above all, treat her gently." With that, he left.

A nurse joined them and quickly outlined the steps Brian needed to take for wound care.

Brian waited for the nurse to leave and for Karina to stand, holding out a sling the nurse had given him.

"No sling." Surely she didn't need it. She hated to look like an invalid.

"No sling…no home," he answered her calmly.

"That's not fair," she said with a gasp.

"The only reason you are going home now is because I promised the doctor I'd do everything I could to make sure you heal properly and quickly. The sling is part of that." He waited, standing in front of her. "Besides, it makes me feel better to know you won't re-injure yourself this way."

Her heart softened. "Fine," she said. "But it won't help any."

The one nurse who'd come in to start cleaning up the room smiled, but stayed silent as she walked past them. By the time they'd made it out to the car, she realized that the stupid thing was helping. That really irritated her. Disgusted with him, herself and the sling, she shot him a dirty look.

He grinned. "Admit it; it helps, doesn't it?"

She didn't answer.

Oh, he loved that. He didn't laugh aloud, but couldn't stop the grin that spread over his face as he helped her gently into the low-slung car.

"Did you call Susan?"

"Many times. They're coming to the house for a short visit later today."

As he fired the car up and pulled out of the parking lot, he suggested she just close her eyes and sleep.

Still irritated over the sling, she fired back, "I'm not tired."

She was out before they hit the main street.

Chapter 13

KARINA WAS STILL half-sleeping when they arrived at home, waking only as Brian opened her car door. She blinked owlishly at him for several moments, trying to clear the wooliness from her mind.

"Let me get out on my own." She eased her sore body up and out. Using his arm to steady her, she stood, her legs shaky. In the daylight, the whole area looked innocent and fresh. Nothing appeared menacing, or flaunted evidence that terrible things had happened there. Maybe the horrific memories would only come after darkness had fallen. She hoped not.

Karina groaned as she moved stiffly toward the front entrance. Everything hurt. Her wrists were light green with bruises where Ian had grabbed her, and she knew there was a big, one on her forehead where she'd made contact with the gravel when she'd collapsed. She couldn't even remember getting the other bruises, which was probably just as well. Her feet screamed with every step she took. There'd be no running barefoot for her for a long time. When they healed, the first place she'd try was the soft sandy beach behind the house.

She hesitated, shuffling uneasily from foot to foot at the front door. She really wasn't looking forward to going in. Brian seemed to understand, waiting silently and patiently at her side. With a deep breath for courage, Karina pushed the door open.

The hallway was bursting with freshly cut flowers. There were bouquets of roses, geraniums, carnations and so many more. Dazed, Karina walked through the house, twisting and turning to see each new bouquet. Even the kitchen was covered with a rainbow of mad, fragrant color.

Tears formed and ran down her cheeks. Brian had done this for her.

Overwhelmed, Karina turned to face him. He was watching her intently. Carefully, she opened her arms, embracing him tightly. She rested against his heart, listening to the strong beat that matched her own. His male scent mingled with that of the fresh flowers to soften the horrible memories she had of what happened here the last time.

"Thank you," she whispered.

"You're welcome." Careful of her injuries, Brian rubbed her back and cuddled her close.

Twenty minutes later, Karina was curled up on a lounge on the back patio, covered with a cotton blanket. The smell of fresh-brewed coffee tantalized her. Contentedly, she inhaled the salty air. The pills she'd just taken left a lingering drowsiness that combined with her surroundings to give her soul a sense of peace.

It was finally over. The stresses of the last few weeks were gone. Ian was out of the picture, and she could finally look toward the future with Brian. Cozy and warm, it wasn't long before she fell asleep again.

The ring of the doorbell jerked her awake, sending pain lancing through her. She froze, willing the ache to fade. Slowly, the trembling subsided enough that she could look around. The sun had moved in the sky and it appeared she'd slept an hour or two. She glanced through the kitchen window and spotted Brian speaking with Susan and Paul in the kitchen.

"I'm awake now. You don't have to stay in there," she called out.

"Hi there. How are you?" Susan bent over and gave a gentle hug. She lifted a lock of Karina's hair, looking critically at the blossoming color on Karina's forehead. "That's quite a bruise you've got there."

Karina chuckled. "I'll have fun coordinating clothes with it, won't I?"

"A perfect excuse to go buy new ones." Susan grinned at her.

"As if you ladies need any excuse to do more shopping." Paul strolled out to join them. He pulled up a couple extra chairs and sat down on one. "Karina, how are you doing?"

"I'm fine." She smiled reassuringly. "Still a little tired and sore, but I'm on the mend. I'm just glad it's all over."

"I still can't believe that Ian actually snapped like that," Susan said. Her red, puffy eyes hinted at long hours of worry.

"Be glad that you didn't see him that night. He was scary in his insanity. I don't even want to think about it."

"So don't. It's over, so let's leave it alone." Brian arrived with fresh coffee and muffins.

Carefully, Karina tried to reposition herself, grimacing at the pain from such a simple movement.

"Susan, are you going to be okay on your own for a few days at the shop?" She turned to her friend. "I was supposed to work yesterday, wasn't I?"

"You were," she answered, her voice cheerful. "And don't you worry about it. We were fine. Janice came in to help out and is available this week so you take as much time as you need to heal. When you're feeling better, come in for a half day and see how it goes." She motioned to the patio and view around them. "This is what you need, though. What a place to recuperate."

"Why don't we wait and see what the doctor says in a week?" said Brian.

"Remember, though, Brian – if I don't work, then Susan has to hire more help to carry my load." Karina reached a hand over to her friend. "And the store is also my income. I can't afford to be off work. Yes, I may possibly take a week, but then I'll be back in the store doing what I can."

Paul smirked. "You might as well give in. Sounds like she's not going to."

Brian chuckled and shook his head. "True enough." He added, his voice quiet and warm, and with a hint of laughter, "She's very stubborn."

The quartet laughed, and the conversation continued on, lighthearted and pleasant.

When it was finally time for her medication, Karina was sore and tired and ready for it. She'd done a good job hiding her discomfort, but now, even that was beyond her.

"You're going to have to excuse me. I need to take my medication and lie down." Karina slowly rose, maneuvering her way into hallway.

"Do you want me to come up and help you?" asked Susan from behind her.

"No, thanks. I'll be fine. I just want to sleep for a few hours. Are you two staying?"

"No. We're going to head back. I'll give you a call tomorrow, okay?"

Karina hugged Susan gently, grateful for her understanding. She wearily continued on to her bedroom. Her cats jumped up on the bed as soon as they saw her.

"Hey, you guys! Are you two all right? Come here, my sweethearts."

Karina carefully stretched out on the bed, cuddling with the cats. Unfortunately, that movement alone sent lightning bolts of pain through her body and hot rivers of tears burning their way down her cheeks. Before too long, the medication finally, blessedly, took her under and away from the pain.

The sky was dark when she opened her eyes. Her stomach gurgled in outrage. Too bad. She had no plans to move. The sleek cats were still stretched out beside her. She'd missed them this last while. They'd always slept with her. Then again, she hadn't slept in her bed the past week. With a start, she realized that she'd returned to *her* room, not Brian's. The reason eluded her and made her uneasy at the same time. Surely, this situation should bring them closer, not separate them. How would Brian read this?

Limping carefully, she made her way to the bathroom. She really wanted a shower but a sponge bath would have to do. And that meant help.

"Brian?" she called over the railing.

"I'm in the kitchen, Karina. Hang on, I'm coming up."

She watched him run up the stairs, two at a time.

"Did you have a good sleep, honey? How are you feeling now?"

He gently wrapped her in his arms, rubbing his cheek against her hair.

"Could you help take off my bandage, please? I desperately need a wash."

He turned on the bathwater for her. "I'll take it off, but

you're still going to need help because you can't get the area wet. You can hop into the water while I get a new bandage for after."

A few painful minutes later, she sat down into the comforting warmth. She closed her eyes as her water soothed her aches and pains. She reached for the soap and wash cloth. Trembling set in before she was halfway done, making her wonder if the bath been such a good idea after all.

She never heard the door open or the gentle voice calling out her name, but relief overwhelmed her as Brian's caring hands gently rubbed the soap over the rest of her body. One muscled arm slid around her ribs, and gratefully, she leaned into his strength and let him take care of her.

When she was completely bathed and rinsed, Brian reached out and turned off the taps. Still supporting her, he opened the door and reached for a large towel. Within minutes, she was bundled up like a fragile parcel. With a second towel, he quickly dried himself. The room tilted as he picked her up and carried her through to her bed. She'd automatically gone into her bathroom and her bedroom. Besides her clothes were still in here.

"Let's get a new bandage on."

"I can get dressed." She struggled out of the oversized bath sheet when his voice stopped her.

"Don't move." He was standing in front of her, his hands full of bandages and ointments. She turned to give him better access.

"Not feeling too good yet, are you?"

"No." Weariness clogged her voice.

Finally, he was done. "I'm sorry. I don't want you to hurt anymore. Here, let's get you into your nightdress." He took over and dressed her.

"I'll bring you up a light dinner. I don't think you're ready for much more than that, are you?"

She smiled at the loving tenderness. A woman could get used to this. "No, I won't eat much tonight."

Just over an hour later, she was fighting to stay awake. Even though she was safely tucked into her own bed, her mind wouldn't stay quiet. Unpleasant memories filled the shadows and made her uneasy. The new dose of medication in her system should have knocked her out but it wasn't having the desired effect.

Brian came into the room to check on her, and the tension in her chest instantly eased. He held her close for a minute before kissing her gently, then turning to leave.

"Brian?" she murmured.

"Yes?" He turned, silhouetted by the hall light.

"You're coming back to sleep here aren't you?"

"I had thought to leave you alone to heal. I didn't want my tossing and turning to aggravate your wounds." He came back to her side and stroked her cheek.

Her stomach clenched. "That doesn't matter. I want you to stay. Please don't leave me alone…not tonight."

IAN WAITED PATIENTLY to be left alone. One nurse kept puttering around as she flirted with the guard standing at the doorway. The guard normally stood outside the door, and only came into the room when someone came in to check Ian or perform some other task.

Of course, Ian was handcuffed to the bed.

Like that would stop him. He couldn't believe just how good he felt. A part of him understood it was the drugs. Another part was the realization that he had several more days here to heal before he was to be moved to the local jail. According to snatches of conversation he'd overheard, he should have been moved already but they had a crowding issue, and given his medical needs, law enforcement had decided to keep him here a few days longer.

And then they'd move him.

That was when he'd make his move. After several more days of healing he'd be that much stronger.

He'd been deliberately friendly and excruciatingly polite with everyone, playing his part to show remorse for his actions. As difficult as that was for him, it was also necessary. He needed them to see his actions as those driven by passion and the loss of his wife. A man who was driven to these drastic actions by his anger and pain due to personal loss.

And he needed them to view him now as a man who'd finally come to his senses. Someone who now understood the damage he'd caused.

They'd ease back the security then. Ease back on the careful vigilance around him. Ease back on their concern that he'd try to escape.

That was when he'd take them out.

And take care of Brian and his bitch forever.

Chapter 14

"SWEETHEART, ARE YOU sure you want me here?" Brian asked. "I didn't want to hurt you during the night. I assumed you'd come to this room to be alone so you could sleep better."

"I wasn't thinking clearly when I came up. It was habit, not conscious choice. Besides, my cats were here and they needed comfort as much as I did." Karina smiled sheepishly at him.

"Then I'll finish up downstairs and come to bed. I'll be quick, I promise."

Just like that, he was gone.

Relieved, Karina curled up on her good side and waited.

She was almost asleep when she felt the bed sink down beside her. "Brian?" she murmured sleepily.

"*Shh.* Go to sleep, I'm here. There's nothing to worry about."

"Thank you." Her drowsy whisper faded from her lips as sleep overcame her once again.

That night was bad. Several times, she woke in pain. Each time, Brian woke too, wanting to help. Unfortunately, in the early hours of dawn, Brian also rolled over and accidentally hit her shoulder as he tried to snuggle closer. Karina woke up in pain, tears streaming down her face.

He'd apologized several times, and though she said she

was fine, he wouldn't listen. Eventually, Karina fell back asleep.

The next night Brian lay down beside her again until she fell asleep but she woke up to go to the bathroom and found herself alone. She'd asked him about it in the morning. She understood he didn't want to hurt her again, she even accepted that reason, but there was no way she liked it.

Another reason to get better and resume a normal life.

Brian drove her to the store the following day.

"Susan. Hi!" Karina burst through the doorway ahead of Brian. By the time he arrived, the two women were deep in excited conversation. Mark and Sandra joined the melee at lunchtime, and in between serving customers and scarfing bites of food, the group caught up on the news in their lives.

It was also Thursday, Brian's lecture night.

Karina stayed behind. She was still too sore to sit through an entire evening. He hadn't wanted to leave her behind, so they'd compromised. Sandra and the twins came over for dinner and to spend the evening with her.

After her day, the soreness in her back increased nearly double, and Karina sheepishly admitted to herself that her half-day outing might have been too much.

Still, she was anxious to resume her life. Their loving relationship had stalled in a state of waiting until she was fully healed. She *was* healing. Not enough to play any sports, of course, but she felt she was certainly healed enough for gentle loving. It was Brian's fear of hurting her that had started the unexpected distancing between them. She didn't know how to bridge that gap.

Since they'd started sleeping apart, she felt awkward and uncertain.

Karina was wondering what to do when the next evening

rolled around. This was the first night that she wasn't completely exhausted at bedtime. It was also the first night that she was fully aware of her loneliness deep inside. She wanted to return to their earlier closeness.

She loved him so much. Her feelings at the first seminar now seemed to be so school-girlish and superficial. The recent pain and horror of everything they'd been through had helped her feelings mature and deepen. That thought brought another to mind. Her erotic letter. It still sat hidden in the drawer of her night table…waiting for that perfect moment.

It occurred to her that if Brian thought she wasn't physically ready, there's no way he'd touch her. He'd be afraid of hurting her again.

It was up to *her* to show *him* that she was ready.

But how?

Should she go to him? Show him how she felt? Tell him?

He would be asleep already; it was past midnight. Maybe she could crawl into his bed and surprise him. That would be fun. She went hot at the thought of what she could do to his luscious, sleeping body. A sneaky grin crept out. Too irresistible. She flung back the covers and headed down the hall.

Karina entered stealthily. The moonlight shone on Brian's sleeping form, illuminating his masculine body just enough to let her appreciate it. Carefully, she slipped naked into his bed. Brian didn't move. She grinned wickedly to herself as she shifted closer. *She'd done it!*

She was filled with nervous excitement.

Lord, it was good to be with him. He shuffled over comfortably, naturally accepting her presence. She wrapped herself, spoon fashion around his muscled length. A giggle escaped. This was so unlike her. However, with his overdeveloped sense of protectiveness, it was going to take forever for him to get the hint and make the first move, especially after accidentally hurting her that first night.

Now, how to start? Hm. Well, that was easy. With their two bodies entwined, it was much too hot. She eased the sheet down to his hips and traced a pattern of kisses on his back. His body was so different from hers. Strong where hers was weak, hard where hers was soft, large where she was small. She stroked and enjoyed every inch of his back and buttocks, before moving on to other interesting areas.

From a kneeling position, she slid the sheet down, to uncover the rest of him. Gently, she nudged his leg over. He willingly shifted onto his back. She smiled. God, he was so perfect.

From his toes, to his feet and calves, then on up to the lean muscles on his thighs, her fingers explored, her palms caressed, her tongue tasted and her lips kissed. It hadn't taken long for parts of him to come fully awake. His erection stood before her majestically, waiting for her attention. She teased and tormented her way along its length with featherlight touches, using her fingertips, lips, and even pieces of her hair.

This was an incredibly erotic experience, and one she was determined to savor. She gave her hands license to do as they willed. Using her hair, she stroked every part of him that she could reach. Kissing a path upward, her lips searched for and found his nipples in the curly hair on his chest. His firm, silky arousal pushed against her belly, bringing a sensual smile to her face as she continued to sway back and forth, touching and retreating, and continuing to tease.

Finally, she straddled his thighs, waiting.

Tiny butterfly kisses on his eyes and cheeks and sweet nothings whispered in his ears gently woke him. Brian moaned, a rich erotic sound like pure black velvet, as his hips surged upwards, searching for her. "Siren!"

Karina smiled triumphantly. God, she loved his stifled groans.

"I want to hear your pleasure," she whispered into the velvet night. "I need to know that you're enjoying this."

Brian didn't answer, as if still caught between dreams and reality, and not yet fully aware that they were now one. His hips lifted, pleading for more of her.

Karina laughed joyfully. How wonderful to have the man of your dreams lie before you, content to await your pleasure. Taking her time, she teased, stroked and explored. She used his moans to encourage her and his whispered prayers to guide her.

His fingers spread out, grasping frantically at the rumpled sheets for strength, muscles tightening and relaxing in the search for control. A fine sheen of perspiration covered his body and a faint musk radiated off him, mixing with her scent. Together it was a heady combination.

"Take me, sweetheart. Get on and ride for both of us," his whiskey-smooth voice pleaded in the dark.

Slowly, she lowered herself, taking him deep into the heart of her. His hands surged up to hold her in place and convulsively he arched, pushing deeper.

At his urging, she rode in a steadily building rhythm. Moving slowly at first, she drew out their passion, until that was no longer enough. Their pace became aggressive, demanding a harder and faster give-and-take, until tremors began to ripple from Karina's center and ecstasy wracked her soul with fulfillment. She cried out with her release.

She could feel Brian holding on, wanting to enjoy her climax for as long as possible, until he too surged upward in his own eruption.

Karina, lying on his sweat-slicked body, smiled in tired satisfaction. She was a little sore, but nothing bad. And it had been so worth it. He was her mate, the other half of her soul. She accepted her fate, smiling, into a dreamless sleep.

BRIAN WOKE EARLY, his body unwilling to move. His heart was so full, his body so satisfied.

Karina. He rolled over and kissed the bare shoulder beside him. He pushed up onto his elbows to kiss her again, and noticed flicks of dried blood on her back.

His breath caught in his throat. Her wound looked angry, puffy, the bandage pulled loose. And he wasn't entirely sure but it looked like maybe one, if not two, stitches had pulled free. There wasn't a lot of blood, but every drop was a reminder that they'd gone too far, too fast.

She hadn't healed enough.

Regrets tore at him.

Damn. She needed her rest; now more than ever. When she woke he'd take her back to the doctor.

He had to get out for a bit. He slid from the bed, dressed quickly and walked down to the beach. An hour passed as he strode the length of the beach in the heavy winds. Ocean spray covered him from head to toe. Rivulets of water ran over his coat and pants. His every step squelched. Yet, Brian barely heard or felt anything.

Ever since Karina had stormed into his world, he'd been off balance. He loved her more than anything on Earth. Yet had he shown her that? No. He'd finally told he loved her, but after she'd said it first. And he hadn't wanted her declaration like that. Hurt and hurting. And now safe. How could she know the truth of her own emotions in that state?

He desperately wanted her love but she'd been right in saying nothing had been normal in their relationship so far. And he wanted this hell to be over. At least they'd survived. Now if he could have just a little time, he could show her how much he loved her. And if he was lucky, she'd know that she really loved him too.

God he hated this insecurity. All these doubts.

Depressed, Brian finally returned to the house and stripped out of his wet clothes in the mudroom, leaving them in a heap on the floor. He pulled shorts and a t-shirt from his 'clean' laundry basket and quickly donned the items. He headed to his study and lit a fire in the tiny fireplace. It was small comfort for the cold inside him.

It came down to the fact that Brian didn't feel worthy. He'd wanted her to heal before taking her back to his bed, to give her the space she obviously wanted after returning to her room. Instead, Karina had come to him. And she'd been hurt. Again.

Well enough was enough. He had to do something to make her understand how he felt.

But what?

TENSE ANTICIPATION THREADED knots along Ian's nerves as he waited for his transfer to the jail.

It was time. Time to finish what he'd started. He'd even figured out where to go after. He could head south to Mexico. He had friends down there. From way back when. He'd planned to go there with his wife this year, but now he'd go alone.

Soon.

"Okay, Ian. Now that you're dressed, we're taking you out in a wheelchair. Out the back way to minimize the impact on the other patients because it's visiting hours."

Back way? Even better. Inside, he smiled. Outside he gave a subdued nod to the guard. Bob was his name. Had a fiancée and was planning to get married in September. Not that Ian planned on Bob making that date.

He shuffled to the wheelchair and collapsed into it, feigning weakness. He reached across and tugged the loose blanket over his body, trying to hide his hands and make it look like he was too cold and feeble to do anything. They handcuffed his hands together. Child's play to undo. His hands were free before they pushed the wheelchair into the hallway.

Bob helped tuck the blanket in around him. "Okay, let's get him moved."

Two officers flanked him as the nurse wheeled Ian down the hallway to the service elevator. Ian gave her a pathetic look of thanks as she backed out of the elevator, leaving him alone with the two unsuspecting officers.

Perfect.

As the door clinked shut, Ian jumped from the chair, spun around and drove his fist into the throat of the closest man. He snatched the officer's gun and spun around, firing off one shot. Bob gave a startled cry, and fell backwards. The other officer struggled to wrap his arms around Ian. Ian gave a coarse laugh as he drove his elbow back into the man's ribs, then spun and kicked, dropping that officer to his knees. Quickly, Ian grabbed his head with both hands and smashed it against the wall. Hard.

When he let go, the officer collapsed to the floor…out cold.

Ian smirked. That was the hard part. The rest would be easier. He took two steps to the door and pushed the elevator button to take him to the basement.

Chapter 15

I T WAS MID-MORNING when Karina awoke, alone.

Still drowsy, she automatically reached for Brian. He wasn't there. She had no idea what time it was. It was too much work to roll over and look at the clock. She wasn't worried, though. He was around, somewhere. She drifted back to sleep, taking with her a dreamy sense of satisfaction about her world.

When she woke the second time, it was late. She sat up, grimacing with the new aches and pains pounding her body. Her shoulder throbbed. In truth, it wasn't just a throb. Needle-sharp pain radiated outward from the wound site. It definitely needed more healing time. She groaned loudly on her way to the bathroom.

Maybe she'd pushed it last night. She instantly rejected that thought. Last night had bridged the coolness between them. That alone was worth any aches and pains she felt this morning. There was such a sense of peace and well-being to her world today.

With hot water sluicing over her sore body, she wondered again where Brian was. She hated waking up alone.

For the first time in days, she took her pain medication. Without it, she knew she wouldn't make it through the morning. She hoped there was no major damage.

She dressed warmly and stared out the window. The day

looked stormy and cold and her body was tired from the strain of getting dressed.

The kitchen was empty. She put on fresh coffee and went in search of Brian.

Just then, the office door opened and Brian walked toward her, an odd look on his face, his shoulders stiff. But he took her in his arms and kissed her. He stepped back and looked down at her. "How are you feeling this morning?" He frowned. "You look tired and sore."

Karina stared at him in surprise. Something was obviously wrong, but what? "I'm fine. Yes, I'm a little sore, but not too bad. Why? What's the matter?"

He walked around behind her and sighed. "There's blood on your shirt. Last night was too much. As a result, you've probably torn your stitches."

Now that he mentioned there was blood, she started feeling lousy. Great. Talk about stupid.

"Let me see," he said shortly.

She leaned forward to maneuver her arm out of the t-shirt. Gently, he pulled her shirt up partway only to drop it after a quick look under the bandage.

"Grab your purse. We'll get this looked at."

On the way into the hospital, she finally asked, "Brian. How did you know?"

"I saw your shoulder when I woke up." He glanced over at her. "I'm so sorry. I wouldn't have wanted you hurt again."

"It can't be that bad or I would have noticed last night," she said. "And I'm not sorry, last night was special."

The wait at the hospital was long. Especially with Brian silent and stoic at her side. She hated that he was upset over last night. Surely it couldn't be that bad. But the longer she sat there, the worse she felt.

When the doctor finally arrived, he seemed to have formed his own idea about the injury. He gave her a shot and checked her over, then told Brian he wanted to speak privately with him. Karina was still reeling from the pain to pay close attention.

However, Brian squared off his shoulders and followed the doctor into another room. The walls certainly weren't very thick. Karina could hear the doctor sharply giving Brian hell. Brian never said a word in his defense.

They were a very subdued pair on the drive home. On her way back to her room, she turned around on the landing. With the last of her energy, she yelled down at him, "I'm still not sorry."

Her outburst finished her and she headed gratefully for bed. The physical pain was easing under the gentling blanket of medication, but the emotional turmoil was gathering speed.

She fell into a troubled sleep.

IAN PEERED THROUGH the closet doors as Karina slept. He hadn't expected her to come in here. Not if they were lovers. Surely they'd share the same bed? That all wasn't perfect in their world made him smile.

He'd barely made it inside the house when they'd returned home. He'd slipped into the first upstairs door he reached and hid in the closet, just in case.

Karina had entered the room shortly thereafter.

It been all he could do to hold back. He stared at her even now. In university she'd been gorgeous. Now she was freaking hot. Somehow she'd started to bloom in these last months. That it could be her relationship to Brian left a dry taste in his mouth.

She should have been his. If she'd gone out with him back in university, he'd have married her. He knew that. Instead, he'd left school bitter and alone.

Kind of like he was now.

His bitterness turned to anger. Then determination.

He held his breath, and opened the closet door.

BRIAN SAT IN the study, his head resting in his hands, his mind churning. *Damn.* He'd done it again.

The phone rang. Picking it up he withheld the urge to throw it against the wall.

Markham began without preamble. "Ian has escaped. I tried to call earlier, and your cell went straight to voicemail. I've dispatched several officers to your house. They should be there in any moment. I have every available officer looking for Blackburn."

Brian's stomach constricted. He could hardly breathe. He was alone in his office but couldn't help himself from spinning around and searching the small space anyway. His worst nightmare was repeating itself.

"When and how, damn it?" he asked in a clipped voice, striding out to the foyer. The door had been locked when they'd returned from the doctor's. But that meant nothing with Ian.

Brian made his way through the kitchen as he waited impatiently for Markham to explain, his gaze searching every corner of the room.

"During the transfer to the new facility. He knocked out one guard and shot another."

So Ian's violence had escalated even more. Not good at all. "And you think he's coming here?"

"I think that's a distinct possibility." Markham sighed. "Ian might have gotten smart and decided to disappear instead, but I don't want to take any chances."

Neither did he. Brian stood at the foot of the curving staircase and stared up at Karina's closed door. The last thing he wanted to do was wake her. She needed to rest after this morning.

"I'll come by in an hour or so. In the meantime, let the officers in to do what they need to do and keep an eye out. Above all, stay safe."

Brian stared down at the receiver in his hand, shaken to the core. Damn, just when he thought they were safe and beyond all this.

The hair on the back of his neck rose.

He spun around as he heard something at his front door.

Chapter 16

Pain kept Karina from getting the benefit of a healing sleep. Pain brought her to the surface once as she tried to roll over and landed on her damaged shoulder. She peered around the room groggily, realized she was alone and slipped back into slumber. But this time she took with her a vague uneasiness.

Fear snapped her awake for the second time only moments later. She lay there, desperately trying to drag air into her lungs. Gasping and shuddering, she tried to calm down.

And couldn't.

"There you are, Karina. How nice of you to wake up for me."

"Ian!" She struggled to sit up, panic overriding the pain. *It couldn't be.*

But it was.

Ian propped himself against the wall. His face was green and black, swollen and puffy and co-ordinated shockingly with the parody of the smile on his face.

He straightened and took a step toward her. He lifted his hand, a syringe held between his fingers.

Karina swallowed convulsively. Dear God, this man was mad. He was here. In Brian's house. *How?* Her panicked gaze searched for a way out. "What do you want?" she asked fearfully. "How did you get in here?"

Ian just smiled, a grotesque parody of the real thing and waggled the syringe in his hand.

"What's in that?" Karina asked staring at the clear liquid. How had he gotten free? He was supposed to be locked up, wasn't he? She couldn't clear her thoughts. The only thing on her mind was escape.

Brian. He should be here.

But he was downstairs. She just had to scream loud enough. And get out that damn door. The door she'd slammed shut.

"Oh, just something to help you sleep. Of course, if you get too much then you won't wake up at all."

"Brian will see you in hell for this."

"I'll take care of him. This way you see, if I don't get an opportunity to deal with him for a little while, I'll know he's living in the same hell that I am."

He lunged.

She screamed at the top of her lungs and threw herself off the bed only to become tangled in the sheets. She stumbled to the floor and pain in her feet screamed through her body. Fire shot through her injured shoulder. But the pain was secondary. Every part of her was focused instead on the maniac coming toward her. Frantically, she wracked her brain for some sort of plan, a way to get out—

Too late!

A brutal hand grabbed her arm and pulled her toward him. Karina burst into nonstop screams, punching and kicking blindly. One punch managed to catch the side of his face, and with the second she struck his injured shoulder.

He bellowed, pulling back slightly in pain.

Good, a weak spot. No mercy. She lashed out with her free foot and nailed his shoulder again.

He roared and grabbed at his shoulder.

Dimly, Karina could hear shouting coming toward them, but she wasn't safe yet. Using all the anger, fear and pain Ian had inflicted on her, she struck out at him repeatedly. She neither knew where her blows were landing, nor cared. She was blind to everything but fighting for her life.

BRIAN PULLED THE door open to see the promised officers standing on the porch hands raised to knock, when Karina screamed, the sound reverberating through the house. He spun and bolted up the stairs, filled with terror. Christ, the bastard was already in the house. "He's upstairs," he yelled. He didn't wait for a response from the officers, but instead focused on getting to Karina.

He threw her bedroom door open and faced his worst nightmare.

And in the midst of it all, striking and lashing out with everything she had, Karina fought for her life. Lunging forward, Brian grabbed Ian by the shoulders and pulled him off her. Something flew from Ian's hands and hit the far wall. He managed to trip Ian, getting him down on the floor. His right fist pounded Ian's face again and again.

This time the bastard wasn't going to get up and run away.

"Stop, Brian. Stop. We've got him."

Only when the words penetrated the red haze in his brain and hands tugged at him, did he relent. Bending over, chest heaving, Brian waited for sanity to return to his mind. He gasped several times.

Brian glared down at the unconscious man. "Keep him under control this time. If he gets to Karina again, I'll kill him myself."

Karina. She'd collapsed into the corner of her room, and was crying uncontrollably. Brian shook off the black wall of rage and raced to her side. "Easy, sweetheart, easy. Ian's gone. The police have him again. It's okay. *Shh,* baby; it's going to be all right."

"Brian—" She struggled to get words out.

"I'm here, Karina. Just relax. It's going to be fine now. The police have Ian. He won't get free again."

She tried to smile, in between her sniffles. "I'm okay. I'm just so glad you were home."

"Yeah, me too."

Her attention moved to something behind him, and Brian turned, surprised to see a room full of men. Foremost in the group, surveying the chaos, was Officer Markham.

"Are you both okay?" Markham asked.

Brian nodded, tugging Karina tighter against his chest. "We will be." He looked down at her. "Won't we, sweetheart?"

"Does she need a doctor? I have an ambulance coming for Ian. If she needs to get to the hospital I can call for another one."

"No." Karina shook her head frantically. "I'll be fine."

Brian tightened his arms protectively around her. "If she needs medical attention, I'll take her in myself."

Karina relaxed in his embrace.

He stood up, tugging her up with him, and then he lifted her and carried her downstairs. They didn't need to be cramped in the same room as the others – and especially Ian. He was unconscious and would hopefully stay that way, but that didn't mean they needed to be there. At least Ian was restrained now, with men standing guard.

In the kitchen, Karina curled up on a chair while he made a fresh pot of coffee.

Markham came in as the pot finished dripping. He refused a cup. "We're moving him out in a few minutes. He's done a lot of damage today."

"Damage?" Karina asked, looking pale yet valiant. "Like what?"

"He severely injured his two guards at the hospital. One is still unconscious and the second is in surgery right now. They're both expected to make it. And you can bet that neither will underestimate another hospital transfer patient. Ian had them both fooled. Even the hospital staff thought he was remorseful and cooperative."

"He's insane," Karina exclaimed. "How could anyone think any different?"

"Because he's very, very clever. I don't know what will happen in terms of the legal system. He'll likely go through testing to see if he's mentally competent to stand trial."

Officer Markham reached out to shake both their hands. He moved to the entryway and paused, turning back to face them once more. "Ian's goal was to stop you two from finding happiness together. If that meant killing you both, he was prepared to do that. You're both very lucky to have survived." He smiled. "You've been given a second chance — make the most of it."

Chapter 17

AS MARKHAM LEFT the house the ambulance arrived. In a swift and efficient manner Ian was transferred to the waiting vehicle and within minutes, the house was empty except for the couple. There would be statements to give but that could happen tomorrow.

Brian looked at her seriously. "If you're sure you're okay, I suggest we sit outside for a bit and have coffee."

And talk. But she didn't say that. Still going out into the fresh air was a good idea. Karina would have to face the disarray of her bedroom soon, but not right now.

They refilled their mugs and wandered outside to the patio. She took a deep breath of the ocean air. The storm had broken and fresh winds swept the remnants of the darkness away, and now warm sunshine streamed down on them. Karina tried to relax but this moment was too important to pass off.

"After all we've been through…" her voice trailed off. She shook her head and sighed, finally feeling the last of the tension ease back. "It's crazy."

"But it's over. Finally."

She nodded. She hoped Ian never saw daylight again, but as long as he was never released, then she'd be happy. She cast her mind back and decided to bring up another subject. "Brian, why were you so upset this morning when I came downstairs?" She paused then looked directly in his eyes. "I couldn't help but feel that I'd done something wrong and that…" she sighed, "makes me think you regret last night. And I so don't want that to be the case."

"You certainly haven't done anything wrong!" He stared at her in astonishment. "Last night was *not* a mistake I'm just mad at myself!"

She stared. "About what?"

Brian carefully put his cup down to fold his arms on the table. He looked at her soberly.

"Karina." He stopped to gather his thoughts. "It just seemed like no matter what I tried to do, it went wrong. All I ever wanted was to keep you safe."

She opened her mouth to speak and he held up both hands, signaling her to wait. She took a deep breath and pressed her lips shut.

"Let me finish." Slowly, determinedly, he continued, "And last night, I loved that you came to me. I hated that you'd gone back to your own room but I understood. Only you hurt your shoulder, tore open the stitches."

Staring off down the beach, he didn't see her close her eyes as she finally understood. Not that it excused his lack of communication. For a professional speaker he was being dense. Idiot, she thought affectionately.

"I didn't need your doctor to tear a strip off me. I'd already castigated myself. He warned me that if your shoulder didn't heal properly then there was a good chance that you wouldn't regain the full range of movement. He made it very clear that I wasn't to touch you again." Guilt filled his expression.

Karina was appalled. "The doctor shouldn't have said that. You're not responsible for me. *I* am. I appreciate you taking care of me, but as for the night we spent together…that's ridiculous."

"Just—"

She held up *her* hand this time, determined to have her say. There was no way she was going to let him feel guilty about something she'd done, especially as she didn't feel the same way. "No, it's your turn to listen to me. Last night I wanted you. And I got exactly what I came for, a night of hot lovemaking."

Ruefully, he looked down at his hands. "Even if you did start it, I should have been gentler. However, once I touched you, I lost the battle."

She covered his hands with her own.

"At no time was I in serious pain. I don't know when the injury happened and I don't care. There was no real damage done. What hurt much worse was waking up alone to find you upset and not know why."

"I felt terrible." His gaze was turbulent with emotion and her heart couldn't help but respond. "You are a special woman, Karina, incredibly strong and valiant. I appreciate and admire who you are."

"And for that I love you," she said.

But apparently Brian wasn't ready for absolution. He smiled gently at her. "And I love you. That's why I want you to be sure. I don't want you to confuse your feelings with relief and gratitude."

She gaped at him. "I know exactly what I feel. I'm not confused at all," she said, frustration beginning to war with amusement.

"Good." He reached for her hand and held it tight. "Then giving us time to get over this nightmare won't make any difference to how you feel."

Karina shook her head. "Of all the things that I worried about when I contemplated telling you how I feel, I never considered that you wouldn't believe me."

She leaned back in her chair and closed her eyes. Now what was she going to do.

THE FRIENDLY GOOD-BYE kisses and good-night cuddles resumed. Much to Karina's frustration, that was all Brian would allow. Every time she tried to ignite his passion to a depth that would carry them both off, Brian firmly reined it in with his control and ended the embrace.

"Not until the doctor says your shoulder's okay," he said several nights later.

"But I feel fine. Besides, there are other things we could do," she said.

"My control isn't up to that." He looked at her disgruntled face and actually grinned at her.

The nerve of the man.

Then he really did it. "Besides, I don't think yours is either."

And that was that.

Under no circumstances was she going to get him into her bed again until she passed her doctor's inspection. With that thought in mind, she phoned to make an appointment. The receptionist said she couldn't get in until the next week, but she wouldn't accept that. In no uncertain terms, she explained what her doctor was keeping her from and that she wanted him to fix it. Now.

The nurse had exploded into gales of laughter, but had gone to see what she could do. The doctor agreed to see her on Thursday. Before ringing off, the nurse asked, "Do you think you can wait that long?"

Karina's face flushed bright red as she replaced the phone. She could just imagine what the visit itself would bring. But embarrassment be damned, she was going. The doctor was going to write Brian a note. She could just imagine his smirk with that request. Tough. This was too important to be faint of heart now.

The doctor's office was packed.

She didn't mind the wait, but it was a little hard to ignore the smirks on the faces of the staff. Obviously, someone had tattled. That was okay. She could deal with their laughter; after all, they wouldn't have Brian in their arms tonight to make them feel better. She would.

The doctor was preoccupied while he checked out her wound. After making her show him the range of movement and muscle activity that she had, he gave her the name of the physiotherapist that he wanted her to go see.

"It looks good, but she can give you some exercises to build and strengthen that area. Take it easy for a while but you should be back to full activity in a week or two." He started to walk out of the room when she stopped him.

The look on his face when he finally understood her request was comical. "Let me get this straight. You want me to write him a note giving him permission to resume your sex life?"

"Yes. You reamed him out so badly the last time we were here that he won't touch me for fear of doing more damage. You created this mess so you'll have to fix it." He could laugh, but even if she was exasperated and embarrassed, the doctor was going to write that note.

And laugh he did. He bent over double, howling in delight. The nurse popped her head in the room to make sure everything was okay, and on seeing Karina there, she grinned and left again. The doctor sat down to regain his breath. With a prescription pad in one hand, he spent a moment staring at the wall, still chuckling softly. He then scribbled something down, while calling out to the nurse for an envelope. He tucked the note inside and swiped his tongue over the strip of glue. After writing Brian's name on the outside of the envelope, he handed it over to her.

"There you go. Give it to him with my best wishes."

Karina narrowed her eyes at him and looked down at the package in her hand. She really wanted to ask what he'd written, but couldn't get up the nerve.

The doctor's chuckles echoed all the way down the hallway on his way out.

IT WAS THURSDAY, and Brian's last evening lecture for his current series of sessions. Their friends were already there when Brian and Karina arrived.

She was handing over her jacket to Mark to hang up when she found the doctor's letter in her pocket. She handed it to Brian.

"What's this?"

"Something for later. I know you're running behind, so don't worry about it right now." But boy he'd better watch out tonight. This time Brian would just get her. Along with passion, honesty and love rolled into her very hungry female body. Damn, she couldn't wait.

After tonight, he wouldn't doubt her feelings at all.

He smiled and dropped a swift kiss on her cheek before heading toward the stage.

Karina found Sandra and Susan and took her seat beside

her friends.

The final lecture was interesting and engaging. Brian seemed to be fully back on his game, and the evening flew by. Although for Karina, who was sitting on pins and needles of anticipation, time couldn't move fast enough. Just before the seminar would normally close, Brian asked for their indulgence.

He opened with a question for his audience.

"Have you ever been sure, even positive, about what another person should do in a certain situation, only to find out later that you were wrong?"

Several heads nodded in amused understanding.

"Change is taking place in all our lives, all the time," he continued. "Often we don't see the inner turmoil in people until they do unexpected things." He paused for effect, his smile inviting everyone to join in on a secret. "It's important to remember that we all need the space to honor our own growth and that of our partners. In our individual ways."

Karina mulled over the simple truth of his words. His next words snapped her back to the seminar.

Brian walked back and forth across the stage, a curious smile on his face. "That is the subject of my next book, titled, *Second Chances.*

"This book is all about giving up our expectations of what we think we know is best for others and for ourselves. Making decisions, admitting you're wrong and doing what's right, are three of the hardest things we face in a relationship with a special someone."

Karina couldn't believe just how true his words were.

"This has been brought home to me in several major ways in my own life these last few weeks. I don't know if you have been following the news, but *my* partner and I have survived some of the most traumatic events a person can go through. We faced danger, were attacked several times and even came close to death." The soberness and obvious truth of his words had the audience gasping. "Yet, we remained strong. Only afterwards did I realize that the real foe was within us. Our insecurities, our fears, led to a distancing between us because we didn't want to hurt each other. Me, in particular. I was so sure of what was right for her… She was more honest, but I wouldn't listen. After all," he gave a self-deprecating smile, "I knew better."

That brought a small ripple of amusement from the audience.

Karina couldn't believe he was actually speaking about this in front of everyone. A gentle hand covered her clenched one. She looked over at Susan.

"Trust, remember," she whispered.

Karina grimaced, but relaxed – somewhat.

Brian continued. "Lack of confidence, fears, and the lack of belief in the other are killers for any relationship. I was guilty of these mistakes more than my partner."

He paused for effect. His honesty captured the audience. Not a soul could say they hadn't made the same mistakes at some time. However, no one expected to hear a speaker of his caliber admit to the same.

Karina sat there reeling. *My God.*

"When my partner and I got together, she was in a state of change. She'd made massive external changes in her life and I was proud of her. Did I remember to tell her? No, I don't think I did. Then we entered this nightmare, during which time she continually surprised me. It's not that I did anything wrong in our relationship."

He smiled, a lopsided, adorable thing that the audience

found contagious. A few muted giggles added to the air of anticipation.

"However, from my perspective I hadn't done anything right either, whereas she outdid herself. The result was that I saw myself as not worthy of this special person. She freely admitted her feelings, but I couldn't see anyone as strong as her wanting to be with me so I dismissed them believing she didn't know her own mind. That her feelings were too tied up with the trauma we'd survived. Again, I *knew* what was right for her when she obviously didn't." His grin was wry. "Based on my own lack of self-confidence at this point, I found it hard to express my feelings. Me, a professional communicator, couldn't communicate in my private life. We were at an impasse, one she decided to break. I was, of course, a willing participant."

His sexy grin at this point hinted at exactly which method the mystery woman had employed. Giggles and gasps abounded throughout the room.

Karina was mortified. She tried to hide her burning face.

Susan reached over and whispered, "Good for you!"

Mark was standing at the back of the room. Karina could feel his stare on the back of her neck. She didn't have to see him to know the look on his face, however, the pull was too strong. She swiveled her head.

He was staring at her, his expression filled with unholy merriment. In an exaggerated gesture, he blew her a big kiss. Hastily, Karina turned away, but not before she realized that several people had noticed the exchange.

Now people were starting to talk and point.

Oh Lord, how could Brian do this to her? She sank lower in her chair.

Brian was speaking again. "However…" Now his grin

widened, his eyes danced. "Not only was this woman confident enough to speak from her heart, she was comfortable in gaining assistance that would help her cause." Brian reached into his pocket and held up the doctor's envelope that she'd given him earlier.

Karina groaned aloud and hid her face in her hands. *She should have stayed home tonight.*

By now, the audience was well clued into the fact that something special was happening here. They were also a very willing audience, eagerly tagging along for the ride and avidly waiting to see how the next scene in this play would unfold.

"She actually went to her doctor and had him write me a note, which he did, even going so far as to seal it in an envelope and address it to me." At this point Brian walked down the two steps of the front podium and moved closer to the audience. He held up the note for all to see.

"She has no idea what he wrote." Pure devilment leapt out of his face as he carried on. "There was, of course, a good reason for that. She never would have given this to me, otherwise."

Karina gasped at that. *Just what had that doctor done?* She didn't know where to look, so she stared down at her lap, fervently wishing she could just sink out of sight.

Brian continued, "Because the doctor actually wrote a poem instead. One that I'm going to share with you." The audience was truly caught in the drama now. Faces turned to follow Brian as he walked toward Karina.

He locked his gaze on her and recited,

> *"Take this woman to bed — that's long overdue,*
> *Hold her close and rejoice in her love for you.*
> *Understand the painful doubts that misconstrue*

Your reasons for not binding her – as you want to do,
She's honest & loving, yet she's single, that's true,
So wed her, bed her and love her each day, anew.
And if you don't take my advice – I'll steal her from
you."

The audience howled with laughter and joyous applause echoed throughout the room. All eyes were on the two of them.

Karina was thoroughly mortified, and too stunned to even think – except for the random thought that she just might have to kill her doctor. Susan and Sandra hugged her tightly, delight shining from each of their faces.

She could hardly feel Brian's hand on her shoulder, but there was no missing his words.

"I'd like you all to meet the special woman in my life. This is Karina. She's made my life blossom in a way I couldn't have imagined. Then again, I couldn't have imagined a doctor's prescription like this one, either. By the way, I'm not an idiot and she'll definitely be getting a new doctor after this."

Hysterical laughter ensued. Karina looked at Brian in disbelief.

As the place started to quiet down, Brian picked up the conversation. "So, on doctor's orders, I intend to make sure this woman is safe, well loved, well bedded…"

He grinned to the audience, lustful anticipation beaming across his face. "And if she'll have me," he ignored the gasp from Karina, "*I'll* keep her happily wed."

He tugged Karina up and into his arms, and then pulled a small golden item from his pocket.

"The only question left to ask is – Karina, will you marry

me?"

There wasn't a sound now from anyone. The audience waited in breathless anticipation.

Karina was in shock, staring down at the diamond ring before her and what it implied. *He'd had it all along.* Her eyes filled with tears, but she beamed with joy. She couldn't speak. Tears clogged her throat and happiness warmed her soul. God, she loved him.

With a tiny nod, she gathered her voice and shouted, "Yes!" She threw her arms around him, wanting to hold him to her forever and ever.

Cheers rang through the room and the applause was deafening. Everyone bounced up from their chairs, hugging one another and shouting their congratulations into the air.

Mark bounded over and pulled both Susan and Sandra into his arms. "About damned time, too!"

Even in the midst of deafening chaos, Karina and Brian barely noticed.

Brian, following doctor's orders, was kissing her soundly and "loving her well."

Epilogue

Ten months later

KARINA SAT IN the sand beside Chelsea, helping the little girl build a sand castle on Salt Spring Island. Her stepdaughter and Sandra's twins were visiting for the weekend. And not for the first time, either. The hot summer was still a few months away but the beach was beautiful all the time.

And with it being spring break, the twins were full of energy. Sandra much less so, but stretched out on a blanket beside Karina, she obviously wasn't suffering too much.

"I was afraid this week would be too hard on you, being pregnant and all," murmured Sandra. "Instead, I'm the one that's exhausted."

Karina laughed. "I'm fine. And I love having you here. I spent so much time alone in Vancouver with just my friends, Cat and Serena, that I'm happy to be surrounded all the time now." She sighed. "And after all that nasty Ian stuff, this is something I don't take for granted."

"I'm grateful Ian isn't competent to stand trial. Saves all of us lots of pain."

Now that was an understatement. But Karina was satisfied *that* part of her life was over. Maybe now Ian could get some help and find peace for the rest of his life. As long as he stayed away from Karina, she'd be happy. As for Ian's wife Mary, she was going through with the divorce apparently but that's all she knew. Karina wished her well in her new life.

"Are your girlfriends still arriving on Friday night as planned? I'm looking forward to seeing them again."

"Yes, they are. Serena is even considering moving here. She says Vancouver just isn't the same without all three of us there. She's also thinking of opening a bookstore herself, preferably one that includes a built-in coffee shop. She's as much an addict as I am," Karina confessed.

"Oh that's perfect." Sandra lifted her head to look at Karina. "We should see if there's an appropriate space in our little mall."

"That's exactly what I told her." Karina laughed. "She'd fit in perfectly."

"And what about Cat?" Sandra sat up, looking for her boys and relaxed as she spotted them building a fort out of driftwood a short way down the beach. "Does she want to go into business, too?"

Karina smiled as she stared down at Chelsea's white-blond curls. There was more sand on her scalp than hair at this point. "Cat is special. She's already got her own business. She's in computers. Very high-tech, hush-hush stuff."

"Sounds exciting." Sandra grinned. "I'm definitely looking forward to their visit."

Thinking back to all she'd gained since making the move to Victoria, Karina realized just how lucky she was. If her friends could find the same happiness, her world would be complete.

Only time would tell.

Author's Note

Thank you for reading Second Chances Books 1& 2! If you enjoyed my book, I'd appreciate it if you'd leave a review.

Dear reader,

I love to hear from readers, and you can contact me at my website: www.dalemayer.com or at my Facebook author page. To be informed of new releases and special offers, sign up for my newsletter or follow me on BookBub. And if you are interested in joining Dale Mayer's Reader Group, here is the Facebook sign up page.
http://geni.us/DaleMayerFBGroup

Cheers,
Dale Mayer

Next is the preview of my latest release called SKIN. Turn the page to read the preview. After the preview are blurbs of other books and my book list.

SKIN

A journey of exploration…
A journey of healing…
A journey of love…

Two people are forced by circumstances into a therapy class to help them deal with their problems. They are strangers. Forced to be partners. Naturally opposites.

Kane is dealing with anger of betrayal at the deepest level, needing to find his way back to forgiveness. Tania is a previous rape victim hoping to deal with her fear of intimacy so she can have a loving relationship.

Tania's medium of expression – her camera.

Her subject – the human body – Kane's physical body.

Looking through the lens of a camera, she learns to find beauty and compassion…and the strength to find wholeness…with him.

To Read a Preview of SKIN turn the page

SKIN is available!

Chapter 1

TANIA TOOK HER seat in the small room. She was early, and the seminar room in was empty. She liked to arrive early in class, because it gave her time to settle before things got started.

She'd been in similar scenarios before. She could do this; again and again, if she had to. Using the meditation tricks she learned, she practiced her deep-breathing techniques to ease back the stress threatening to choke the breath from her body. Therapy was good for her. She was getting better. She could do this.

This particular program was special, a university workshop type of thing. Intensive. Invasive. Guaranteed to help bring about change.

She could do this.

Liar. She so sucked at this.

She stared out the large windows, her nerves raw, hot. Morning sunshine shone through the curtains, giving a muted look to the bright light. Kind of like her own life. As if she were living only a shade of the life she could be.

And that was precisely what she was doing.

Several other attendees entered and took their seats. Special group, special problems, and they'd all signed up to do this willingly; had even paid for it. More than that, once committed there was no quitting. They were all students here at the University of British Columbia in Vancouver. They were all associated in one way or another with the professor who'd be leading this week-long session. She was friends with one of the participants and recognized most of the others from Jenna's lectures on internal healing.

In her case, her best friend had paid the hefty deposit to hold Tania's place while she convinced her to get help. Five days in a hotel at the edge of campus. Workshops in the mornings, assignments in the afternoons and therapy sessions dotted the rest of the evening. Even those who lived locally weren't allowed to leave at the end of the day; it was all-inclusive. She wished it were otherwise, and then she could return to her normal life instead of this intensive, no-hiding type of session. Which was, of course, the purpose of the seminar.

She was scared, but she was more scared of staying caught in this limbo forever.

It was stupid. She shouldn't need help. Not after all this time. It had happened years ago. She should be over this.

But the sad fact was – she wasn't. And if she didn't do something about it, her life would never go in the direction she wanted it to go. Her dream of a small house and white picket fence with the perfect two kids was never going to happen if she didn't find a way to let a man into her bed-room. *Sure*, she thought moodily, *I could adopt*. She had actually seriously considered it.

But she wanted the loving relationships she saw so many of her friends enjoying. And to get there, she had to heal herself first. So not easy.

She smiled as her friend, Robin, came in and sat down beside her. Robin said, "Hi. How are you doing this week?"

Tania smiled wider. "Fine. As long as I avoid men, as

usual."

"Ha." Robin grinned. "Defeats the purpose, doesn't it?"

"It's what I can do." Tania shrugged. "Leaving that safety net is not easy."

"I hear you." Robin settled in beside her. Tania's scars were inside, but Robin's were outside. She had been in a horrible accident and was dealing with reconstructive surgery and the fact that she might never be 'normal'. She had trouble going out in public and had barricaded herself in a secular life of school. Robin was here to deal with her fears and how she looked now and to find the strength to get out in public where she'd be ridiculed and stared at. After children had run from her screaming in a park almost a year ago, she'd gone home. And stayed home. It had become the safe haven that she didn't want to leave, but that also made it a prison. She had to force herself to go to class. Had to force herself to come to this seminar.

Tania understood.

They were all here to deal with issues – big issues. Whatever issues stopped them from living full lives. Their professor was a special woman who'd walked their path and had healed herself. Now, she was on a journey to help others do the same.

Just then, several men walked in, loud and boisterous. There was just something about that big, dominant energy as it filled the small, casual lounge. It was the same three men that had arrived as a group last night, the first day of the seminar, and the same way they arrived at Jenna's classes on campus. Every week, the quiet disappeared, and Tania and Robin became even quieter. This wasn't a normal therapy group; she'd been to those. This one demanded a commitment to complete the session and participation at all times.

There was homework, assignments that forced participants to step out of their comfort zone.

Everyone knew something about each other, but the details had been offered at the discretion of the person. They were all here for a week. One week. Working together, pairing up for various assignments.

She *could* do this.

Then *he* walked in and sat down beside her.

Her stomach dropped and her blood heated. She could hardly breathe. She straightened and shifted ever so slightly closer to Robin like she always did. Like a moth to a flame, she knew better than to get any closer to Kane, a huge muscled guy that seemed too rough and…angry for her to be safe. But, just like the moth, the attraction went at the cellular level and she was helpless to resist.

God, she wanted him.

And she'd never wanted a man in her life.

He terrified her. She wanted to want a small man. Someone her size. Someone…she'd have a chance to escape from if he turned abusive. Someone gentle, tender, understanding.

Kane oozed strength, power, bitterness.

Not at all what she wanted. Or needed.

Kane crossed his arms, his muscles bulging beside her. She shuddered. How could she want to stroke her fingers across his skin at the same time that she wanted to run away from him? He could pound her into the ground with one punch. Why? Why would her body want anything to do with him? It made no sense.

And only reinforced that she was crazy.

"Ah, Tania? Can you move back over slightly?" Robin gave her a concerned look then nudged her shoulder and, using her chin, pointed to Tania's half-empty seat.

Tania realized she'd damn near crawled into Robin's chair with her; she was that close. With a sideways glance at Kane, Tania flushed and settled back into place. "Sorry," she whispered to Robin.

"Don't worry about it."

Two voices said the same thing.

She wanted to yell 'snap', that silly remnant from her childhood, but was too busy staring in surprise at Kane. He gave her a stone-faced look. She'd never considered how her constant avoidance of him must look. He was no monster; in fact, he was stunning – to her. He had a lean face full of angles and planes. She thought of granite when she contemplated him. Strong. Infallible. Unyielding.

She had no basis for such an assessment. She didn't know him outside of seeing him the odd time in Jenna's classes. They were of a similar age, she thought, but he seemed older. It was his demeanor; slightly off-putting in that he almost always had a sneer on his face. As if he was here under duress, but he didn't truly belong.

But then, she'd been like that in her last therapy class. That she wasn't now meant she'd grown a little. Maybe he just needed a bit more time. Accepting one had a problem was a hell of a start – and often the most difficult step.

He might not want to see himself as one of the participants here that needed help, but that's what he was. And being here meant he had issues regardless of his attitude. So he was no better than she was.

But his attitude needed some adjusting if he was going to get any benefit from the class. And considering the money he'd dumped into this, he'd better.

She couldn't help but wonder at his story. That he had a

chip on his shoulder was obvious, and that there was that thin layer of bitterness just below the surface. She had to think relationships were involved. From what she'd seen, there were some pretty screwed-up people in the world, and those here for this session had taken a hit from some of the worst.

It had been good for her to come here and see she wasn't alone in dealing with her problems, or that her problems were by no means the worst. One of the men was young, like nineteen…maybe. Or possibly younger, considering the sparse bristles on his chin. He had a raunchy humor and dead eyes. Another, Sean, was tall and lanky and seemed seriously-old on the inside. He both scared her and struck a deep cord of sympathy inside. He'd been horribly abused by his mother for years before she finally OD'd on drugs, and he'd been left with a legacy of pain.

And like so many others here, he'd been working on his healing for years. He hoped this retreat would get rid of his last stumbling block.

Tania wasn't so sure it would be. Or that it could be. That look in his eye…

She shuddered, grateful she'd come as far as she had.

Now if only she could kick this fear and go all the way. Yet another school idiom that made her want to chuckle. What was wrong with her? It was as if she had a delayed teenage-hood. Maybe she had. She certainly hadn't spent it dreaming over movie stars or giggling in groups waiting for the special guys to walk by.

The door opened, admitting Jenna Price, their professor and therapist. She was a mix of ruthless compassion and steely resolve. She was determined that everyone here get something useful from this session. They weren't randomly accepted into this workshop; there had been a long list, which grew even longer every term, apparently. Money hadn't been the only criteria. The problems you were dealing with had to be something she felt would work in a group setting and that she could help you move past. That the other participants could help you to deal with your issues, too. She wasn't about everyone getting along, more about how the interaction would work to benefit everyone involved.

Jenna walked to the empty chair, her hand wrapped around a large china mug with a lid. She was a tea drinker. Apparently, at any time and any place she could always be seen with the mug. She was a stately woman, anywhere from her late thirties to mid forties. Tania had no idea, just that she appeared to be competent. Now if only she held that magical key to getting Tania's life back on track…

"Good morning." Jenna placed the mug on the floor beside her. "Last night was basic. Today, we are going to get into the nitty-gritty stuff, and you are going to hurt. It's hard dealing with the issues we don't want to look at. It's painful to step out of our padded cloud and deal honestly and openly with what needs to be dealt with." She cast that warm but determined gaze around the room. "Remember, none of you are here by accident. You came because you want to deal with something, and you want change for yourself. Today is Day 1. You will have changed by Day 5; I guarantee it." Her gaze landed on Tania and Robin, a slight softening warming her chocolate-brown eyes. "We'll be working together as a group all morning. But after lunch, you will be put into groups of two with your week-long assignment."

Week-long assignment? That was the first Tania had heard anything about that. As long as it was in pairs, she was probably okay with that. She could work with Robin. That would most likely suit both of them.

Taking a deep breath, Tania turned her attention back to the morning's work.

A long time later, Jenna opened a folder she'd brought with her and handed out sheets of paper to everyone. "This is the outline of the assignment. You will be given all afternoon every day for the rest of the week to work on this, with my help if need be. But let's make no mistake here: the assignment is not a cerebral one. Each of you must deal with people, the public, and yourselves for this to work."

A small knot of dread formed in Tania's stomach as she realized how very difficult such an assignment could be. Poor Robin; she'd have the worst time with this. Already, Tania's mind was wandering, looking for ways to make it easier on her, and came to a full stop. No. That was not the answer. She'd be enabling Robin. Better for her to deal with the issues that surfaced than to have Tania automatically assume she couldn't do it.

Tania would have her hands full herself.

She accepted the sheet of paper from Robin and handed the last one over to the silent Kane. At least he'd lost the bored look. She studied his body language, seeing him sit a little straighter and lock his jaw. He wasn't as comfortable as he was putting on.

Interesting. So, control was important to him. She filed that tidbit away and turned her attention back to class. Jenna had been taking pairs of people off to one side and speaking with them privately. She'd watched as Robin and the abused young male walked out of the room together. Tania was surprised at the compassion on Robin's face. And on Sean's. What was going on?

She turned her attention back to the paper in her hand. The project was intended to push her out of her comfort zone while being within the scope of what she needed to learn to do. Given the private nature of her problem, she really didn't want to have to do anything really uncomfortable. It would be embarrassing and potentially crippling. As another pair of attendees left the room, she realized Jenna was speaking to two more. Leaving her and Kane.

Her insides twisted in on themselves. Please, let her be wrong. She wanted Robin as a partner, not Kane. Maybe this had nothing to do with the project. But God, it really felt like it did. The longer she sat there waiting for her turn, the harder her fingers clenched the paper in her lap and the tighter the steel band around her chest constricted. She stared almost blindly as her knuckles turned white, and her chest struggled to relax enough to let air in.

Oh, God.

If she had to be partners with a man, let it be with a small one. Not Kane. Please, not the six-foot-four, 240-pound man that looked like he belonged with his mitts wrapped around a jackhammer all day.

She had nothing against construction workers, but she so didn't want anything to do with Kane where her problems were concerned. She was looking for so much less of a man.

And her mind called her on it. *Liar. You so want to have something to do with him.*

She had to correct herself. *No, I want to be able to do something with him. But I'm not there yet.* She slid a sideways glance at his massive thighs encased in tight jeans as he sat relaxed in the chair beside her. *And,* she repeated, *I might never get there.*

Then it was her turn.

"Tania and Kane." Jenna walked over to them and tugged a chair forward so she sat in front, making a triangle of their positions. "Sorry for making you wait."

It was on the tip of Tania's tongue to say 'no problem', but she couldn't get the words out. Feeling like a mouse caught in a horrible sense of knowing it was about to get pounced on, she sat, frozen…and waited.

And knew her fate was as bad as the mouse when Jenna said, "Let's discuss your project."

Tania felt more than saw Kane glance her way, but she heard his comment clear enough. "Are you sure this is a good idea? Maybe Tania would do better with someone else."

His smooth-as-chocolate voice sent waves of want through her, but the actual meaning sent rods of steel down her back, making her straighten in outrage.

"I'll be fine," she snapped and widened her gaze as she realized she'd just agreed to work with him. Oh, shit. That damn stubborn temper of hers…

"Good. I think you'll do just fine. Besides, your partner-ship isn't a spur-of-the-moment decision. I've been working on these pairings since you both confirmed you'd be here, and I think you'll work perfectly together." She studied the papers in her hand for a moment, as if unconcerned at the reception of the other two.

Tania knew she had to be perceptive to the change in the air, the tension. But she also had to assume the woman knew what she was about. Except Tania had been to some crazy therapists who should have dealt with their own crap before trying to counsel others.

She didn't *think* Jenna fell into this same category.

But who could know?

Hunkering down in the chair, she tried to open her

mind to the concept of a team project, actually managing to laugh at herself. It was just for a few days. *Like, how hard could this be?*

Then she listened in growing horror to Jenna's explanation.

When Jenna fell silent, Tania could only stare at her in shock.

Thankfully, Kane appeared to have a handle on this and blasted Jenna with her sentiments exactly. "You want us to what?"

He stood up and stormed around the room. "Are you nuts?"

Tania couldn't agree more.

With his hands out, he said, "Look, I'm here and willing to do the work to deal with my stuff, but you're putting Tania in danger."

She what? Tania straightened. "Excuse me? What kind of danger?" Because she wasn't up for any; not in any way. She wanted a safe, controlled project that would allow her to open the door to her comfort zone and put her big toe in to test the water; that was it.

Danger? Hell no. She'd had enough of that when she'd been raped over ten years ago.

She wasn't going to be in any kind of danger – ever again.

*   *   *

KANE HAD SAT through enough today. Watching Tania's tiny body shift away from him from the moment he'd sat down – hell, probably from the moment he walked into the room, he knew she had some big-time man issues. He didn't get man-hater vibes from her, but a tiny woman like that would be easy prey for the wrong man. Unless she was a black belt in something, she had no protection from a man's anger. That she was here in therapy, he'd bet his years of experience that she'd been in an abusive relationship. She was a creampuff for any guy over sixteen. For someone like him, hell, no way could he be around her.

He felt like he'd be slamming a tea cup against the wall if he said anything in a harsh tone.

She was way too delicate for this class. For him. For this project. The damn shrink had this one wrong.

There was no way anyone with his anger issues, his hatred of his ex, should be around someone who he could break in half with two fingers.

As he realized Tania was nodding her head in emphatic agreement, a tiny part of him was sorry for it. In the old days, he'd have loved to have been the knight in shining armor and help her deal with whatever issues she had. He'd seen enough sad cases in his years in law enforcement that he had some idea of what she might have gone through. It could be something completely different...but his instinct said he was close. Damn close.

The shrink smiled at them both, with that damn compassionate warmth that made him wonder if she lived with sunshine and pussy cats all her life to have given her outlook a rosy tinge. Because that wasn't the reality as he knew it.

She had to know that. They all interviewed to come here. Every one of them had spoken to her privately about their issues, and then they'd all attended her lectures at the university alongside their regular classes. While he might not know all of Tania's issues, he knew that Jenna did know.

And still she'd paired them together. Wondering what she could possibly be thinking, he slowly sat back down.

And wondered why?

Chapter 2

TANIA WATCHED SILENTLY and a bit regretfully as Kane blew through his temper and back into calm. Her father used to do that; blow up, cool down, and then refuel for the next blow. Her mother had always loved to get him going. They'd fought like cats and dogs all the time, but it hadn't weakened their relationship. They'd argued, debated, and made up with the same passion. Because they blew up often, bad feelings and irritations didn't build up to the point that they caused damage. They shared what they felt all the time – good and bad. It hadn't been the easiest childhood, but she'd always known where she stood on any issue. Bottom line – they loved each other and her.

Even after their divorce, she'd never doubted it. They were still friends today.

Kane looked to be of similar ilk.

It made him a little easier to understand. Except, in this instance, she wished he'd blow a little harder, a little louder. And get them out of this.

"It's only a project," Jenna was saying in that smooth, what-could-you-possibly-be-worried-about tone of voice.

And that just made Tania terrified. She'd been through too much therapy to believe that. And from the look of him, Kane hadn't been through enough. He appeared to be falling for Jenna's line of bullshit.

Tania wasn't so easily swayed. She leaned forward. "Jenna, you know our history. I'm not sure what Kane's issue is, but you know mine."

Jenna smiled warmly at her and waited for her to continue, expectancy on her face for a favorite student about to give the right answer. That should have been enough warning, but just in case Jenna really didn't get it… "Surely," Tania added, "I could work with Robin. I'd love that." And she beamed with relief at the smile on Jenna's face. This would work. Tania had always managed to get things to work at university and at work. People were accommodating; no one wanted discord.

And then she saw the look in Jenna's eyes and realized there was to be no easy exit from this one.

"Fine. How hard can this be?" Tania glared at Kane, who just raised an eyebrow at her. He flicked something off his thigh, but it was the mocking look that made her ask. "What?"

"Oh, nothing; just flicking away an irritating mosquito."

She shot him a narrow-eyed look before turning her back on him to glare at Jenna. "This is a really bad idea," she said in a dark tone.

But Jenna was laughing. "Maybe and maybe not. So let's go over what you are going to do."

And that was when Tania realized she was getting a camera.

She couldn't stop the smile that broke free, the relieved laughter that rippled throughout the room. "Oh, my God. You should have said something in the beginning." She laughed and laughed.

When she could stop the giggles, only the odd hiccupping laugh still escaping, she realized Jenna had a wry smile on her face. Kane wore a thundercloud.

"I'm glad this isn't quite as impossible as you'd first been afraid it was," Jenna said gently.

And that, of course, had been the crux of the issue. Settling down and realizing she'd let her fears completely override rational thought here, Tania relaxed.

She loved photography, and of course, Jenna knew that. They'd discussed it several times. She wasn't sure why or how, or if the sensation was real or just another mirage she put up in her world to make something doable, but being behind a camera put distance between her and a situation. Gave her a buffer from the uncomfortable, the too-intense insights, and the world at large.

It gave her a sense of security. Of safety.

Jenna was seriously bright to have done this. And that relief was something that let Tania sit down and let herself settle inside. She was safe. This wasn't going to be something that was super scary. Super intimate. In fact, she had to wonder if it would do anything for her at all. But her mind immediately clutched at the straw offered and said she could deal with the other stuff later. Down the road, like in ten years' time.

"Okay. I'm really going to love this project." Her mind wandered through the camera gear she'd brought with her, wondering what to use first. It all depended on what they had to photograph. And then another tidbit fell into place. "That's why you told me to be sure to bring my camera gear, isn't it?"

"Yes, it is." Jenna nodded, but she didn't look at Tania. Instead, she kept her gaze on Kane.

Realizing she'd been awash in her own satisfaction and joy at what she would be doing, she'd put no thought to

Kane's role in all of this. It's not like she needed him to carry stuff. It was all small, and she'd been packing her gear for a long time.

She frowned as she took in the hard gaze between Jenna and Kane.

And realized she'd missed something.

"Uhm, what's going on?" She studied the tick on Kane's jaw and realized instead of a blow-up, he'd gone super quiet. In her dad's case, that meant he was seriously pissed. She winced. Kane was going to have a monster of a headache after this. Clenching his jaw, his neck was corded, and as her gaze slipped down his chest, she realized his fists were almost white at the knuckles.

"Jenna?" No one could miss the signals in the room right now. She cleared her throat and tried again. "Maybe you could tell me what Kane and I are going to photograph?"

Kane, his voice like silken steel, answered instead. "Go ahead, Jenna." His voice deepened dangerously. "Tell us."

Shit. Tania's gaze raced from the one so furious she couldn't believe he was holding back to Jenna, who sat calmly, returning his stare in apparent unconcern. But Jenna was no fool; everyone knew you didn't turn your back on a dangerous animal.

And right now Kane was one hell of a dangerous animal.

"Why don't you tell her, if you think you know," Jenna said smoothly.

"Kane?" Tania wanted this tension to break. Even tensile strength had a breaking point.

"It's not what you're going to photograph," he snapped. "It's who."

Tania didn't understand, but at the approving curl on Jenna's lips, she figured Kane just got the favorite student award.

"Who am I supposed to photograph?" she asked, bewildered.

"Me."

*   *   *

KANE CLOSED THE door to his room with a very controlled click. He stood stock-still and let the anger ripple through him. He didn't dare let loose or there'd be a hole in the door. He splayed his fingers wide with as much force as he could manage. When the tension finally drained, he relaxed slightly. Then he took several steps toward the bed, where he threw himself down on the cushy surface. He leaned his head back and groaned out loud.

"What the hell am I doing here?" He could blame his brother for this damn session, but that wasn't fair. Sure, Jerry had pushed and prodded to get Kane to sign up, and it had been a good idea initially. Sounded like just what he needed. He'd been nursing that grudge of his for far too long.

Time to move on before he screwed up other relationships.

He groaned again, lifting both hands and scrubbing his face. He only had an hour's lunch break. Everyone had split immediately after their meetings with Jenna, taking off for their own silent spaces. He needed food, but he'd needed space and time to regroup more. He could do a stupid camera project with Tania.

So what if she took a picture of him? Big deal.

Then why was he damn near shaking? It's as if he were stressed to the max. And if that was the case, why? He'd been fine first thing this morning. Fine since he'd arrived. He'd been disdainful as the process started. It gave him that bit of buffer in case he started to feel too involved, or they got too dangerously close to his own hurts.

It was easier to come to something like this if he kept himself separate from the others. And of course, the therapist's purpose was to stop him from that disconnect. He didn't know when he'd started to feel a fine edge of anger or bitterness to put more distance between them, but it was somewhere around the time he noticed Tania flinching away from him. This morning, she'd damned near crawled into Robin's lap.

It made for a tough few hours when every time he shifted, he felt her response like a scared rabbit. He'd wanted to reassure her he wasn't planning on hitting her or hitting on her. But he'd known that would have made it all worse.

It was too bad.

She was tiny, delicate-featured, and curvy. He hadn't been able to stop thinking about her. Then with every breath he took, he was intimately aware of her reaction – just as she was aware of his every action.

To have that level of awareness with someone…someone who was terrified of him…was just wrong. No… he pulled that thought. He hadn't gotten the impression that she was terrified of him…she didn't know him. He was a stranger to her. It was more that she was terrified of what he represented.

His mind played with that.

What did he represent? Maleness. Strength. Power. He'd caught her gaze on his biceps. His thighs. He studied his arms; he kept in shape, worked out, had a stocky build. No one would ever call him a toothpick, that was for sure.

From any other woman, he'd take her glances as interest. And there could be a touch of that here, but he knew it wasn't the main part. Given they were in therapy, chances were good she'd been beaten up by someone bigger and stronger than her and most likely someone like himself – male.

And that made it tough to sit beside her.

Because he didn't have the same issues. At least not over sex. He *was* interested. Then again, he was male, so of course he was interested.

He grinned, his good humor restored. It would be a cold day in Hell before any healthy male wasn't interested in Tinkerbelle.

But to put the two of them together for hours on end was just asking for trouble. He wasn't sure he could stay calm and cool around her like she needed him to be, and he didn't want to terrorize her by blowing up in front of her.

She didn't need that.

He just didn't know what she did need. And it was none of his business. That was for Jenna to sort out. He needed to tell her privately to forget about this project.

Feeling better, he hopped up to his feet, prepared to go down to the restaurant for a quick bite, when it hit him. He was making a big deal over nothing.

This was a class project, just a few hours when he had to be in control. Calm. Detached. Even cop-like would work. He was a cop. He was just back finishing his degree so he could move up the ranks.

She could take a few pictures he'd learn a little patience, and he could go home.

Feeling better, he ran down the stairs, hoping to get a bite to eat after all.

Surprisingly, his appetite had returned.

Chapter 3

W HILE WORKING HER way through her lunch, Tania realized it was stupid to feel so relieved. She was here to face the parts of her she'd been keeping locked away. But there was no doubt that finding out she got to hide behind the lens of a camera made this an easier assignment than she expected.

That Kane was going to be her subject filled her with mixed feelings. She adored playing with light and dark. The camera would love him. His muscles. That build. There was just so much about him that excited her to be able to do this.

And with that camera, she didn't feel in danger. He was no threat to her. She'd be able to keep a lens between them.

She knew photography. She understood images.

But she didn't know him. But she *would* know him by the time this assignment was over. There was no way she couldn't. Photography was a tool to study something. To learn about something she hadn't been able to access before. The lens brought her closer, highlighted the focus, and forced everything to drop away yet lift the subject for closer inspection. Almost as if he were standing naked. Alone. Vulnerable. Reachable.

That gave her pause.

She laid the fork back down beside her plate and stared off in the distance. Was it coincidental? Or had Jenna understood this could help Tania in a big way?

"Something wrong?" Robin asked across from her.

Tania shook her head. "Not really. Just thinking about the assignments."

"Oh. Those." Robin sighed heavily. "Yeah, so not sure about that."

Part of the assignment instructions had been to keep the assignments private from the rest of the group so as to not be influenced by anyone else's thinking.

Robin attacked her fries with more force than necessary. She'd sat where her scarred face would be out of the public eye. Not that the restaurant was full. It rumbled in a nice enough way to say it was busy but lacked the overpowering-noise element of being bustling.

It suited Tania fine. She could be lost in her own thoughts without anyone noticing.

Then Kane walked in. No, Kane didn't walk anywhere. He strode in, determined, loose-gaited, and ready for anything. Her photographer instincts kicked in. Kane definitely had presence. She could imagine screen producers loving him. He didn't just take over a space, he owned it.

Her fingers itched to run to her room for her camera.

Her hands actually clenched the table to hold herself back. With an inward shudder, she dragged her gaze away and caught Robin's wide-eyed stare.

She flushed as heat raced up her cheeks. "Sorry," she muttered.

"Oh, don't be. I would love an explanation, though." Robin looked at her expectantly.

Tania shook her head. "Wish I could. It's part of the assignment we're doing."

"Uh-huh." Robin snorted lightly and dove back into her

French fries. "Must be one hell of an assignment."

The teasing tone made Tania's cheeks heat again. She stuffed her mouth with salad so as to not have to answer. Lunch finished quickly. By the time they made their way back to the seminar room, Jenna was already getting the first groups started.

When it was Tania's turn, Jenna said, "Kane is going to maintain what would be his usual routine for the afternoon. This is where you will start. You need to come up with a title, a theme, and a series that you can explain to me – if an explanation is necessary – of what and why and how."

Kane snorted. Tania spun around in surprise. She hadn't heard him come in. She frowned up at him, and he stared back, one eyebrow raised.

She wanted to ask what the hell he'd be doing for his half of this assignment besides lazing around all afternoon while she worked but held back. She had to trust that Jenna, who knew why Kane was here, had plans that would help him, too.

"We'll check back here at four. If you need any help, you can text or call me. I'll be in the morning room working." And Jenna gave them a bright smile and walked away.

Damn.

Kane never said a word. Actually, she rarely heard him speak at all. She cleared her throat and said, "I have to get my camera from my room. What are you going to do?"

He stared at her then looked around. "If I were at home, I would be doing yard work. Here at a hotel, that's not my own space, so I might do a bit of sightseeing, watch a movie, go to the gym…"

"And your choice right now?"

He ran his fingers through his short, wavy hair and

sighed. "I think I'd like to get the hell out. So a walk around the university sounds about right."

She brightened. "I love the university grounds. Perfect. I'll go get my camera and meet you in the lobby."

And took off.

*   *   *

KANE WATCHED HER run away. She was brighter, happier than he'd seen her yet. How bad could wasting a few hours pretending to be a tourist be? Especially with Tinkerbelle at his side?

He had no idea how this assignment was going to help him.

As he turned to stare at the empty room, he realized Jenna stood off to the side watching him. Waiting. As if she knew.

What the hell was he doing here? He looked at her. "How does being a model help me?" The derision in his voice brought a smile to her face, which was not quite the reaction he was hoping for.

"I think it's going to help a lot, actually." The serious tone surprised him.

"So me going out and being a tourist is going to help me deal with my anger issues?" He shook his head and started to walk away in disgust. "What a waste of time."

"Really? Except look at where your anger issues sprang from."

He stalled and leaned his head back to stare at the ceiling. "I prefer to *not* think about that time of my life, thank you."

"And that's why the anger. You need to examine it. The pain is more painful because you keep it alive…whereas the anger is a blind…. for something else." She paused then added gently, "Maybe for fear."

He spun around, feeling the familiar anger vibrating through his system. He glared at her. "I have to keep it alive, or else I will forget."

"No," she said, her voice gentle but determined. "You need to realize you are keeping the anger as justification for not letting anyone else get close. Not that close. Never again."

He stared at her, hating the resonating truth to her words. "Easier said than done," he muttered.

"Not easy. None of this is easy. But for a full life that you can enjoy again, it's necessary."

"And playing the tourist is going to do that?"

"Interesting you chose being a tourist. Casual. Distant. Disconnected."

He reared back. "What? You said to do what you would normally do. I can hardly go mow the lawn, now can I?"

Those all-too-knowing eyes studied him. He wanted to squirm and held himself strong against it. He was no schoolboy.

"There are other activities you could choose, and you don't have to play tourist all afternoon."

She reached out and patted him on the shoulder "You'll figure it out." And she walked away, leaving him wondering what the hell she was up to.

He pulled out his phone and texted his brother. *Waste of time and money.*

As he closed his phone, an overly-bright, I'm-determined-to-do-this voice called out to him, "Are you ready?"

Knowing she couldn't see him, he rolled his eyes and

turned around to face her. He could only hope she wasn't going to be wearing a half-dozen cameras around her neck, or they'd really look like a pair of damn tourists.

Instead, she had a single black fanny pouch on that tiny waist and a single camera around her neck. He knew nothing about cameras, but it didn't look to be a cheap, casual deal. She just might be a serious photographer, and for some reason, that made him feel better. He didn't know what she did for a living or what her education program was. He'd never seen her on campus except at Jenna's lectures. Still, she put her money into good equipment, and he could respect that.

If he had to play the gallant knight for a couple of days, whatever. And if a part of him wanted to give the no-refund policy of the damn contract a closer look, he pushed it to the back of his mind. What Jenna asked was impossible, but his pain didn't have to dim whatever problem Tinkerbelle was working on. He'd always been good at playing the stoic role. He could do this.

He nodded. "Let's go."

Chapter 4

TANIA UNDERSTOOD THE camera, just not the subject. Kane was difficult. A man of secrets. Getting him to be natural was key. He was doing the posing-tourist role, and she wanted nothing to do with it. Still, that was normal. It would take some time to find him under all of that.

She let him walk ahead on the cobblestone. There were intricate patterns worked into the street, and her camera loved them. Whenever he looked away or something caught Kane's eye, she tried to capture him.

But she didn't like the results. She'd have to ditch most of them at this rate.

"Coffee?" he asked hopefully, pointing to a small bistro off to the side.

"Tea?" she suggested, not knowing what they'd talk about.

He shrugged and led the way over. "I'll go in and order."

Happy to let him take charge, she nodded and took pictures of him walking into the tiny shop. He had a hell of a butt. What she wouldn't do to get him in tight boxers. The magic her camera could work then… And that thought was immediately by shock. Had she really just though that? About a perfect stranger?

He returned in a few minutes with two mugs. "Hope this is okay. Black tea and black coffee."

She fished the tea bag out quickly, not wanting to have it too strong if there wasn't milk and not wanting to go in and get milk even if it was available. For a therapy seminar, so far she'd cried no tears and had yet to feel under the gun with questions or swamped by emotions. She felt odd, not herself. Normally, she'd have just asked him to get the tea the way she liked it, but not this time.

Was it doing any good?

As if reading her thoughts, Kane said, "Weirdest therapy session I've ever done."

She laughed. "Exactly what I was thinking. I feel like this assignment is supposed to do something, but we are completely missing the mark."

"Are we?" Moodily, he stared into the deepest, blackest mug of coffee she'd ever seen. "Seems like a complete waste of time so far."

She leaned forward. "That's what I mean. We're out here sightseeing when we should be working on healing."

He leaned back at her emphatic comment. "You think we shouldn't be out here."

She shrugged and looked around. "I can't help but feel like we are deliberately avoiding something. Or aren't ready yet to get too close to the real issues."

"Really?" he snorted. "What real issues? I highly doubt you want to share your issues with me. And I know I'm not taking that step. So what else are we supposed to be doing here?"

She stared at him, realizing she *could* share, but she didn't want to. And he was right; if they weren't going to help each other, what was the point? Unless one of them could help the other, and maybe in the helping, the other healed a little, as well.

"Did you research Jenna's seminar?" She smiled at his emphatic nod.

"Hell yes."

"And read the comments, reviews people had left?" When he nodded again, she said, "And do you recognize that our conversation is similar to many that were written on her website? And I quote, 'I started the journey expecting to find the opposite of what I got. Thank God.' Or 'When I first started this seminar, I thought I'd signed up for the wrong one. It was nothing like what I'd expected.'"

He stared at her then leaned back, dropping his gaze to his cup. Speaking slowly, he said, "The one that resonated with me was, 'I don't understand the how or the why or the process in which it happened, but healing has started…'"

"Oh, I like that." Contemplative, she stared around as the traffic picked up slightly as more people came looking for sustenance. "I'm supposed to find a journey with you as my subject. I don't understand that really, but I'm willing to trust a little here. Outside, it feels like it's an impersonal journey." She stopped and frowned. "I'm not really sure where I'm going with this, but say we were at home and you had the week off – what would you be doing?"

"Refinishing my bathroom."

The answer came so fast it surprised her.

He grinned with real humor, and his face came alive. She stared, entranced, as he spoke. "It's been the plan for a while. Now if you were to say, if I had a couple days off, what would I be doing, I guess I'd be working out, catching up on yard work, lazing around the house, and watching some classic movies."

As his mouth moved, her eyes caught on the lean muscles that formed and reformed in perfect symmetry. He was

lean and hard and spoke about a world she didn't understand. And she was suddenly afraid she just might know
what Jenna had been thinking.

And hoped not.

She raised her gaze to Kane's and watched light play
across his features as his eyes darkened. He leaned closer, his
whole body language shifting, softening. Damn, she wanted
to photograph him.

"What's up, Tinkerbelle?"

That startled a laugh out of her. "Tinkerbelle?"

He waved an arm at her. "You're tiny, delicate, and look
like a good wind would blow you away." He shrugged. "It
just came to me."

And something just came to me, she thought. Sending up a
prayer that she had this right and Kane wouldn't find her off
the wall, she said, "I know this might sound a bit weird,
but…" she took a deep breath, then added, "You have a very
photogenic face." She motioned to his biceps. They bulged
and relaxed almost as if he was bunching to a tune in his
mind. "In fact, your muscles are really interesting." As his
eyebrows shot up to his hairline, she quickly corrected, "For
the camera I mean."

She looked away for a moment before forcing herself
back on target. "I guess what I meant to say is that skin and
muscles, how people move, have always fascinated me. If you
are okay with it," she took a deep breath before she dropped
her gaze to the table, wishing it were wider, deeper, higher –
anything to increase that barrier – and said in a rush, the
words tripping over themselves before she could take them
back, "I'd like to take pictures as you work out."

Her shoulders and chest collapsed, completely empty.
There, she'd done it, and he hadn't laughed yet. She took a

peek at him from under her lashes to see him still staring at her. Shock turned to consideration, then to contemplation. She watched him throw down the napkin clenched in his fists. "Sure. Whatever."

Whatever? Did that mean he didn't mind? Or he was okay with her off-the-wall request? Or that he'd do anything to get through this assignment so he could go home? And did any of his reasons matter?

He did need to be comfortable with her doing this, or else it wouldn't work. The camera would pick up every nuance of his moods, his emotions. That was the thing about the images. They didn't lie.

Raw footage caught the truth. Sometimes more truth than anyone cared to have revealed. "I wouldn't want to make you uncomfortable, so if it's not okay, I'd rather hear the truth now."

He was watching the coffee swirl in his mug. After a moment, he raised his gaze to hers. There was a blind over his feelings, a sense of detached mockery coming through. She winced. "Okay, so it's not a good idea. Forget I mentioned it."

"No." He reached out to stop her as she'd instinctively pushed her chair back. "Wait."

She stilled as the heat of his hand soaked into her chilled skin, and she slowly sat back down. "I'm not trying to push your boundaries. I just thought this would be something I could do that would be within the parameters of the assignment and be something I would like to do. But I don't want to make you do something you don't want to do."

"And you can't." The corner of his mouth lifted. "But isn't doing what we're uncomfortable doing part of why we're here?"

"True."

"Are you taking an easy way out by doing something like this?" he asked. "Where's the uncomfortable part in all this for you if you want to do it?"

"I don't know. I hadn't actually realized I'd enjoy documenting the process until I realized how much my eye is caught by your muscles." She reached out and laid her finger on the cord, tightening and relaxing on the back of his hand as he tapped the top of the table. "You're very mobile. And that means muscles shift, skin moves, light plays over all of you in different ways." She gave herself a mental nudge to pull back.

She was fascinated by what she was seeing, and she desperately wanted to do this project now that she had a topic she could hold on to. She hated to admit it, but there was a solid chance she needed to do this. Maybe Jenna was right. "But it's your body, and it's your personal space. I didn't mean to intrude." That she had was already incredible. She was normally the mouse at the door waiting to run at the first hint of discord. Instead, here she was actually asking this super-male physique to do something he didn't likely want to do.

"It's a stupid idea," she said suddenly. "Forget it."

"No, I won't forget it." He motioned to her tea. "Settle down and drink your tea while I mull it over."

She picked up her cup and waited. Impatiently.

*　*　*

KANE STUDIED THE disgruntled look on Tania's face. Tinkerbelle had a temper. Well, so did he. She'd seen him blow at Jenna earlier, but that had merely been a trickle to what it could be. Still, she hadn't seemed phased by it. He'd half-expected her to have run from the room screaming, but instead, she'd sat there with a grin on her face.

Someone around her had a temper for her to be so blasé. Interesting.

Now, did he have a problem with her taking pictures while he lifted weights? He couldn't think of a decent reason to stop her, especially when she'd lit up at the idea like she'd been covered in fairy dust. He hadn't ever been photographed working out. It was hot, hard, and sweaty work. He didn't go to the gym to look for girls. He went with a trainer for some serious, anger-releasing work until he was dead-tired from the workouts, and there was nothing pretty about that.

He stared morosely into his empty mug. There was nothing pretty about any of this bullshit. As much as he couldn't say he was comfortable with the concept, he'd had a few friends who had participated in similar photo shoots, so it was more his comfort level at question here.

"As long as you don't post these pictures online and they are only for the project, then I am good with it." He looked up to stare into her eyes. "That goes for all the pictures you're taking. I'm the model, but I'm not giving you the rights to the images beyond the scope of this class."

She smiled, and the relief in her eyes was obvious.

She said, "I won't. These pictures are just for the project, and if there are one or two I really like, I'll ask you for permission if there is anything I want to use them for." She laughed. "What am I talking about? I don't do anything with my photography. I don't post them online at all." She pursed her lips. "Maybe it's something I should consider."

"I'm surprised you haven't. You appear to be serious about it."

Her hand instinctively went to the camera around her neck. "It's just a hobby, something to keep my mind and hands active."

He stood up. "Kind of like my workouts. Come on let's hit the gym at the hotel. You can take pictures, and I can work on some of this restlessness."

She bounced to her feet and dashed ahead of him.

Eager much? Still, there were worse things in life than having a beautiful woman sit there and watch him lift weights.

Chapter 5

INSIDE THE HOTEL lobby, Tania stopped her headlong rush. Belatedly, she realized how it must have looked. She'd raced back to the hotel as he'd strolled behind her. She turned her head to see him just now approaching the front doors. How idiotic.

On the other hand, she couldn't remember the last time she'd been this excited. And it was photography related the last time, too. Too bad she couldn't make a living that way.

Working part time with preschool children had brought her from the dark ages into the light. The laughter and light of the little children had reminded her of the good things in life. The joys in the mundane. The reason for living.

And it reminded her why she was here. So she could heal to the point of having a relationship and having children of her own. Just the thought of those tiny chubby arms wrapped around her neck and snuggling close brought tears to her eyes.

Kane moved past her toward the elevator. When she didn't fall into step behind him, he turned and asked, "Have you changed your mind?"

"No."

"Then come on. I have to get changed and the gym is in a different floor."

She ran into the elevator behind him and realized how

stupid she must have looked. Of course the fitness room was on a different floor, as were the other amenities. She stayed quiet until the door opened, then followed him into the hallway. He unlocked his room and pushed it open. She leaned back against the hallway and said, "I'll wait for you here."

"You can come in. I won't be a moment." He motioned for her to enter.

It felt stupid, but for some reason, her feet were obeying her mind and not her heart. She entered a man's bedroom for the first time in her life. Sure, it was a hotel bedroom, but it still counted…

"I'll get a few things."

And he disappeared from view, which gave her a chance to look around. Essentially, it was the same as her room, but slightly larger. There was a similar layout and look that spoke of the two rooms belonging to the same hotel, but that was where the differences lay. His room had a suitcase and a large gym bag open on the bed, a few casual pieces of clothing lying around. He rummaged in the gym bag and pulled out a few things, including what looked like a pair of gloves that startled her, and then an outfit. "Back in a moment." And he disappeared into the bathroom. She sat down on the edge of the single spare seat and lifted her camera to look through the lens.

Immediately, she felt better. That slight distance eased the discomfort of a new and uncomfortable situation. Inside, she was exultant. If only her friend, Jillian, could see her now. In fact, she'd take a few photos as proof. Quickly, she snapped a couple of shots of the male domain before he returned.

When the door opened, she'd retaken her seat and was

making adjustments to the zoom. Looking around, she caught sight of him.

Her breath caught in her throat. A muscle shirt had been designed for men like him. Holy Hannah.

And she might be afraid of having sex, but apparently there was nothing wrong with her libido. He wore pants that clung to his massive thighs and as he walked past her in the hallway, she barely restrained her hand from reaching out and grabbing his ass to see if it was as rock-hard as it appeared. She shuddered.

He was to die for.

He pulled open the door, sighed, turned back her way, and said, "Are you coming?"

Heat swept through her. Her mind screamed, *I wish!* Her mouth mumbled, "Sorry. Lost in my thoughts."

"Whatever."

She scooted past him, careful not to touch him.

He shook his head slightly and locked the door behind her. "This way."

She followed along, lost in the rosy haze of lust, and wondered how people survived days of this. She'd never been one to moan over men in any size or shape, and now all she wanted to do was crawl up his frame.

Except, as soon as she touched him or he touched her, the situation would all change. There was no way it wouldn't.

And that was a sobering thought.

Cooler and more composed, she walked beside him, happy when he chose to take the stairs. He ran down lightly and she followed. She was in good shape, but she wasn't fit as in *fit* fit. She didn't work out, and she didn't do any crazy spin classes. She walked a lot and did yoga for stress relief.

For some reason, twisting her body into crazy-ass positions always loosened her muscles. Probably because she stretched them past the point they'd normally go, so when she finally released them, they were like rubber and sagged in relief.

He pushed open the door to a lower level and led the way inside. It was a small but perfectly-acceptable space as far as she was concerned. From the disgusted look on his, she figured the amenities were not up to his standards. Then again, a heavy fitness enthusiast probably needed more than the bits and pieces of equipment here. For her, it was fine. There were a few decent-sized mats leaning on one corner. She wouldn't mind doing a few yoga poses while she was here. She glanced down at her sandals and Capri pants. Not good. She wouldn't be able to maneuver in these clothes. Why hadn't she thought to get changed herself?

Stepping back to give him room, she watched him open the bag he'd brought down with him. There was a tub of chalk in the bag and with a cloud of dust in the air, he pulled on his gloves.

He started with a few simple stretches to loosen up. She used that time to walk the room and change her settings for the interior light. There were no natural windows, and from the number of stairs they'd walked down, she had to assume they were below ground level. In spite of that, the room was bright and open and boasted a full wall of mirrors. She took several pictures and adjusted the setting again. She shifted to a different lens and another one. Finally satisfied, she turned back to Kane, watching as he performed a series of sit-ups, followed by pushups before locking into a nice, steady plank.

She might not work out, but she could certainly appreciate the ease and smoothness by which he switched from exercise to exercise. By the time she walked back over, she could see a thin shimmer of sweat on his skin. She immediately lifted her camera and clicked then again and again. She was lost as she tried to zoom in and capture that sheen to his skin, the effervescent glow that made his muscles shine. She shifted around him, moving carefully as he worked just as hard at what he was doing.

She hoped she wasn't disturbing him. He was a serious machine in motion. His gaze was inward, as if working on controlling his breathing and counting his movements. His muscles shifted and rippled as they answered his demands.

And boy, was he demanding.

He was doing different reps of different intensities in the floor-exercise portion. She almost laughed. She was good at sitting down and doing reps of eating cupcakes just as seriously. This man was definitely working out!

She was lost in bemusement as he crunched and lifted and flipped and did it all over again. She was exhausted just watching him.

Then she watched a bead of sweat roll down his forehead, and she went into action. She stared from where she stood and zoomed in as many stages as she could go, trying to capture that single drop as it stood poised on the pulsating cords lifted along his temple. Then it dropped.

She couldn't stop. She moved as close as she dared, clicking away as his jaw twitched and clenched and that chin firmed and the cheekbone locked down.

"He's something," she murmured to herself.

And then realized he'd stopped and was staring at her.

She lowered the camera, tilted her head slightly, and asked, "Is there a problem?"

He stared at her as if she'd asked a seriously-stupid question then shook his head and silently went back to work.

She was left wondering what she'd done. Or what he'd thought she'd done.

*   *   *

REALLY? SHE THOUGHT he was something. Intriguing. Tinkerbelle just might be interested. Except he wasn't sure she even knew what she was doing. She certainly hadn't appeared to realize that she'd spoken her thought out loud. Most women he knew would never be so honest.

And he suspected she hadn't meant to be.

Sure, she was comfortable around a camera, but he had to wonder if she'd ever been around a man – not a boy but a full-grown, adult male – because she certainly wasn't acting like it. For someone her age, she appeared damn innocent.

At first, he'd managed to block her out as he got into the swing of it. He loved setting a rhythm and working his body through the paces. It felt good. It felt natural. It felt right.

And he managed to get through most of his warm-up until she fixated on his face. What the hell was she doing? She'd been quiet, taking the odd picture before she had suddenly gone click-happy, her fingers moving at a speed he could only guess at. Then she'd moved closer, and he realized she'd locked onto his face. And she appeared to be studying his forehead. It completely disconcerted him when he realized that a drop of sweat had fallen from his brow to the padded floor and she dove after it to take a picture.

What was that about?

Why would she even think to focus on such a thing? He always worked up a sweat. Had she been taking pictures of his shirt as it slowly soaked up, too? He wanted to make a sarcastic remark then figured he better not bring attention to it – just in case she hadn't seen it yet.

He couldn't imagine what interest any of this would have for her, but she appeared enthralled. He closed his eyes and pushed his body through several more reps. The whirling click quickly became background noise. Then he stopped and rested. His body thrummed with energy and fatigue had hit the muscles – that was a good thing. He stretched his arms up over his head and sighed gently.

"Feel good?" Her voice held an odd note. If he didn't know better, he'd say she was doing that whole mixed-signal thing. He also couldn't get rid of the feeling that she had no idea what she was projecting. Or what she thought she was projecting.

She was like Tinkerbelle in the innocence department, too. He had to wonder if she could be, but her age and the fact that she was in university made it hard to believe. She wasn't beautiful in the sense that she had the look of a model, but those huge, haunted eyes were enough to bring any man to his knees. It certainly brought out his protective instincts.

Another guy could easily use her as a punching bag. He'd assumed from her original trepidation around him that had been her problem, but the camera had completely changed her.

It fascinated him.

He also assumed it was a surface change only and that if he made a move on her, she'd bolt like lightning in the opposite direction.

There was a part of him really wanting to push that issue, too. Make her fess up to being as terrified as she really was. And that would be a shitty thing to do. He really wasn't that kind of guy, unless he was fucking pissed.

Then everyone was that kind of guy.

Chapter 6

S HE GOT THAT she'd done something off, but for the first time in a long time, she was able to brush it away. She was doing something she loved with a subject that was fascinating. Even better…this activity was encouraged. Necessary, even.

A part of her wanted to squeal for joy. She'd wanted to take pictures of people for a long time, but there were rules and regulations and laws and…of course who she'd been interested in taking photos of versus the ones who were willing weren't the same, either.

Kane fascinated her.

And he was male. In the beginning – was that only last night – he'd been imposing. Scary. Forceful. She knew he could break her in two within seconds. She'd done a mess of self-defense courses and she'd have an edge if he tried anything, but there was no doubt that strength won out.

She'd spent the better part of the day capturing who he was, and although those fingers clenched into fists and his jaw clenched into stone, there was an element of control to him. As if he were afraid he'd cross the line…one day…but hadn't yet.

Not for the first time, she wondered at his story. Curiosity ate at her, but she didn't dare ask. Everyone struggled with personal boundaries in therapy. Some stories were meant to be told, others told in parts, and even more would never see the light of day.

Hers was in the middle category. They used to be at the end. Progress.

In Kane's case, he was a cop back finishing his degree so he could move up and do more. There was an awareness, an alertness to everything going on around them at all times, as if he never rested. Never relaxed that guard of his. When they were at the coffee shop, there'd been a softening in his gaze a few times. She tried to capture them, but she wouldn't be able to tell if she'd succeeded unless she could take a closer look on her laptop.

The first time, he'd been looking across the harbor at a group of colorful sailboats drifting by, their sails billowing in the wind. A lazy afternoon on the water. There'd been something wistful in that gaze. She hoped she'd caught it, and also hoped she'd caught what she'd understood of him in that moment – the dreamer in him.

As they'd been getting ready to leave, there'd been an older couple walking on the street. They'd been holding hands. She'd instinctively taken pictures of the couple, although she had hundreds already. It was her dream future. She wanted to grow old together with someone special. She couldn't think of anything nicer than to sit on a veranda with her partner, together in rocking chairs, enjoying the passage of time, full of memories of their life together.

She'd caught sight of Kane's gaze on the same couple as they walked away. Sure, there was a bit of wistfulness there, but his gaze held more than a hint of regret for something just out of his reach. She'd been unable to resist taking several shots. A man like him had to have had a full and rich relationship history, but chances were also good that something had gone wrong with one of them. And that whatever had gone wrong had been the major reason he was here.

There was a fury inside this man, but not for everyone. She definitely felt like it was directed at one particular person, most likely at his last relationship.

Or possibly…at himself.

As she sat there, waiting for him to walk around and cool down from his last set of exercises, she wondered what could have gone so wrong as to send him to this place. It wasn't exactly AA therapy, but a specialized type of session for those that needed a different approach. As she hadn't been able to see the benefit for herself and had needed Jillian, her best friend, to point out how this could be her answer, she wondered who had shown Kane that this was the next step in his journey.

Because he didn't look like he could see it for himself—especially not here and now.

She was due for a one-on-one session with Jenna this evening. She had to admit, she was looking forward to it. She had something to say, some new insight into her life, her mind, her way of looking at the world. And as much as she didn't want to dwell on Kane, some mention of her inscrutable partner was inevitable. She didn't want Jenna to know there was a definite physical attraction to Kane but thought the therapist would be able to figure it out within a few moments of Tania opening her mouth.

And that would be embarrassing.

She could feel her cheeks heating up at the thought of trying to explain herself. Now her friend Jillian would be screaming for joy, and she was tempted to text her friend and mention the hottie partner, but that would also start a long string of questions that would demand answers.

And she didn't want to go there right now.

Or ever.

This was special, kinda like the first stirrings of long-dead hormones. Tania had tried to find other men attractive, but one couldn't force something like that. She didn't know why now. She couldn't submerge the constant need to look Kane's way and see what he was doing. That need to wonder about his story, his life, or any number of other issues going on. That awareness…that heat…that instinctive knowing where he was at any given time.

This was new for her, and she felt rubbed raw, super-sensitized to his presence. He must know. Maybe he could sense it. How humiliating was that? She felt like an over-grown teenager with awakening awareness of him.

She knew it had to be the circumstances. The setting. The project throwing them together in close proximity. It couldn't be real. She shook her head.

She smiled, feeling a release of tension across her shoulders.

This was just a moment in time. A passing thought.

"What's up?"

Startled, she looked over at Kane, now with a towel around his neck and wiping the sweat off his red face. He'd been working out while she'd been lost in thought.

She hopped to her feet. "I am so sorry. I was daydreaming."

"Yeah?" He tilted his head to study her. "About what?"

Willing the heat to stop its rapid climb up her neck, she stood up and fiddled with her camera. "Just life. Things that brought me here. Things I want to take away from here."

He raised an eyebrow. "Glad you're getting something

out of this."

"So are you." She grinned. "You're getting fit."

"Ha." He dropped the towel. "I am fit. There's no *getting* in this equation."

"Yeah, well, it seems to me you missed one rep on that last round."

He stared at her in mock outrage. "How would you know? You were sitting there like some kind of decoration, daydreaming. I'm the one working out here."

"And you'd better get back at it and make up that set," she said smoothly. She lifted her camera. "And this time, I'll be sure to catch every grunt and muscle movement."

He froze, a look of horror on his face. "You don't have audio on that thing, do you?"

She laughed. "Nope. Just kidding. But I run a mean camera, and that means I'll catch every little trick you try to avoid in your full workout."

Good-naturedly, he returned to the huge set of weights and, starting with his right arm, he lifted a barbell she'd never be able to lift with two hands and started bicep curls.

She grabbed her camera and went to work herself.

When he stopped the next time, she noticed a change in his attitude. The look on his face. She bent closer, not quite understanding but wanting to – at least from behind the camera. It's as if he was exhausted but determined to continue. To force his body past this wall.

She didn't understand the will to do this. Why? Why would anyone, male or female, *want* so much physical pain and do yet more damage? She didn't understand how muscle-building worked at this level. She understood it had something to do with creating tears in the fibers and having your body rebuild bigger, better, stronger.

But at this point…no, way earlier…she'd have walked away.

Instead, he was heading into this next set as if this was now…finally…serious business! As if everything else was a warm-up to this.

She leaned closer.

His face twisted with concentration, and his gaze flattened – those don't-mess-with-me cop eyes she'd seen flicker in the dark-chocolate depths. And he reached deep inside and pulled those damn weights up again.

She could see his pain. Hear his pain. Feel his pain.

And still he pushed himself to reach for that goal.

In the end, she was so absorbed in the intensity of his own moment that she completely forgot to take pictures at that final point before he hit the wall…and went over it. She lost her balance and fell on her butt, camera in hand, mouth open as she stared at him.

He ever-so-slowly lowered that massive weight as if everything in him wanted to drop it and he wouldn't give in to it.

He was all about control.

And goals.

And making them.

Pushing himself, forcing himself to face his own weakness was everything to him.

And she knew in that moment, in ways she couldn't understand, that this man would never allow himself to hurt another person through a moment of weakness. It was not to say that in an equal fight in a boxing ring he wouldn't enjoy pulverizing his opponent, because she thought he would love that.

But he'd never take advantage. Never hit a woman, a

child, or another man in anger.

She knew he'd never abuse that trust or take advantage of his superior strength.

But she wasn't sure *he* knew that. That when he lost it, that when red took over his emotions and rage replaced the blood in his veins, he might shove his fist through a wall, but he'd never mistake a woman's face for that wall.

And he'd never, ever use force on a woman in other ways. He wouldn't have to. He would naturally see a lot of action, if he wanted it, but he wouldn't force a woman. He was a protector, not a predator.

With that thought, a band loosened around her chest, and the tension from just being this close to him eased back into the realm of normalcy. She'd been keeping a safe distance between them, being sure to avoid his touch, even accidentally. Something she'd done for years. Something she wasn't consciously-aware of doing.

She sat quietly, contemplatively, while he collapsed and worked to regain his breathing.

How foolish she'd been. Walking the safe road may have been the way to go in the past, but she'd hit a turning point. She could trust her instincts that said he was safe to be around, or she could continue on this safe pathway and not give herself a chance to get a little closer to a strong, sexual male.

Her body said to jump his bones, but she was light years away from something like that. And so was he. He'd given no sign he was interested in her at all, and he had a lot more experience with sexual attraction than she had. He didn't seem to notice she was acting any differently.

So maybe she wasn't.

She lifted the camera and captured the sense of satisfaction, glowing exhaustion…pride.

Click. Click. *Click.*

*   *   *

WHAT COULD SHE possibly find to take pictures of after so many shots? She'd been going crazy with that damn thing. He'd blocked her out as he put himself through the pacing. He needed this workout, and all the more now because of her bouncing around. She'd gotten quiet once or twice. She'd called it daydreaming. He wasn't so sure, but it was weird.

Still, he needed to focus, needed this release of tension, of the uncomfortableness of the situation. He wanted to be home. In his space. In his gym. And work…

He had homework to do, cop work to do, getting that degree to do. He loved being a cop. He just wanted to do more. That's why he was here. Right? No, it was one of the reasons. His temper had been blowing louder and hotter. His personal issues had bled over into his work life, and that was when he'd realized he couldn't hold off doing something about this. He wanted a personal life, but he needed to work. And he couldn't afford to give his personal issues any more time to do their own thing on their own time – not once it had crossed into his work arena.

And then there was his brother.

Jessie had convinced him to take this step, to commit the time, energy, and intention to make this happen.

No one had warned him about the other people in the session – like Tania.

Then how did one prepare for such a thing?

He reached up and rubbed his face. The workout had done its job. He was exhausted. He was mentally and physically done, and he was at the calm place where he was fine. Everything in his life was going to be okay. God, he loved this space.

It felt like home.

Centered. Balanced.

Peaceful.

Some people would say he was a gym junkie. That it was an addiction. If it was, he didn't want to get over it. There were truly few places he could go to get this feeling, and even fewer ways to get there.

He needed this.

And now he felt like he could handle the world again.

Even Tinkerbelle.

"Surely you have enough pictures by now?"

She froze. "If you're done, then I do." She straightened and busied herself putting away her gear.

"Well, I need a shower," he joked. "So, unless you're planning to document that…"

There was a tiny gasp. He spun around and realized she'd frozen in place, her eyes huge. But it was what churned in the back of those eyes that made him add, "Hey, I was just joking."

She blinked once again…and then she started babbling. "Sorry, I'm late. Need to go…back to my room. It's almost dinnertime." The whole time the words tumbled out of her mouth, she was backing up to the door, putting as much distance between them as she could.

At the door, she opened it and turned around as if to say something. Her face worked while he stood there with his mouth open, then she closed her lips and bolted.

The door slammed closed behind her.

SKIN is available!

Dear reader,

Thank you for reading the free preview of SKIN. I hope Tania and Kane's story interests you. The full story is out! If you'd like to read about other books I've written, please turn the page.

Cheers,
Dale Mayer

Tuesday's Child

Book 1 of the Psychic Vision Series

Get this book at your favorite vendor.

What she doesn't want…is exactly what he needs.

Shunned and ridiculed all her life for something she can't control, Samantha Blair hides her psychic abilities and lives on the fringes of society. Against her will, however, she's tapped into a killer—or rather, his victims. Each woman's murder, blow-by-blow, ravages her mind until their death releases her back to her body. Sam knows she must go to the authorities, but will the rugged, no-nonsense detective in charge of tracking down the killer believe her?

Detective Brandt Sutherland only trusts hard evidence, yet Sam's visions offer clues he needs to catch a killer. The more he learns about her incredible abilities, however, the clearer it becomes that Sam's visions have put her in the killer's line of fire. Now Brandt must save her from something he cannot see or understand…and risk losing his heart in the process.

As danger and desire collide, passion raises the stakes in a game Sam and Brandt don't dare lose.

For a short preview – please turn the page

Tuesday's Child

Chapter 1

SAMANTHA BLAIR STRUGGLED against phantom restraints. No, not again.

This wasn't her room or her bed, and it sure as hell wasn't her body. Tears welled and trickled slowly from eyes not her own. Then the pain started. Still, she couldn't move. She could only endure. Terror clawed at her soul while dying nerves screamed.

The attack became a frenzy of stabs and slices, snatching all thought away. Her body jerked and arched in a macabre dance. Black spots blurred her vision, and still the slaughter continued.

Sam screamed. The terror was hers, but the cracked, broken voice was not.

Confusion reigned as her mind grappled with reality. What was going on?

Understanding crashed in on her. With it came despair and horror.

She'd become a visitor in someone else's nightmare. Locked inside a horrifying energy warp, she'd linked to this poor woman whose life dripped away from multiple gashes.

Another psychic vision.

The knife slashed down, impaling the woman's abdomen, splitting her wide from ribcage to pelvis. Her agonized scream echoed on forever in Sam's mind. She cringed.

The other woman slipped into unconsciousness. Sam wasn't offered the same gift. Now, the pain was Sam's alone. The stab wounds and broken bones became Sam's to experience even though they weren't hers.

The woman's head cocked to one side, her cheek resting on the blood-soaked bedding. From the new vantage point, Sam's horrified gaze locked on a bloody knife held high by a man dressed in black from the top of his head down. Only his eyes showed, glowing with feverish delight. She shuddered. Please, dear God, let it end soon.

The attacker's fury died suddenly. A fine tremor shook his arm as fatigue set in. "Shit." He removed his glove and scratched beneath the fabric.

In the waning moonlight, from the corner of her eye, Sam caught the metallic glint of a ring on his hand. It mattered. She knew it did. She struggled to imprint the image before the opportunity was lost. Her eyes drifted closed. In the darkness of her mind, the wait was endless.

Sam's soul wept. Oh, God, she hated this. Why? Why was she here? She couldn't help the woman. She couldn't even help herself.

She welcomed the next blow – so light only a minor flinch undulated through the dreadfully damaged woman. Her tortured spirit stirred deep within the rolling waves of blackness, struggling for freedom from this nightmare. With one last surge of energy, the woman opened her eyes, and locked onto the white rings of the mask staring back. In ever-slowing heartbeats, her circle of vision narrowed until the two soulless orbs blended into one small band before it blinked out altogether. The silence, when it came, was absolute.

Gratefully, Sam relaxed into death.

Twenty minutes later, she bolted upright in her own bed. Survival instincts screamed at her to run. White agony dropped her in place.

"Ohh," she cried out. Fearing more pain, she slid her hands over her belly. Her fingers slipped along the raw edges of a deep slash. Searing pain made her gasp and twist away. Hot tears poured. Warm, sticky liquid coated her fingers. "Oh. God. Oh God, oh God," she chanted.

Staring in confusion around her, fear, panic, and finally, recognition seeped into her dazed mind. Early morning rays highlighted the water stains shining through the slap-dash coat of whitewash on the ceiling and the banged up suitcases, open on the floor. An empty room – an empty life. A remnant of a foster-care childhood.

She was home.

Memories swamped her, flooding her senses with yet more hurt. Sam broke down. Like an animal, she tried to curl into a tiny ball only to scream again as pain jackknifed through her. Torn edges of muscle tissue and flesh rubbed against each other, and broken ribs creaked with her slightest movement. Blood slipped over her torn breasts to soak the sheets below.

The smell. Wet wool fought with the unique and unforgettable smell of fresh blood.

Sam caught her breath and froze, her face hot, tight with agony. "Shit, shit, and shit!" She swore under her breath like a mantra.

Tremors wracked her tiny frame, keeping the pain alive as she morphed through realities. Transition time. What a joke. That always brought images of new age mumbo jumbo to mind. Nothing light and airy could describe this. Each blow leveled at the victim had manifested in her own body. This was hard-core healing – time when bones knitted, sliced ligaments and muscle tissue grew back together, and time for skin to stitch itself closed.

Sam understood her injuries had something to do with her imperfect control, paired with her inability to accept her gifts. Apparently, if she could surmount the latter the first would diminish. She didn't quite understand how or why. Or what to do about it. Her body somehow always healed, the physical and mental scars always remained. She was a mess.

The physical process usually took anywhere from ten to twenty minutes – depending on the injuries. The mental confusion, disconnectedness, sense of isolation took longer to disappear. She paid a high price for moving too soon. Shuddering, Sam reached for the frayed edges of her control. It wouldn't be much longer. She hoped.

Nothing could stop the hot tears leaking from her closed eyelids.

This session had been bad. Apart from the broken ribs, there were so many stab wounds. She'd never experienced one so physically damaging. Nervously, she wondered at the extent of her blood loss. If she didn't learn how to disconnect, these visions could be the end of her – literally.

Just like that poor woman.

Sam hated that these episodes were changing, growing, developing. So powerful and so ugly, they made her sick to her soul.

Several minutes later, Sam raised her head to survey the bed. The pain was manageable, although she wouldn't be able to move her limbs yet. Blood had soaked the top of the many Thrift Store blankets piled high on the bed. Her hollowed belly had become a vessel for the cooling puddle of blood. Shit. The stuff was everywhere.

The metallic taste clung to her lips and teeth. She rolled the disgusting spit around the inside of her mouth, waiting. She wanted to run away – from the memories, the visions, her life. But knowing that pain simmered beneath the surface, waiting to rip her apart, stopped her. Weary, ageless patience added to the bleakness in her heart.

Ten more minutes passed. Now, she should be good to go. Lifting her head, she spat the bloody gob onto the waiting wad of tissue and noted the time.

Transition had taken fifteen minutes this morning.

She was improving.

Oh God. Sam broke into sobs again. When would this end? Other psychics found things or heard things. Many of them saw events before they happened. She saw violence – not only saw, but experienced it too.

Occasional shudders wracked her frame from the coldness that seemed destined to live in her veins. The odd straggling sniffle escaped. She couldn't remember when she'd last been warm. Dropping the top blood-soaked blanket to the floor, Sam tugged the motley collection of covers tighter around her skinny frame. Warmth was a comfort that belonged to others.

She wasn't so lucky. She walked with one foot on the dark side – whether she liked it or not. And that was the problem. She'd been running for a long time. Then she'd landed at this cabin and had been hiding ever since. That was no answer either.

Her resolve firmed. Enough was enough. It was time to gain control. Time to do something. This monster had to be stopped. Now.

Christ, she was tired of waking up dead.

Touched by Death

Get this book at your favorite vendor.

Death had touched anthropologist Jade Hansen in Haiti once before, costing her an unborn child and perhaps her very sanity.

A year later, determined to face her own issues, she returns to Haiti with a mortuary team to recover the bodies of an American family from a mass grave.

Visiting his brother after the quake, independent contractor Dane Carter puts his life on hold to help the sleepy town of Jacmel rebuild. But he finds it hard to like his brother's pregnant wife or her family. He wants to go home, until he meets Jade – and realizes what's missing in his own life.

When the mortuary team begins work, it's as if malevolence has been released from the earth. Instead of laying her ghosts to rest, Jade finds herself confronting death and terror again.

And the man who unexpectedly awakens her heart – is right in the middle of it all.

Vampire in Denial
This is book 1 of the Family Blood Ties Saga

Get this book at your favorite vendor.

Blood doesn't just make her who she is…it also makes her what she is.

Like being a sixteen-year-old vampire isn't hard enough, Tessa's throwback human genes make her an outcast among her relatives. But try as she might, she can't get a handle on the vampire lifestyle and all the…blood.

Turning her back on the vamp world, she embraces the human teenage lifestyle—high school, peer pressure and finding a boyfriend. Jared manages to stir something in her blood. He's smart and fun and oh, so cute. But Tessa's dream of a having the perfect boyfriend turns into a nightmare when vampires attack the movie theatre and kidnap her date.

Once again, Tessa finds herself torn between the human world and the vampire one. Will blood own out? Can she make peace with who she is as well as what?

Warning: This book ends with a cliffhanger! Book 2 picks up where this book ends.

Dangerous Designs
Book 1 of the Design Series

Get this book at your favorite vendor.

Drawing is her world...but when her new pencil comes alive, it's his world too.

Her... Storey Dalton is seventeen and now boyfriendless after being dumped via Facebook. Drawing is her escape. It's like as soon as she gets down one image, a dozen more are pressing in on her. Then she realizes her pictures are almost drawing themselves...or is it that her new pencil is alive?

Him... Eric Jordan is a new Ranger and the only son of the Councilman to his world. He's crossed the veil between dimensions to retrieve a lost stylus. But Storey is already experimenting with her new pencil and what her drawings can do – like open portals.

It ... The stylus is a soul-bound intelligence from Eric's dimension on Earth and uses Storey's unsuspecting mind to seek its way home, giving her an unbelievable power. She unwittingly opens a third dimension, one that held a dangerous predatory species banished from Eric's world centuries ago, releasing these animals into both dimensions.

Them... Once in Eric's homeland, Storey is blamed for the calamity sentenced to death. When she escapes, Eric is ordered to bring her back or face that same fate. With nothing to lose, can they work together across dimensions to save both their worlds?

About the Author

Dale Mayer is a *USA Today* best-selling author, best known for her SEALs military romances, her Psychic Visions series, and her Lovely Lethal Garden cozy series. Her contemporary romances are raw and full of passion and emotion (Broken But … Mending, Hathaway House series). Her thrillers will keep you guessing (Kate Morgan, By Death series), and her romantic comedies will keep you giggling (*It's a Dog's Life*, a stand-alone novella; and the Broken Protocols series, starring Charming Marvin, the cat).

Dale honors the stories that come to her—and some of them are crazy, break all the rules and cross multiple genres!

To go with her fiction, she also writes nonfiction in many different fields, with books available on résumé writing, companion gardening, and the US mortgage system. All her books are available in print and ebook format.

Connect with Dale Mayer Online

Also by Dale Mayer

Published Adult Books:

Psychic Vision Series

Tuesday's Child

Hide'n Go Seek

Maddy's Floor

Garden of Sorrow

Knock, Knock…

Rare Find

Eyes to the Soul

Now You See Her

Shattered

Into the Abyss

Psychic Visions Books 1–3

Psychic Visions Books 4–6

Psychic Visions Books 7–9

By Death Series

Touched by Death – Part 1

Touched by Death – Part 2

Touched by Death – Parts 1&2

Haunted by Death

Chilled by Death

By Death Books 1–3

Second Chances…at Love Series

Second Chances – Part 1

Second Chances – Part 2

Second Chances – complete book (Parts 1 & 2)

Charmin Marvin Romantic Comedy Series

Broken Protocols

Broken Protocols 2

Broken Protocols 3

Broken Protocols 3.5

Broken Protocols 1-3

Broken and… Mending

Skin

Scars

Scales (of Justice)

Broken but… Mending 1-3

Glory

Genesis

Tori

Celeste

Glory Trilogy

Biker Blues

Biker Blues: Morgan, Part 1

Biker Blues: Morgan, Part 2

Biker Blues: Morgan, Part 3

Biker Baby Blues: Morgan, Part 4

Biker Blues: Morgan, Full Set

Biker Blues: Salvation, Part 1

Biker Blues: Salvation, Part 2

Biker Blues: Salvation, Part 3

Biker Blues: Salvation, Full Set

SEALs of Honor

Mason: SEALs of Honor, Book 1

Hawk: SEALs of Honor, Book 2

Dane: SEALs of Honor, Book 3

Swede: SEALs of Honor, Book 4

Shadow: SEALs of Honor, Book 5

Cooper: SEALs of Honor, Book 6

Markus: SEALs of Honor, Book 7

Evan: SEALs of Honor, Book 8

Mason's Wish: SEALs of Honor, Book 9

SEALs of Honor, Books 1–3

SEALs of Honor, Books 4–6

Collections

Dare to Be You…

Dare to Love…

Dare to be Strong…

RomanceX3

Standalone Novellas

It's a Dog's Life

Riana's Revenge

Published Young Adult Books:

Family Blood Ties Series

Vampire in Denial

Vampire in Distress

Vampire in Design

Vampire in Deceit

Vampire in Defiance

Vampire in Conflict

Vampire in Chaos

Vampire in Crisis

Vampire in Control

Vampire in Charge

Family Blood Ties Set 1–3

Family Blood Ties Set 1–5

Family Blood Ties Set 4–6

Family Blood Ties Set 7–9

Sian's Solution – A Family Blood Ties Short Story

Design series

Dangerous Designs

Deadly Designs

Darkest Designs

Design Series Trilogy

Standalone

In Cassie's Corner

Gem Stone (a Gemma Stone Mystery)

Time Thieves

Published Non-Fiction Books:

Career Essentials

Career Essentials: The Résumé

Career Essentials: The Cover Letter

Career Essentials: The Interview

Career Essentials: 3 in 1